IS HE WORTH AFFECTION...

IKE OKORIE

IS HE WORTHY OF HER AFFECTION?

IKE OKORIE

Typeset by **Omega Prints**, Port Harcourt, Nigeria

ISBN: 978-179-291-7202

Published by **Corinna Books Ltd**
48, Old Aba Road, Rumuobiokani, Port Harcourt
Rivers State, Nigeria
+234 813 544 4109, +234 808 404 2890
E-mail: enquiry@corinnabooks.com
www.corinnabooks.com

1

Strange and tragic things happened last night. Steve showed a reckless disregard for his own safety. His death last night was attributed to reckless driving. All agreed that the wide and tarred roads of Abuja, Nigeria's capital held a seductive appeal to motorists. This morning Rosemary was still in shock over the death of her husband. She was dressed all in blue. A large diamond ring sat on her ring finger. It was a gift from her uncle when she turned twenty-five. Occasionally, she twisted the diamond ring when she was nervous. For three years Steve and Rosemary had lived in Tom's house. Tom, her late husband's friend was already in the dining room when she came downstairs for breakfast. And as she came into the dining room, Tom stared at the diamond ring as if he was seeing it for the first time. Tom's big house located at number 35, Zik Boulevard looked grim and dreary today.

The Boulevard was one of the beautiful tree lined roads in the sprawling city of Abuja. Rosemary waved a friendly greeting and then sat down to breakfast. Breakfast consisted of a mixed grill of scrambled eggs, sausages, tomatoes and mushrooms. They ate in silence. With eyes downcast, she nibbled at her breakfast. Tom observed her closely and concluded she was overcome with grief. He felt that she was most likely suffering from bereavement crisis. He could see she was gazing at her plate through a mist of tears.

She was lost in thought. Try as she might, she could not conceal the deep resentment she felt at the way she had been treated by Steve's family when they returned to Nigeria three years ago. That was why last night she had felt a sense of alarm when her husband did not return. She had waited in an agony of suspense until she and Tom watched the news on TV. Apparently Steve had died before help could get to him. She had stared at Tom in disbelief, clutching her cell phone. He could see there was a feeling of restlessness deep in her soul. What happened next was totally out of character. She lay quietly, enfolded in Tom's arm. Impulsively, she threw her arms around his neck and moaned; "Tom help me. I'm shocked and confused. I don't know what to do."

Suddenly, she got up, grabbed his hand and dragged him behind her out of the house, dazed and her eyes misted with tears. Tom got behind the steering wheel of the Estate Mercedes Benz. She hopped in and they drove in silence to the National Hospital Morgue, Abuja. They got a shock when they saw the body of Steve on the slab, cold and dead. Downcast and overcome with grief they returned home at midnight. Eventually, they fell asleep in each other's arms. Last night Rosemary looked very vulnerable sleeping in Tom's arm. When he turned on the double sofa in the sitting room and saw her sleeping like a baby in his arms, it was with an effort of will that he resisted the temptation of making love to her at her most vulnerable period in her life. Although he had admired her from a distance he cautioned himself not to take undue advantage of her.

And now Tom felt there was nothing to it, strange though it was. He told himself it was all a mistake. He watched her quietly as he ate a hurried breakfast. He was about to leave to visit the family of his late friend, Steve when Rosemary held him and said; "I'm hurting inside. Stay close to me. Don't leave me all alone by myself," She sighed. Quickly, she added, "You've been on my mind all night." She stood up and held his hand. She fluttered her eyelashes at him. "Don't bother me this morning. I've got a lot on my mind." Tom said, gently pushing her away. "What a heartless thing to say!" She blurted out. "Listen, I know you're hurting and I want to help you. It breaks my heart to see you like this. What happened last night between us was a mistake. We were caught in a whirling vortex of emotions," Tom explained. He smiled nervously. Beyond any shadow of doubt, he knew it was a hurt that would take a long time to heal. In any case, he sounded more confident than he felt. "I admit that I mistook your intentions. But I need a shoulder to cry on at this point in time. Don't misunderstand me. I am grateful for all you've done for me and Steve since we returned from the States." She said pleadingly. "I don't mind admitting that I find you irresistible. We get along just fine together. What do you say?" she asked, touching his arm. It was clearly an offer that came from the heart. "I'm sorry, Rosemary. My heart bleeds for you. Shall we go for a drink later in the day?" Tom asked, looking into her eyes. "No, thanks; I have to go shopping this afternoon." she said. "Rosemary, I suggest you give your mind to the arrangements for the burial of Steve. It's too early in the day for us to be thinking about ourselves. We must respect the memory of the dead," he admonished her.

"You think I might be out of my tiny mind! I went to sleep secure in the knowledge that I was not alone in this house. Since Steve and I returned from the States three years ago, you've been a pillar of support to us. Is it wrong to have strong feelings for you?" she said, obviously agitated. "Love is a stimulant. There's no point stoking the embers of romance at this moment. After all, your family has always been well thought of around here and elsewhere. Regain your self-control." Tom said, patting her on the shoulder. "I've had a wonderful life. I'm proud of my family background. I don't regret a thing." She said as she gave a self-deprecating shrug. "I regret that I am unable to accept your kind invitation to consort with you. Perhaps someday I may fulfill your yearning. You've always comported yourself with dignity," Tom stated. "I agree. Dignity is a sense of your own importance and value. It's difficult to preserve your dignity when you have no job and no home. Yet you urge me to stand on my dignity." She moaned. Tears were streaming down her cheeks.

"This is your home. My home is your home. For three years, you've lived here with your husband," he said consolingly. At that her face went pale as his words hit home. He continued, "You're fortunate in that you have friends to help you." "True, I fell in love with your house when Steve and I returned from the States. Then, unconsciously, I fell in love with you, even though you neither recognised it nor reciprocated it. I was attracted to you the first time I set my eyes on you." She said, sobbing openly now. "Hold yourself. Pull yourself together. It's a fluid emotional situation. You speak with great fluidity of tongue." He counselled her. A pink flush spread over her face. A well bred lady; Rosemary was too well bred to show her disappointment. Tom thought. He, however, found her preoccupation with romantic feelings irritating. He had a premonition that he would lose her friendship if he did not give in to her. He also observed that she had been drinking heavily since she lost her job. Worse still, she had erroneous impression that someone was dogging her steps. Yet his total disinterest in romantic relationship puzzled her. Little wonder he sought to dismiss her overtures from his mind. In many ways, he believed she was a truly remarkable woman. It would amount to indecent haste if he did not rein in his emotions tightly. He felt such action might offend the sensibilities of his friends. The memory of the dead was held sacrosanct among Africans. She was reluctant to admit she was wrong and sought to justify herself.

From the look on her face, he surmised that she had an argument. "Tom, I want to be in control of my own destiny. I believe there's some force guiding us - call it God, destiny or fate. I want to love and to be loved," She said, without much enthusiasm. Tom was silent. He knew she was spurred on by a strong sense of destiny and ambition. And there was a note of desperation in her voice. But of late his increasing financial difficulties, had forced him to take desperate measures to live frugally, although he had always been working."I'll skip the usual preliminaries and come straight to the point. Is everything we do preordained? Are you suggesting that you and I are being pulled by force of destiny?" Tom asked. A smile flitted across his face. "You're too preoccupied with your own thoughts to notice any overtures I make to you. I find your preoccupation with money irritating." She spoke slowly, in a state of preoccupation. "Your assumptions beg the question that we are in a romantic relationship. I beg to differ; I hold the view that our meeting in the first place was not preordained." Tom stated, clearing the dishes. He took them to the kitchen sink. She joined him in the kitchen

"You're so concerned with your own thoughts that you don't notice what's happening around you." She accused him as she clenched her fists to stop herself from trembling. Tom looked for the entire world like a school boy caught stealing mangoes. "I wouldn't hurt you for the world. You feel the world is against you. You lost a husband last night and I lost a friend. We've suffered irreparable loss." He said touching her arm. She gave him a worried look. He began to worry at the knot in their friendship. There followed a short silence. When Steve died last night Tom knew her entire world was turned upside down. He had tried to offer a few words of comfort. Surprisingly he had comforted himself with the thought that her state of shock would soon be over. It had comforted her to feel his arms around her. She had even tried to cultivate an air of satisfaction. Even while Steve was alive their marriage was finished. They were just tagging along. To all appearances, they were content to tolerate each other. As he dried the dishes, he fixed her a sympathetic smile. He was fully aware that the first 24 hours after bereavement were the most critical. It was apparent from her face that she was really upset. "Tom, it's time we were getting along. Steve is dead. It's frustrating to have to wait so long to love again. I need a shoulder to cry on." She said slightly leaning on him. "I don't want to belabour the point, but it's vital you understand how important this is. You're not responsible for the tragedy which snuffed out Steve's life last night. I know you're going through a time of crisis..." She interrupted him. "Strangely enough, I don't feel at all nervous. You've been acting very strangely this morning. A strange thing happened last night. We slept in each other's arms." She said, and then she suddenly realised the oddity of her remark and blushed.

He did not offer any explanations for his behaviour. He was very orthodox in his views. But his body language was different. When he looked at her now, tears had blurred her eyes. She marched off, seething with frustration. He followed her to the sitting room. He felt his efforts to persuade her to drop her romantic designs on him were proving fruitless. "You really have to sell yourself at a job interview. You need to apply for a new job. Many women are in part time jobs. By the way, did they offer you the job you applied for last month?" He asked with genuine concern. "I don't think my private concern is the issue here. Because I grew up in a happy family, love is important to me. It seems to me you're incapable of love. That what's in issue, Tom?" She said as she bravely blinked her tears.

A look passed between them. "Your ankle is swollen - I think the doctor ought to look at it." Tom pointed out. Silence descended over them again. Obviously she was in love with him. But he was in love with his work. He had always thought of their relationship as strictly platonic until last night. Now she was unable to think clearly in a sensible way because she was in love with him. But he was not in love with her. Suddenly she got up and sat on Tom's laps. "When the going was good Steve was the love of my life. Back in the States, we had a lovely time. By degrees, we noticed cracks in the wall of our relationship. We couldn't mend the cracks as repairs require skills. So, it was only consequential that I should fall in love with you when we settled in Abuja, even though you didn't notice it." She confessed unashamedly. "Relatives need time to grieve over loved ones they have lost. I know you're still grieving for Steve. You seem to have a very low opinion of your own abilities to cope without Steve. Your Morales is at low ebb." He said consolingly. Rosemary thumped the table in frustration. "You can mock me, but I'm willing to have a try! Your cold response has made a mockery of my love for you. Yet you seize the moral high ground to claim that your side of the argument is morally better than my side. It's clear that you don't love me," she said, touching his cheek.

"I love you, Rosemary not as a lover but as a brother would a sister. My argument hinges on moral fibre. We need inner strength to do what we believe to be right in this difficult situation. The issue is one of manners rather than morals." He explained. "Are you insinuating that I'm suffering from low morale? Are you accusing me of being a woman of loose morals?" she asked angrily. She stood up and began pacing the floor.

"Please calm down. We must give Steve a befitting burial as tradition demands. We can't be expressing romantic feelings when the dead has not been escorted home. That's the point you seem to be overlooking, Rosemary." Tom admonished her. "So that's the point? Steve is as dead as a door nail. I wish I could bring him back to life. There is no such thing as a love for life." she said in a flat monotone. "I'm afraid; this crisis won't be easy for us to cope with in the days ahead," he said with concern. It grieved him that he could do nothing to help her. "I know that in Africa life can be hard. Steve had a good life; but when he became a movie star in the States, his daily life changed and I was left in the cold, shut out of his life, emotionally..." she trailed off with tears welling in her eyes. "Life isn't like in the movies, you know. We have lessons in drawing from life. Flowers can bring a dull room back to life in the same way our inner resources can pull us through a crisis," he said stoically. "I feel pretty grim this morning. Go ahead and spill it out. I can take it," she challenged him. "I know it was a big change in lifestyle when you moved to Nigeria. But romantic feelings are not exactly life enhancing stimulant which can make you feel better and happier. Embrace reality and be sober," he advised as he rose up, picked his car key and started for the door. "I'm not finished with you yet," she shouted hoarsely after him.

Her eyes were full of fire. She stared moodily at the TV, seething silently in the corner of the sitting room, quietly chewing over the words Tom had spoken to her. She seldom watched TV these days. Her emotions seesawed from anger to fear because she found his remarks deeply wounding. Her rejection by Tom had made her feel worthless and unwanted. She felt she was not worthy of him in the same way no composer is considered worthy of the name until he had written an opera. As she moved to the open window, she gazed down in wonder at the city spread below her. For the first time she realised that Abuja was one of the beautiful cities of the world. The Zik Boulevard was a wide city street with trees on either side. Tom's house overlooked the Freedom Park and several buildings. The entire place, she noted silently, was overlaid with memories of her secret longings for Tom. Suddenly she sighed, overwhelmed by feelings of guilt. She had feelings of guilt about her inability to mourn the death of Steve. She wanted to tell Tom the whole truth- that she was no longer in love with Steve even before his death- but she had checked herself. She had felt it was not the right moment.

She moved restlessly from one foot to another because she was unable to stay still. Quickly, she left the house, and locked the door securely behind her. Soon it was getting dark. When Tom returned home, he found the door locked. He used his key to open it. Once inside, he went to the refrigerator and took a bottle of water. Returning to the sitting room, he switched on the TV. For several hours, he sat glued watching the movie showing on the TV. It worried him that Rosemary had not come home yet. Where people were concerned, his threshold of boredom was low. Nevertheless, he did not have to wait long as he heard Rosemary drive into the compound. When she entered the sitting room, she was clutching two shopping bags. "Where have you been? I was worried about you," Tom said, getting up to help her with the bags. "Don't worry about me. I can take care of myself," she replied, smiling. She was friendly, but a bit excitable. "Where have you been? I've been worried sick. You had me worried for a moment; I thought you were going to do something stupid." Tom said, taking the bags to the kitchen.

"Can I sit down? I'm worn out," she said as she sat on the sofa. She did not have the strength to talk any further. "How would you like your steak done?" Tom shouted from the kitchen. She did not answer. She looked vulnerable sitting there on her own. Suddenly, she felt a presence behind her as she bent down to shake a pebble out of her shoe. Looking at her shoe, she remembered she took a size 5 in shoes. Although from time to time she glanced at the TV, she pretended an interest she did not feel. The sitting room was preternaturally quiet for her in spite of the movie showing on the TV.

She uttered a wordless sound of despair as a deep sense of despair overwhelmed her. She knew that one harsh word from Tom tonight would send her into the depths of despair. For the profundity of her misery was not lost on her. Yet she believed that everything in life was fated. Because she felt that fate had been unkind to her, a sense of fatality gripped her. She reasoned that Tom's abrupt change of attitude had left her floundering helplessly. Reflecting upon this, she left the room with a flounce. Her rejection, she thought, was expected but it was hurting nevertheless.

2

Tom was in the kitchen preparing dinner when he heard the sound. It was a shrill voice. "Wait for me!" Rosemary shrilled. He made a rush for her room. When he entered her room, he could see she had been crying. "I should have seen it coming," he muttered to himself. Immediately she saw Tom, she let out a piercing shriek. "You ought to see a doctor about your condition. I hate to see you unhappy," Tom said without emotion. Rosemary shuffled her feet and blushed with shame. "Are you seeing anyone?" she asked suddenly. He did not see the joke if the question was intended as a joke. Quickly, she shrugged him away angrily. Turning away he called an ambulance to come to number 34, Zik Boulevard immediately. Soon the paramedics arrived. Rosemary was shrieking abuse at him as the paramedics carried her away.

When he resumed preparation of dinner in the kitchen, he refused to lose control of his emotions. He only felt betrayed by Rosemary. The event of this night tested both his physical and mental endurance. What should he do now? He wondered. For, he knew without a shadow of doubt that he could not depend on her to deal with the situation all by herself. He was very conscious of the problems involved. He had always tried to keep a sense of proportion. Tonight he was afraid that his excuses were wearing a little thin because Rosemary had heard them so many times before.

He did not eat much dinner. Of course, he rarely ate a big dinner when he had a crisis sitting on his lap. Tom even admitted that the meals he cooked were always nourishing but never particularly appetizing. His appetite had almost gone tonight when it became apparent that Rosemary had finally flipped under the pressure of her emotional weight. He was aware that he was in no-win situation. Was he right to be cautious in his relationship with Rosemary? Was he right to have told her right off what he thought of her? As he stared rigidly ahead, he sighed and muttered, "If only I could have helped put matters right. Is it ever right to reject a woman's love?" He knew he had made a terrible mess of the situation. And he was acutely aware that nothing could make up for the loss of true friendship. In Steve he had lost a friend and now he was about to lose the friendship of Rosemary. He had to make it up with her tomorrow.

Thus resolved, he slept on the sofa for four hours. The next day, early in the morning, Tom got dressed and drove to the hospital to see Rosemary. He arrived at an inopportune moment. Rosemary was last night being kept under sedation in the hospital. He waited for several hours before she was woken by the sound of someone moving around. "Hello, Rosemary, how are you feeling now?" Tom asked cheerfully. "I'm just fine, sweetheart," she replied, smiling. She still had a lot of feeling for him. He reached out his hand to touch her. His fingers closed around the soft flesh of her arm. In response she called up her last reserves of strength and sat up. A fleeting moment of happiness crossed her face. She edged towards him and suddenly she kissed him with unusual fervour. "What did you do that for?" he asked, feeling idiotic at his own voice. She only replied with a smile. But he loved the way she smiled.

"What is the diagnosis of your case?" Tom asked, slowly withdrawing his fingers from her arm. "I'm waiting for the result of the doctor's diagnosis. An accurate diagnosis was made after a series of tests last night," she replied confidently. "In any case, try to get some rest." Tom advised her. "I know. The doctor told me to rest. I can rest easy," she replied. "Sleep is the best restorative there is. You need to get some sleep. By the way, I must be getting home," Tom said, rising up from the bed. "I'll like to go home with you. I don't want to be away from home for too long, Tom," she said, sitting back in the bed. "The final decision whether to go home or not rests with the doctors. Just relax. I'll check-up on you tomorrow," he reassured her. As he turned to leave, she drew him back, pointed to her cheek and said, "Give me a peck." She smiled broadly. "I wish you get –well- soon," he said, trying to move away from her. But she held close to him and pressed her cheek to his.

Tom knew the chemistry between them just wasn't right. Conflicting emotions churned inside him. His feeling for her was close to pity. Without a word, he left the hospital with almost indecent haste. With the way she was going, he felt she needed intensive care for several days. His car purred away as he drove through the IBB Boulevard. One of the beauties of living on the IBB Boulevard was that it was so peaceful. Trees lined both sides of the wide street. Dotted everywhere on this Boulevard were beautifully painted houses. The essential character of the Boulevard had been carefully preserved by the Abuja Development Authority. Suddenly Tom remembered he had not checked his emails for a couple of days. The internet had become part of his everyday life. He drove to a nearby internet cafe. Adjacent to the cafe was a restaurant and he decided to have his lunch as well.

The next day he visited Rosemary again in the hospital. This time around he brought some apples, mangoes, oranges and cakes for her. He also bought flowers. "I just love it when you bring me presents!" she said, hugging him warmly.

"You're going to love these fruits," Tom said, placing the fruit basket on the bedside table. "What seems to be the matter with you?" he asked with concern. "The doctors found nothing. The results of the tests were all negative." She replied as she took some cake from the fruit basket and nibbled at it. "Did you hear the storm last night?" Tom asked. "Yes, I did. I lay awake all night; thinking about you," she said with a smile on her face as she edged closer to him. "I'm getting you a job in a newspaper. I think you'll like it," Tom said as he looked her in the eye. "That'll be splendid. What's the position?" she asked excitedly. "Advice Columnist," he replied. "Oh, I see. That means I'll become an agony aunt who writes in reply to people's letters about their personal problems," she elaborated. "Precisely," he concurred.   "That's Ok. Please proceed with the application process," she said. "Don't get excited yet," Tom cautioned her. "I'm really excited at the prospect of working again. I think I'll find the job exciting," she enthused.

He did not argue with her. He knew she had been going through a bad patch recently. She had constantly been strapped for cash ever since she lost her job and had to depend on Steve for handouts. The prospect of getting a new job filled her with joy. Suddenly she looked at her hands. The skin on her hands was soft.

She remembered it all. She was very bitter about losing her job. It was indeed a bitter disappointment for her. The employees whose appointments were terminated had prepared to fight for their rights. They had complained about the unfair termination of their jobs. Rosemary had wept bitterly when she returned home that fateful day. Now as she gazed into vacancy, she realised how much she needed a job. Tears streaked her face. Tom immediately noticed and edged towards her. "You're crying again. You need something to cheer you up. I know just the thing you need," Tom said soothingly. "You don't know how much a new job means to me. Life seems so unfair," she said blinking back tears. He held her hand in a vice like grip. "Recent events seem to confirm your opinion. I'm expecting Julia, my secretary, to bring some documents to me for signing." Tom said. "Here or at home?" she asked with interest.

"At home, of course," Tom said innocently. "I feel sick with jealousy," she said, slowly moving away from him. "There's no need for you to feel jealous, Rosemary. You know I live an entirely virtuous life," Tom replied. "You don't understand women at all. Jealousy is the working capital of every woman whose love is scorned," she said, pressing the bell to get the attention of the nurse on duty.

Tom realised that his remark had jolted her into action. His asking Julia to come to his house was in her judgment the wrong thing to do. For the first time, he admitted that they were both caught up in a whirling vortex of emotion.

When the nurse entered her private ward, Rosemary was gathering her things. "Nurse, please tell the doctor to discharge me. I'm going home," she said in a commanding tone. "No, Madam you're not strong enough to be discharged. All the same, I'll talk to the doctor about it," the nurse said as she hurriedly left the room.

Tom looked at her in the eye and said, "Don't be so childish!" "There's no point complaining now-we're leaving immediately in any case," she replied. "Don't be ridiculous!" Tom retorted. "I've made up my mind, Tom. Don't try to persuade me to retract my words." she said with a note of finality in her voice.

"In that case, there's no point discussing it." Tom said indignantly.

Soon the nurse returned with a note. The nurse handed the note over to Rosemary. She read it. The note in effect stated that she had discharged herself against medical advice. "Damn it. It's none of your damn business!" she retorted.

Turning to the nurse, Tom quietly said, "Send the hospital bills to me, please." "Shall we go? I'm ready when you are!" she said as her eyes flashed with excitement. Tom picked up the fruit basket and made for the door.

They got a flat on the way home. They had to stop to fix it. It amazed her that he could be so calm at a time like this. As she watched him from the corner of her eye, she noticed his face was etched with tiredness. Her heart went out to him.

Four days after Steve's death, she still felt empty. The void left by her husband's death was yet to be filled. In the shade of a pine tree, she stood staring emptily into space. Her emotions veered between fear and anger. She wondered at her mood swings. At the moment she knew there was an aching emptiness in her heart.

"Please get into the car. I've fixed the flat," Tom said. She got into the car. "Please use your seat belt," Tom directed. They rode in total silence all the way home.

"Go inside the house, dear. I'll get your things and the fruit basket," "Thanks," she muttered as she alighted from the car.

A smile lifted the corner of his mouth. Not long after their return from the hospital, Julia announced her arrival with a knock at the door. Rosemary eyed her jealously. Panic seized her as she realised that Julia was dazzlingly beautiful. She appeared to be in her early thirties.

Eagerly she stood and moved towards Julia. "It is a pleasure to welcome you to our home," she greeted Julia, smiling. "Sit down and make yourself at home." Tom said to Julia. "Here are the documents you requested for, Sir," Julia said edging towards Tom.

Rosemary watched to see what would happen next. Her expression was watchful and alert. Tom showed no visible sign of emotion. Rosemary looked at the bundle of documents. As if she was struck by thunderbolt, Julia turned to face Rosemary. "My condolences go to you on the death of your husband. May God grant you the fortitude to bear the irreparable loss," She said with emotion laden voice.

"Thanks for your concern," she replied, as she snuggled her head on to Tom's shoulders. She was on the verge of tears. "I had no appreciation of the problem you faced," Julia consoled her. "I'm feeling a whole lot better," she replied as she now lay pliant in Tom's arms. It was a knee jerk reaction on her part. It was meant to send a strong signal to Julia. As if that was not enough, she traced the contours of his face with her finger. His face was contorted with embarrassment.

At this point, Julia felt her stomach knot with resentment. She pranced out of the sitting room on the pretext of going to the ladies. "I don't know what you think you're doing," Tom rebuked her. "You don't have to pretend. Didn't you notice anything suspicious in her behaviour?" she retorted. He found himself cornered by her on this point as he had no ready answer to give to her.

When Julia returned to the sitting room, she made an empty gesture aimed at pleasing Rosemary. "I'm really pleased that you're feeling better," Julia said with a hint of sarcasm in her voice. "There's no need to be sarcastic," Rosemary replied as she disentangled herself from Tom's arms.

Turning to Tom, Julia said, "It really annoys me when people forget to say thank you. I'd better slap some make up on before I go home."

Rosemary struggled to articulate her thoughts. Her mouth was contorted in a snarl. "Don't insult me, Julia," she said spitefully.

"I'm sorry that your husband lost his life in that accident. Stop feeling sorry for yourself and think about other people for a change." Julia advised her. "Is this a social visit, or is it business? Tom, I hold you liable for this insult she's pouring on me," she said as she turned to Tom. He hardly dared to venture an opinion. Instead he merely shrugged his shoulders.

"Tom, I'm ashamed of you. You've shown yourself to be ready to make compromises in matters of the heart. You shouldn't be seen to have any affection for your secretary, it's quite demeaning, to say the least," she said, letting her hair loose and it fell around her shoulders. She was in a vile mood.

Tom was embittered that she had dared to cast a slur on his character. When he spoke, his bitterness showed through. "You need to build your self-esteem. Most of your problems are self inflicted," he said smiling, but his eyes retained a look of solemnity. He rose from the sofa and left the sitting room.

Rosemary exercised all her self-restraint and kept quiet. The recent death of her husband and the rejection of her affections by Tom were two events which left her on the verge of having a nervous breakdown. Veins showed through her pale skin. Quickly she went to the refrigerator and took a bottle of red wine and poured a generous quantity in a wine glass. She gulped it and quickly refilled her glass.

"The dangers of what you're doing are self- evident," Julia pointed out.

She retorted, "Don't dare you judge me! You don't know how I feel."

Unperturbed, Julia continued, "I know exactly how you feel..." Rosemary interrupted her, "Oh, no, you don't. You don't know what it is to lose your husband, job and on top of that a man you love resents you. So, don't tell me you know how I feel. So stop patronizing me. Get it into your damn skull!" she said angrily.

Tom soon returned to the sitting room. "You're drinking again, Rosemary. I don't know what you think you're doing. Responsibilities are not sloughed off so easily," he cautioned as he resumed sorting out the documents Julia had brought. "Look, Sir, I have to go now. A letter arrived for you this morning," she said handing it over to Tom. Quickly he tore it open. It was a notice of interview for the position of Advice columnist in one of the dailies. He had applied for the position through a very close friend of his. He had made the application on behalf of Rosemary.

"It's for you, Rosemary. Your interview notice," he announced cheerfully. He handed her the envelope with mock solemnity. There was a sparkle of excitement in her eyes. She unfastened the belt loosely around her waist. Tom noticed that she was both charming and susceptible. As she received the envelope, she held on to his arm for support. She knew opportunities such as this did not come every day.

"I feel almost ashamed that I've been so lucky. To whom should I address my letter of availability for the interview?" she asked no one in particular.

"Would she take it amiss if I offered to help?" Julia asked Tom. "Honestly, I do not arrogate to myself the right to decide for her," he replied without commitment. Turning to Rosemary, Julia promised; "I'm going to help you again. In any case, you're sadly mistaken about me." Tom knew he could trust Julia. He had always thought of her as pliable. She was a sensible lady.

In the meanwhile, Rosemary was prancing around with the interview letter. "This is just the opportunity I've been waiting for. I'll be famous one day, just you wait!" she asserted as she accidentally knocked her drink flying. Taking the cue, Julia started for the door. Tom followed her. "Are you trying to say you want to rid of me? My marriage to Steve was a mistake, if you ask me. I hated the label housewife back in the States. My life now seems empty without you. Let your heart rule your head, Tom." she shouted as she heard the door close.

Rosemary had longed to find somebody who understood her problems and in Tom she thought she had found such a person. She wore a scarf loosely knotted around her neck. As she sat on the floor, overwhelmed by her sense of misery, she began to sob. Her sob soon turned to sniffs. This twist of fate was certainly a crisis for which she was totally unprepared.

When Tom returned that night, he handed her a pack of dinner he brought from a Chinese takeaway. In her lucid moment, she came to Tom.

"I'm sorry; I shouldn't have lost my temper. I was in the gall of jealousy when I saw your new secretary, Julia. She is an absolute knockout. You can be married and still be plenty lonely. It's the plain unvarnished truth." She said with mouthful of food.

"Some things are better left unsaid. Who knows what changes tomorrow may bring? Sleep well. Goodnight, Rosemary," he said as he went to his room.

3

The day had dawned bright and clear with the promise of warm, sunny weather. Rosemary wore her hair loosely knotted on top of her head. She had an interview this morning for the Advice Columnist job. Her gaze drifted around the sitting room as soon she entered, fully dressed for the interview. Tom was sitting on a sofa going through the papers.

"Hey, dude, what's up? Can I have a drink? I mean soft drink. I drank far too much last night," she said, beaming with smile. "Don't be deluded into thinking that you are out of danger yet. It's not a healthy thing to go against the weight of medical advice or opinion," he spoke so slowly and without inflection as he went to the kitchen. She observed that he was casually dressed in jeans and a T-shirt.

He quickly fixed breakfast for her. Breakfast consisted of three slices of bread and a cup of tea. She went into the kitchen in search of a drink. She took a drink from the glass and then put it down. Hurriedly she ate her breakfast. As his eyes lingered on the diamond ring on her finger, she gave him an imploring look. "Prejudices can easily become implanted in the mind," she said lamely.

Quickly he navigated the discussion to another subject. "I'm confident that you'll get the job," he said sincerely. His sincerity impressed her. Suddenly his cell phone rang. As he took the call, Rosemary's curiosity was aroused by the mysterious phone call. "It's your mum. She couldn't reach you on your cell phone. She'll be arriving in the evening. My car is overdue for a service," he said.

"I have to go and get her from the airport after the interview," she said. "Hurry up and get dressed. The company has a strict dress code," he advised her. "I'm fully dressed," she replied as she took her handbag and headed for the door. At the door, she lingered for a few minutes and took a perfunctory glance at him. "Don't drive so fast. Drive carefully. I wish you great success. Come out of the interview in flying colours," he cheerfully said. "Trust me, sweetheart, I'd like to take this employment opportunity," she replied as she stepped outside the sitting room, closing the door gently behind her. The faint smell of her perfume lingered in the room several minutes after she had gone.

She got to the venue of the interview in good time. Taking her courage in both hands, she opened the door and walked in. She seemed outwardly composed. As soon as she entered the interview room she observed an interview panel of five; three women and two men.

"Please sit down and let's get started. We have been deluged with over two thousand applications for this job," one of the panelists told her. Another member of the panel sized her up. "You have a good sense of dress code. This company has a strict dress code. Briefly tell us about yourself and why you think you are the most qualified and suitable candidate for this position of Advice Columnist."

"I'm a focused professional who will like to add value to the stakeholders of this organization. To give advice in reply to people's letters about their personal problems, I believe such advice should come from the heart. I've just lost my husband barely a week ago. I've suffered contradictions of life. I've become stronger to give advice to people who may be hurting as I do because my job entails sharing my life experiences with others. Back in the States, I worked for the **New York Times** as a freelancer covering living conditions in the ghetto. Both my qualifications and experience make me eminently qualified for this position," She answered confidently.

"In a word or two tell us what you think about absolute personal freedom and why you need this job." Another panelist put the question to her.

"The idea of absolute personal freedom is an illusion. Compromise is an inevitable part of life. Work is basic to the human condition; it's both biologic and social," she stated brilliantly. "What's your chief motivation when you write?" another panelist asked. "I'm concerned to write about situations that everybody could identify with," she answered the question with confidence.

"Let's test your knowledge of the information communication technology. Describe the typical computer equipment." "The computer has a processor and random access memory and a hard disk capacity which comes with modem and speech recognition system. The multimedia system includes a sound card and a graphics card for high resolution colour display." Rosemary explained.

"Tell us how you can get started when using the computer." "PC users should log on to the network before entering their username and password. Next you load the programme into the computer. Save your files onto your hard disk and back them up into flash drive. You should store important data on the central file server." She summed up.

"When things go wrong, tell us or describe the steps you'll take to sort them out," another panelist cut in. "If you're not able to log in, simply shut the server down. You'll lose all your files if the system keeps crashing. You'll need to switch off and reboot. The computer will indicate error if user name contains invalid character. Virus in the software can corrupt the hard disk," she answered.

"Tell us about User interface," one of the ladies on the panel chipped in. "Click on the window to make it active. You can run several applications at the same time. You should select New from the File menu when you want to create a new document. Always insert the cursor at the beginning of the line and use the mouse to drag the icon to a new position. By clicking on the scroll bar, you'll scroll up or down the text." Rosemary spoke in a confidential tone, her voice audible.

"Tell us what you do with your time on the internet," the Chairman of the panel asked as he looked Rosemary in the eye. "I spend my free time surfing the net, making use of search engines. I also check my emails. I can also read feature articles on the net. The social media is there for me to use in my social interactions," she answered boldly. When the Interview Panelists asked questions which were of private nature, Rosemary refused to answer such questions that infringed on her private affairs.

The Chairman of the interview panel summed up: "I think we should tell you that imperfect articles are rejected by our quality control. You may do as you wish outside working hours. You'll have to review your training needs with your line manger. We are pleased with your performance and our legal department will have you sign a confidentiality agreement with us. On behalf of my colleagues here, I say congratulations. You may resume a day after tomorrow." As members of the panel filed out of the room, Rosemary sat down to conceal the fact she was trembling. She was overjoyed at her success. Tears of joy streaked her face. She knew that a whole new world of possibilities was ahead of her.

Regaining her composure, she rose and left the room. She tried in vain to keep her emotions tightly reined in. Climbing inside her car, she powdered her face and put on her lipstick. Thereafter, she reversed around the corner and headed for the airport.

When Rosemary returned that evening with her mother, Tom immediately noticed that her mother was a pleasant woman in early middle age. He guessed she would be about 65 years.

"You're welcome, Ma," his voice was pleasant and cultivated. "Thank you, my son. Rosemary has told me how kind you've been to her, especially in this trying moment," she said. Tom helped get her suitcase from the car. He reached out to Rosemary and gave her a peck. She felt overwhelmed by his kindness.

Inside the sitting room, Mrs. Brown, for that was the name of Rosemary's mother- was taking in the scene. Tom could see that Mrs. Brown had been a beauty in her day. "Get a drink for Mama," Tom told Rosemary. She went to the refrigerator and brought a bottle of wine. She also fetched three wine glasses. "Tom, how is your business?" Mrs. Brown asked. "Business isn't good but we are managing to hold our own," he replied pleasantly. He drew the cork out of the bottle.

Turning to Rosemary, he asked her, "How did the interview go today? Why are you so bright and cheerful today?" "They told me informally that I had got the job." He was overjoyed at her success. "Let's toast to your success," he said. The ladies exchanged confidences. A smile brightened Rosemary's face. Tom quickly interposed himself between Rosemary and her mother. He filled the glasses and handed a glass each to Rosemary and her mother. "To your success, my lady," Tom gave the toast. They clanked their glasses as they all drank. Her heart was brimming with happiness. She needed the drink badly. Her mouth felt as dry as a bone.

"Tell me more about the interview," Tom prodded her. "They signed a confidentiality agreement with me today. I'm resuming a day after tomorrow," she announced cheerfully as she emptied the glass the second time. Her mother noticed. "My daughter, be careful. Wine is not good for women. As a retired senior nursing officer I've seen the evils of alcohol," she cautioned.

Tom seized the opportunity to declaim against the evils of alcohol. "Even though you've just got a new job, it's important you don't get drunk. Your drinking is getting to be a problem." "I have a right to be happy. I'd like to take this employment opportunity. Exciting possibilities will open up for me in this new job. No one should begrudge me my happiness. And you, Tom, I know you don't want to see me happy," she blurted out.

Tom didn't reply. Instead, he turned on his heel and left the room. Mrs. Brown was alarmed. "Nobody hates you. It's all in your imagination. Tom is such a handsome and pleasant young man," her mother said soothingly. Rising from the sofa, Mrs. Brown hastily left the sitting room. She met Tom in the kitchen.

"Have you tried patching up things with her? I think she loves you." Mrs. Brown said. Looking Tom in the eye, she hinted; "My daughter has no inner resources and hates being alone. She needs a man in her life. There is an aching void in her heart. Give her a shoulder to lean on, my son. By the way, nothing beats home cooking. What are you cooking for dinner, Tom?" Mrs. Brown cajoled him.

"Do you like cooking, Mama? Rosemary still hasn't learned how to cook. Dinner won't be long. It's cooking now. I'll just add the meat and let it cook for ten minutes," Tom said, beaming with smile.

Just then Rosemary sauntered by, looking as if she had all the time in the world. "I don't mind helping, but I draw the line at doing everything myself," she offered. "You can boil the vegetables, eggs and rice. Simmer the carrots in a large pan of water," Tom directed. "Don't tell me what to do!" she retorted. "Rosemary, watch your tongue. I think we're owed an apology," Mrs. Brown said. "I'll steam the fish. Rice is usually prepared by steaming. I'll fry the onion and garlic for five minutes. You know, Tom, the smell of frying bacon makes my mouth watery. And you, Rosemary, tender your unreserved apology to Tom, right now," Mrs. Brown ordered as she looked Rosemary intently in the eye.

"Mum, Tom drives me crazy," she protested. "Do what I tell you," Mrs. Brown insisted. Rosemary said nothing. Her silence infuriated Tom even more. "Mama, I don't need her apologies," he said and shrugged indifferently. Rosemary was left feeling inept and inadequate. "My grandmother always used to bake on Saturdays. You know, you can bake cakes or potatoes in the dry heat of an oven or a fire. I'll bake cakes tomorrow. Turn the heat down or what you're cooking will burn," Mrs. Brown lectured. Tom scrubbed out the pans and left them to drain. Then he turned the heat down. Rosemary leaned forward to scrutinize their faces. She was reluctant to confess her ignorance.

"Dinner is ready. Rosemary, go and arrange the dinner ware on the dining table," Mrs. Brown told her daughter. Dinner was served. They huddled together around the dining table, eating and conversing. Rosemary did not eat much dinner. "My dear, are you full?" Mrs. Brown asked her daughter with concern in her voice. "I never eat a big dinner, Mum," she answered politely.

"It's your turn to cook dinner tomorrow," Mrs. Brown told her daughter. As Rosemary rose from table, she turned to Tom. "I'm sorry, I was rude to you. I think I'm suffering from mood swings," she apologized. "I understand. I don't bear any grudges against you. It's easy to oversimplify the issues involved," he replied coolly.

"My Children, please take your seats. I've come to see the family of Steve, my late son-in-law. Tell me if you've heard the arrangements for the funeral." She looked from her daughter to Tom. "I understand the funeral service is slated for next week at VGC Chapel Lagos. Rosemary isn't in the know of the arrangements because she suffered shock and was treated for it." Tom said as he stopped and watched Rosemary's reaction. "Oh, poor Child! Why didn't you send for me?" Mrs. Brown asked with concern.

"You can never entirely eliminate human error and oversight. But my gratitude goes to Tom. He's been a pillar of support to me. I don't know what I would have done without his support to me. On a serious note, I don't know what I would have done without his support," She said. She didn't worry overmuch about details. Looking at Tom, Mrs. Brown was full of gratitude. "Thank you, my son. May the good LORD bless you," she said. "Now my daughter, don't overdo the salt in your food when you cook for us. By the way, I'll stay with you, looking after you until you're well. By next week, I'll fly down to Lagos with you for the funeral. Go wash off the plates, before you retire for the night," Mrs. Brown finished at last. She smiled.

Tom observed that Mrs. Brown had a dimple which appeared whenever she smiled. As Rosemary took the dirty plates to the kitchen sink, Mrs. Brown confided in Tom; "My daughter lived a sheltered life in England. When my husband was alive, Rosemary was the delight of his eyes. He worked in a Specialist Hospital, actually St. Andrew's London. I worked as a senior nursing officer at St. Jude's Infirmary."

It was Tom's turn to inform Mrs. Brown about the recent behaviour of Rosemary. "Ever since her husband died, Rosemary has been behaving funny. She's completely infatuated with me. It isn't love. It's a passing infatuation. Our views are diametrically opposed on this issue. She has been driving me nuts with her amorous advances which I've vigorously resisted." He paused to gauge the impact of his words.

"Poor you! You don't know anything about the heart of a woman. A woman's heart is an open wound. Only care and tenderness can heal it. In the matters of the hearts, feelings are magnified beyond and above reason. We are first and foremost emotional beings. Reasons have no place in our hearts. Reasons reside in our heads. It's our hearts which make us human, tender, caring and loving. Out of the heart are the issues of life. Have a change of opinion of her and let your heart rule your head," Mrs. Brown lectured Tom, her maternal instincts fully activated.

"I'll remember that, Mama. Your room is next to Rosemary's. Good night, Ma." Tom responded as he rose and went to his room. "Goodnight, my son." She intoned. Mrs. Brown knew she had to do something to help her daughter regain her fractured dignity. She would talk to her in the morning. As for Tom, she would steer him to appreciate the delicate nature of matters of the heart.

Rosemary threw back the covers and leapt out of bed as she heard a knock on the door. She drew back the curtains and let the sunlight in. Just then her mother opened the door, peeped in and politely asked, "May I come in?" "Yes, mother. Good morning," she replied. Mrs. Brown moved a step closer to her daughter who sat on the edge of the bed. Rosemary looked at her mother with admiration. She observed that her mother's hair was close-cropped. Her parents were very close way back in England. They were a very close family. Mrs. Brown sat on the bed.

"My daughter, we need a clear understanding of the problems involved in your relationship with Tom. In any relationship, you have to make compromises," Mrs. Brown paused for a moment, and then said: "You're a woman inflamed with love. A woman feels with her heart."

Rosemary looked at her mother and smiled. "We can't make rules about our feelings. Can we?" she asked with her arms spread. A smile spread slowly across her face.

"No, we can't. We are emotional creatures," Mrs. Brown replied. "I love Tom intensely. I have no illusions about my feelings for him. Mum, I love him." Rosemary made a full confession of her love for Tom. There was a look of surprise and incredulity on Mrs. Brown's face. "My dear girl, you're too hasty," She cautioned her daughter.

"Mum, don't judge me harshly for the feelings of my heart. Perhaps I spoke too hastily. True love can never go wrong. Nothing evil can proceed from love," she stated as she lowered her voice reverentially.

"Yes, I know. We can't sit in judgment on our true feelings," Mrs. Brown reluctantly conceded the point. "Does Tom love you with equal intensity?" Mrs. Brown asked as she put a protective arm round her daughter's shoulders. "I'm not sure, Mum. He has no respect for my feelings," she responded. "Everyone has a right to be treated with respect. Maybe he'll reverse himself. Has he ever reversed himself? Mrs. Brown asked, puzzled.

"He has reversed himself on a dozen issues, Mum." She said without emotion. "Can you rely on him when it matters?" Her mother prodded. "Mum, you can rely on him to respond to a challenge." She stated confidently. Mrs. Brown chewed over the words in silence. She scanned her daughter's face anxiously. Tears blurred her daughter's eyes. Rosemary, she knew was a lovable child. Yet she was clearly in a lot of pain. She hoped with all her heart that things worked out for her daughter. It was heartbreaking to see her daughter wasting her life like this. She reached out to her daughter as she took her hands. "It's well my daughter. The storm would soon pass. Let me wipe away your tears," she said consolingly.

They were jolted out of their reverie as the door opened. Tom popped his head around the door and said hello; "Would you like tea or coffee?" Mrs. Brown replied, "Tea." "Do you take sugar in your tea?" Tom asked Mrs. Brown. "Yes," she responded. As he withdrew his head, Rosemary quickly added, "Two teas, please." She smiled at her mother. "See what I mean? Tom is a pleasant chap," Mrs. Brown said to her daughter.

"Mum, I need a shower- I won't take long," Rosemary said as she left the room and got into the shower cubicle. Soon Tom brought in the tea set with tea cakes. "Where is Rosemary?" He asked. "She's in the shower." "Of course, she is. I can hear her singing," Replied Tom pleasantly.

"I'd like to talk to you about a personal matter, Tom," Mrs. Brown said as she lowered her voice. "Please take a seat, my son." "Go on – I'm all ears," Tom said as he sat on a chair. Both tea set and tea cakes were on a side stool. Mrs. Brown added a teaspoonful of sugar to her tea. She stirred her tea.

"It's about Rosemary," she began. "I think she's in love with you. A woman's heart is a deep well. You must make efforts to draw water out of it. You ought to reciprocate her affections for you," she paused to let her words sink in. Tom kept twirling his moustache. Rosemary had showered and dressed. As soon as she entered the room, she had a silly grin on her face. At that moment she felt the first twitch of anxiety. She seemed anxious about the conversation between Tom and her mother. Tom admired her white blouse with frills at the cuffs. She twirled around in front of the mirror. Spontaneously, Tom got up, held her hand and twirled her around. She twisted a scarf around her head. Her eyes twinkled with merriment.

Nervously she twisted the diamond ring on her finger. She gave Tom a small twisted smile. In return he gave her a thin smile. Tom was conscious of the fact that she exuded sexual magnetism. "Your friendship is very important to me." Tom confessed. This was an attempt to appeal to her finer feelings. "You're my friend, Tom. You're a friend in need. Your support is greatly appreciated," she said and turned to look at her mother. Her mother was beaming with a smile.

Tom stepped back and his eyes coolly appraised the young woman before him. With a satisfied smile on his face, he said: "I love you, Rosemary. I'll always love you." "I feel as if my head is going around and I can't balance," she said. He spun around to face her. "Can I sit down? Your words have taken my breath away," she pleaded. He smiled sweetly and walked quickly away without further word.

She sat there on the bed, paralyzed with emotions. She could feel her heart pounding in her chest. "Come on, drink up your tea," her mother intoned excitedly. "Mum, is it wrong to love even when we are hurting inside?" she asked innocently as she edged towards her mother. Putting a protective arm around her daughter, Mrs. Brown said: "To love is to live. To love is to let go of our hurts. It's bliss. When we love truly we can never go wrong. For love is the aroma of life."

Rosemary turned and looked out of the window. She twisted the diamond ring on her finger. Her thoughts turned to her dead husband. She sighed regretfully; she had a twitch in her right eye. Turning to face the tea ware, she stretched to pour tea for herself.

4

Rosemary bore herself with dignity throughout the funeral. The funeral procession made its way to the VGC cemetery where the body of Steve was laid to rest. All through the funeral ceremony she was sidelined by Steve's family. The family had felt that her marriage to Steve was marriage of convenience. But she despised herself for being so cowardly when she had the opportunity to challenge them. Now some malicious rumours were circulating about her getting married soon. Whenever she remembered the attitude of Steve's family towards her when she and Steve returned to Nigeria, she groaned at the memory, suffering all over again in the excruciating embarrassment of those moments.

All she wanted now was to move on with her life. She looked back on the past without regret. So when the funeral was over, she hurried past without stopping. She noted that a week went past following the death of Steve and nothing had changed in their estimation of her. She concluded that the events of today were just a blur on her new found happiness. As she reflected on everything relating to her marriage, her eyes brimmed with tears. Her mother noticed her tears. "Take this handkerchief and dry your tears. It's all over. Pull yourself together my dear." She consoled her daughter.

All through the funeral Tom had discreetly stayed away from Rosemary as he was quite aware of her marital designs on him. Malicious rumours had even spread that he had designs on her. It happened that when the two of them were left alone after all the others had gone, she felt a surge of love and desire for him.

Now she felt an overwhelming desire to return home. She felt betrayed by her late husband's family; for she got nothing of value out of the marriage. No child. No property. No money. In her estimation it was a complete fiasco, a total failure. Even before Steve died she had become estranged from Steve's family.

As far as she was concerned, she had shown great courage and resilience in fighting back from a losing position to win the game of life. The difficulties in her way up merely strengthened her resolve to become the best she could ever be. In the last resort what really motivated her were her personal convictions about life. Her heart was a precious thing and she was determined to give it to the man who could cherish and keep it safe. In Tom she had found that man. But Tom would have to prove himself worthy of this trust. Her uncle in Lagos would acquaint Tom with the demands of her family tradition.

She made a resolution to visit her uncle and cousins while she was in Lagos. As they headed for the exit gate of the VGC Cemetery Lagos, Tom admitted silently that Rosemary had undergone an amazing metamorphosis from the awkward school girl whose pictures he had seen to a beautiful woman who was now walking beside him.

Nudging him a bit, she said, "Tom, Let's stop for lunch at my uncle's, I'm hungry." "That's all right. Tell your mum, OK." Tom advised. "She's aware of the arrangement to visit my uncle in Ikoyi," she responded. Outside the VGC Cemetery, he stopped and bought some flowers for her. Her eyes brightened. "You remember that day you told me, 'I love you, Rosemary. I'll always love you?'" She asked beaming with a smile. "Yes I remember it clearly. What happened?" He asked. "I felt as if my heart had stopped." She said and gave him a thin smile. They called a taxi and gave the address in Ikoyi.

Robertson Street was a highbrow residential area of Ikoyi, Lagos. There were large compounds with tree branches overhanging the buildings. Residents of the area were mostly retired senior government officials, judges, army generals and business moguls. Visitors to the area would scarcely hear any noise. The standby electricity generators were soundproof.

Chief Ote and his family lived in a six bedroom duplex on Robertson Street. For one heart stopping moment, Rosemary thought they were too late for the lunch. Mrs. Ote stood in front of the duplex, waiting for their arrival. "That's Aunty Maggie standing over there!" Rosemary said excitedly. As soon as Aunty Maggie saw Rosemary alight from the taxi, she spread her arms and Rosemary ran towards her. She held Rosemary in a warm embrace. "Oh my daughter, what heartache you've had to endure! Welcome." She said, looking over the young woman.

Releasing Rosemary from her embrace she reached over to Mrs. Brown and gave her a peck on the cheek. "Welcome, my dear," she said. "Please come into the house." She nodded welcome to Tom as she led her guests into the sitting room.

Chief Ote was lying sprawled in an arm chair, watching TV. He sat up as soon as the guests entered the sitting room. He got to his feet and held both Mrs. Brown and Rosemary in a warm embrace. "Welcome, my dears." He said pleasantly. Turning to Tom, he nodded welcome to him. He tried to disentangle his fingers from Rosemary hair. Mrs. Brown gently disengaged herself from his embrace. "Please sit down. Make yourselves comfortable." He said to the guests. He sat back in his arm chair.

"Edward is coming to lunch." Aunty Maggie announced cheerfully. Edward was their son. He became a doctor barely five years ago in England. At the moment he was working with the Lagos University Teaching Hospital, popularly called LUTH. Mrs. Ote was always proud of Edward. Arunma her daughter was a chartered Accountant with one of the big commercial banks.

"What shall we have for lunch?" Chief Ote asked, taking his eyes off the TV. "Rice, stew, roasted chicken and boiled potatoes. We'll just micro wave them for three minutes," Aunty Maggie said, dragging Mrs. Brown and her daughter towards the kitchen.

Chief Ote turned to look at Tom. "How do you find life in Abuja?" he asked. "My day to day life is not exciting. But I'm coping with the challenges." Tom said, noticing that the house had been lovingly restored. "We've lived here since we returned from England. You know my late brother, Dr Brown and I lived in England for years. I'm sorry; we should have started off by introducing ourselves." He said as an ingratiating smile spread across his face.

"Well, then I'm Chief Ote. I'm the chairman of Arunma Group of Companies and a father of two. I'm the younger and surviving brother of the late Dr Brown Ote who incidentally dropped Ote from his name to avoid the prejudiced and racial attitude of some Britons when he wanted to become a consultant physician for St. Andrews Specialist Hospital, London. Now let me hear you, my son." Chief Ote said.

Taking the cue, Tom cleared his throat and began. "I'm Tom Allison, a Principal Partner of Allison Associates, a firm of Estate Surveyors and Valuers based in Abuja. My father is late. He was until his death the Permanent Secretary in the Federal Ministry of Mines, Power and Industry. I'm single but seriously searching for my missing rib." He said and gave a small twisted smile. He kept twirling his moustache.

"Talking about searching for your missing rib, don't you find my little niece, Rosemary, attractive enough?" he asked as he gave a thin smile. Tom was startled by his question. He looked at Chief Ote with startled eyes. The first part of Tom's plan was to ingratiate him with the members of Rosemary's family.

"You look startled, Tom. We shouldn't be ashamed of the matters of the heart. The heart is a precious thing, especially the heart of a woman. We must handle the affairs of the heart with respect and tenderness," he said flatly.

Just then, the women came in with the prepared lunch. They set the dining table in order. Chief Ote and Tom lowered their voices to a whisper. "Where is Arunma?" Aunty Maggie asked her husband. "She is not down yet." He replied. He turned away and looked out of the window. "Arunma, Arunma!" Aunty Maggie called out to her daughter. Arunma rushed downstairs and burst into the kitchen. Her hair flowed down over her shoulders.

When she saw her cousin, Rosemary, she held her in a warm embrace.

"I think we can dispense with the formalities. Your boyfriend is charming." Arunma said smiling broadly. She lowered her voice to a whisper. "Do you love him? If you love each other, why not get married? Arunma asked excitedly. Rosemary and her cousin took some water from the refrigerator and some cutleries to the dining room where the rest were waiting for them.

Chief Ote said the grace and they began to eat lunch. "Edward called to say he would not be able to join us for lunch. He's on call this afternoon." Aunty Maggie announced. "Hey, you get a job yet?" Chief Ote asked Rosemary. "She's just started a new job," Mrs. Brown announced proudly. She quickly added, "She's an Advice Columnist in one of the dailies." "What's your standpoint as an Advice Columnist?" Aunty Maggie prodded Rosemary. "I'm writing from the standpoint of someone who knows what life is like in person." She responded. Eyes downcast, she continued eating and did not speak again.

Turning to Tom, Chief Ote asked, "How do you keep fit? Do you play tennis?" No, I don't. I do aerobics once or twice a week. I also play football on Saturdays," Tom said as he chopped off some pieces of meat from the roasted chicken. "I go swimming twice a week," Chief Ote said as he pushed a spoonful of rice into his mouth.

"Mum, let me have the melon to start with. I'll take some apples later." Arunma said to her mother. Aunty Maggie passed the plate of melon to her. "Can I help you, love?" Mrs. Brown asked her daughter as she stretched for the plate of potatoes. She then passed the plate to Rosemary.

"Do you like bananas?" Aunty Maggie asked Tom. "Thanks. I'll rather have pineapple," he responded.

When they had finished eating lunch, Chief Ote picked up his newspaper and started glancing through it. Suddenly all the lights went out. Quickly the security guard went out and put on the standby electricity generator. "Do you want a drink?" Chief Ote asked Tom. "Have you any idea where the rumour started?" Aunty Maggie asked Mrs. Brown. Chief Ote lowered his newspaper and looked around. "Get us some red wine, please," he directed his daughter, Arunma. She quickly fetched a bottle of red wine and two glasses. She drew out the cork, poured wine into the glasses and returned to the dining table where the rest of the women huddled together. Chief Ote sipped from his glass.

He turned to Mrs. Brown, "Your daughter is still hurting inside. I suggest you stay with her a couple of weeks before you return to Enugu." He advised. Quickly Aunty Maggie added, "It was brave of her to stand up to those bullies from Steve's family."

"Is it true you're in love with Tom, Rosemary?" Chief Ote asked in a tone of seriousness. Rosemary got up and jumped back like a startled rabbit. She was silent. Arunma looked at her cousin and her shoulders heaved with laughter. She quickly added, "My lovely cousin, tell us if you've lost your heart already to Tom." Rosemary turned away and looked out of the window.

Undaunted, Chief Ote proceeded to say, "Don't let me influence you either way. The belief that we should do our duty is deeply ingrained in most of us. We have a family tradition. If any man wants to take any of our daughters as a wife, he must fulfill the demands of our family tradition. When that's done, then, he may formally ask our daughter's hand in marriage." He paused to gauge the impact of his words.

"Uncle, what are the demands of the family tradition? How much are we talking about here?" Rosemary asked with interest. "Our family tradition does not necessarily involve money. After all your late father has a fortune stashed away in various bank accounts in England and Switzerland." He paused for effect. "Uncle, you mean my father left me a fortune and all these years you didn't tell us? Why, uncle?" Rosemary asked her uncle. She looked at him with startled eyes.

"Your late father left instructions to the banks directing when they should release the money to you and your mother. It was kept in time deposit accounts. Those deposits are now mature. It's all there for you and your mother. I will tell you about that diamond on your finger. I don't want any gold digger to come after your fortune. Any man who claims to love you must show himself worthy of you, my dear." He reassured Rosemary. She nervously twisted the diamond ring on her finger. She blinked back tears.

'My dear young man, you'll have to participate in the Oso festival held every November in our hometown, Ozu Abam. Until you've done that, I want you to stay away from my niece. We have a guest room if you want to stay over," Chief Ote finished as he dropped the bombshell. There was a deafening silence.

Arunma put her arm around Rosemary's shoulders and said, "I hope with all my heart that things work out for you." Tears ran down Rosemary's eyes. Nervously she twisted the diamond ring on her finger.

Tom comported himself with great dignity. He frowned, making an effort to compose himself. He seemed outwardly composed. With an effort of will he resisted the temptation of criticizing the family tradition. He quickly summed up the situation and took control. "Trust is a vital component in any relationship. To give someone else your heart is a function of trust. I haven't yet plucked up the courage to ask Rosemary to marry me. I'll like to sleep over it. I have a flight to catch this evening," he said, standing up to shake hands with Chief Ote.

"Don't take offence at what I said. No decision will be taken on the matter until you're ready to fulfill the demands of our family tradition. In the meantime you have a standing invitation to visit the family anytime," Chief Ote said in a calm voice.

There were tears and embraces as he said goodbye to them. He looked at Rosemary and walked slowly away from her. Arunma opened the door and Tom walked away. Outside he hailed a taxi. "Take me to MMA2," he said flatly. He wallowed in self-pity and despair. He felt self-pity because he thought the family would henceforth see him as a gold digger now that it had been revealed that Rosemary had inherited a fortune from her late father. His despair arose from his inability to ask Rosemary to marry him. From his standpoint the stakes for asking Rosemary's hand in marriage had been raised a notch higher. What was this Oso festival all about? What was at stake here? Perhaps one day he might return to Chief Ote to find out what it was all about.

The memory of that day still haunted Tom. It had been two years since that incident happened and he had already moved on with his life. Rosemary had come to despise him as a man without courage. For, she felt that a man, who could not stand up for the woman after his heart, was unworthy of her affection.

As he got up from the sofa he called Esther on his cell phone; "Hello Sweetheart, I'll attend your birthday party tomorrow. Goodnight." She drowsily responded, "Ok. See you tomorrow, dear." He went to the kitchen to fix himself dinner.

Tom woke up with a really bad head this morning. He awoke early after a disturbed night. He looked tired, disheveled and pale. He was acutely aware that Rosemary had loved him at a distance for years.

He picked his cell phone and wished Esther "Happy Birthday." He promised to bring her a birthday card and present at her birthday party later in the evening.

He cooked a breakfast of bacon and eggs. It was a light breakfast that he ate. Nowadays he was overworking himself as he recently pulled his firm back from the brink. He quickly drained the last of his tea. He got up and got dressed in suit. He had a lot to do in the office today. He had appointments with several clients. And he knew he was driving himself too hard.

There were two cars parked in the drive. He climbed into the **Ford Escape** and drove to the office. Tom Allison Associates had its offices in a high rise office block in the Central Business District of Abuja. He sat behind his desk and approached his work with total concentration. The phone call from Esther really made his day.

"Rosemary is coming to my birthday party this evening. It wasn't easy to persuade her to come. I'm expecting you too. Akon will also be here. See you later," Esther said as the line went dead. His office was the room at the other end of the corridor. Julia, his secretary had gone on leave for two weeks. So he juggled a lot of things in the office.

It was a long tiring day. He went home and refreshed himself with a cool shower. As he drove towards the Central Business District, Abuja, a Mercedes Benz B-Class car swept past with Rosemary at the wheel. Close to the Shehu Musa Yar'dua Centre, venue of the birthday Party, he could hear sounds of revelry.

Esther was clearly reveling in all the attention. She wore a print blouse and jeans. Tom walked across the hall to say hello to her. After exchanging the usual pleasantries, they got down to serious discussion. The hall reverberated with the sound of music and dancing. He gave her a birthday card and an envelope containing some money. She thanked him for his kind gesture. At the far corner of the hall he saw Akon chatting with some acquaintances. He excused himself and made his way to where Akon stood.

"Hello Akon, you're here," Tom greeted. "I'm glad you came, Tom. Tell me what's happening to property value in Abuja." Akon enquired.

"Property values have suffered another reverse," Tom replied. "Is the trend towards privatization reversible?" Akon asked. "I don't know, but it's an idea that may be worth revisiting at a later date. Opinions diverge greatly on this issue," Tom opined. Akon nudged him gently. Rosemary and her friend, Susan sauntered by, looking as if they had all the time in the world.

"Don't pay any attention to her- she's just being difficult." Akon advised. "We have our differences, but she's still my friend," Tom pointed out. "Why don't you settle your differences and be friends again? Akon retorted.

"It's different now than it was two years ago. She looks different from what I'd expected," Tom stated. The loudspeaker seemed to distort his voice. "I hate to disillusion you, but not everyone is as honest as you," Akon said as he took a glass of wine from the waiter who was carrying a tray.

"This is confidential, but I know I can rely on your discretion. I think I still have some feelings for her," Tom confided in Akon. There was a distant look in his eyes; his mind was obviously on something else. "My good friend, follow your heart," Akon said turning to chat with a friend.

Rosemary and Susan stood in a corner sipping fruit juice. Suddenly Susan cast a fleeting glance at Tom. "I don't like Tom, and it would be dishonest of me to pretend otherwise," Susan said, her attention still trained on Tom. "We should cherish pleasant memories of the past. Deep down in my heart, I still love him," Rosemary confessed. "If you take my advice you'll have nothing more to do with him," Susan advised.

Rosemary dug her hands deeper into her pockets. She wore a revealing blouse and flared trousers. The MC's voice reverberated around the hall; "Help yourselves, everybody! Dig in. The birthday buffet is ready. We have enough food and drinks for everyone."

Tom dug his fork into the steak. He ate appetizingly. He sipped wine from his glass. As Tom turned, his eyes locked with Rosemary's. They looked at each other with distrust. At the same moment, Rosemary sipped fruit juice and nibbled at a slice of cake. There and then Tom decided to break the ice. He summoned up his courage and went over to where Rosemary and Susan sat at a table.

"Hello Rosemary, I'm sorry to disturb you, but can I talk to you for a moment?" Tom asked. Her eyes burned darkly. It disturbed her to realize that she was still missing him even after two silent years. "Stop dithering and get on with it," she said calmly. The coldness and distance in her voice took him by surprise. "Sometimes reality and fantasy are hard to distinguish." Tom said pleasantly. His voice was quite moderate but every word was distinct.

"How do you mean?" Rosemary challenged. "Newspapers are often guilty of distorting the truth. Your writing sometimes is really difficult to read. What was the genetic profile you alluded to in your writing in the last edition of your column?" Tom prodded. He spoke slowly and with great difficulty. She overcame her natural diffidence and spoke with great frankness.

"You recall I was writing in response to a paternity question put to me about a young lady. DNA is the biological blueprint of living organisms, including human beings. It is the genetic material that is present in nearly every cell of the human body. Irrespective of the cell or tissue source, DNA from any particular individual is consistent throughout the body of that individual. It is extremely unlikely that any two individuals will have the same genetic makeup unless they are identical twins. This property of our genetic profile is utilized in identifying the source of DNA in forensic investigations," She finished at last. She dug into her bowl of pasta.

"Does the time we spent together mean anything to you?" Tom asked pointedly. "The time we spent together is now a distant memory," she stated flatly. "How can you easily forget the time we spent together? You're mistaken, Rosemary. I'm not just one of your friends; I'm your only true friend," he said excitedly. He laughed, revealing a line of white teeth. Her emotion rose in revolt. "What do you want from me?" she asked with concern.

"There are two points which I wanted to make; first, our friendship should be kept in constant repair. Second, our present relationship is in want of a total review," Tom spoke slowly and with great difficulty. He took her hand. "What do you take me for?" she retorted, withdrawing her hand. He straightened himself up to answer the question. "I want to meet your family. I want to participate in the Oso Festival. I want to ask your hand in marriage," He revealed.

Rosemary looked him in the eye. "Are you playing straight with me? She asked incredulously. "I'll do it straight away," he pledged. "Are you serious?" She asked again. "Yes, I am. You're a jewel of inestimable value. I'm ready to sell what I have in order to lay my hand on this precious jewel which sits before me," once more he pledged his readiness to fulfill the family tradition. Tom's confession took Rosemary by storm. She looked at him with dark staring eyes. "In that case, I'll call my uncle to book appointment for you to see him immediately on this matter," she promised. She looked at him intently and felt he sounded genuinely interested in her.

"How is your mother keeping?" He asked. "She's OK." She responded, beaming with smiles. Her hair was straggling over her eyes. She brushed it back. She twisted the diamond ring on her finger nervously. "Do you want to dance? He asked politely. "Yes, I want to dance with you, Tom." She replied. "Let's dance." He said rising to his feet and holding her hand. She nodded her head in agreement as she rose to her feet. He gazed deep into her eyes. As they danced, all eyes were focused on them. Esther was overjoyed at their reunion. But Susan was in the gall of bitterness. She felt her friend had lost her reason and she was going to give her a piece of her mind at the appropriate time. Rosemary and Tom danced close to thirty minutes.

As they were dancing, Tom gazed deep into her eyes, holding her tightly close to his body and said, "I love you, Rosemary. I'll always love you." Smiling she responded, "I love you, too. Take my heart and fill it up with your tenderness and affection."

"What should we do now about our marriage?" He asked in the heat of passion. "There's nothing we can do except digging and waiting." She said as her face glowed with happiness and joy intermingled. When the music stopped, there was a standing, thunderous ovation for the couple as they disengaged from their embrace. Rosemary and Tom each returned to their seat.

"I don't know what you're into, girlfriend. What are your interests?" Susan asked rudely. "My interests are diverse." Rosemary responded with sarcasm. "I think you're making a mistake; I don't think Tom is the right man for you." Susan remarked spitefully. "Deep down I still love him," she confessed pleading with her eyes for understanding. "Love my foot! The guy is after your money. He's a gold digger," Susan said accusingly. "Shut up! You're doing my head in. I don't want to discuss this anymore!" her voice reverberated across the hall. The discussion had deteriorated into an angry argument. Rosemary took her handbag and took an angry look at Susan with frown on her face, "Lets head home," she said and headed for the door.

Tom and Akon watched in silence as Rosemary stormed out of the hall with Susan following behind. "I think the problem can be got over without much difficulty. Rosemary seems completely divorced from reality." Akon said lowering his voice. "You judge her harshly and unjustly. The point is that you don't understand her at all." Tom said defensively.

"The truth is sometimes difficult to get at especially if one is not a disinterested party." Akon said with a hint of rebuke. "What are you getting at? I must have my hair cut. I have to see Chief Ote this weekend in Lagos." Tom stated unequivocally. His face darkened. "I get the message; you don't want me to come with you to Lagos. I understand that Rosemary was warned to keep her distance from you if she didn't want to incur the displeasure of her family," Akon teased with mischievous undertone.

"I had hoped that you would at least be happy that I got off with Rosemary at this party. It seems the reverse is the case. It may interest you to note that I asked her to marry me." Tom revealed. "You did what?" Akon asked with disbelief. He quickly added, "What did you do that for?"

"I pity you. You don't seem to understand matters of the heart. For a woman to offer you the custody of her heart is the highest honour any man should be eternally grateful to God to have been the humble recipient of such honour." Tom said with poetic declaration. "That is to say, you've danced to her tune at last. I hope things work out for both of you." Akon said wishfully.

"I must be getting home; it's past midnight," Tom said heading for the door. Inside the hall, the music and dancing continued.

5

Tom had a smooth flight from Abuja to Lagos. When he knocked on the door of the six room duplex on Robertson Street, Ikoyi, Arunma opened the door for him with a flourish. She smiled. "Welcome, Tom. I'm glad to hear that you and Rosemary had patched up things. My dad is in the swimming pool; come, let me take you to him," she said. She led him through the back door. At the far corner of the garden was the big swimming pool. Chief Ote was floundering around in the deep end of the swimming pool.

"Did you have good weather on your trip?" Chief Ote asked as he stepped out of the water. He fetched his towel and began to dry himself. "I had a smooth flight. The weather was good." Tom responded pleasantly "Arunma, take our guest to the sitting room. Make him feel at home. I'll join you shortly." Chief Ote directed his daughter.

"Let's go to the sitting room, Tom," she said leading the way. Tom followed in tow, clutching his small travelling bag. "Guess what, Tom: I'm reading an interesting novel. The main character is a journalist in flight from a failed marriage. I'm sure that character does not have any correlation with my cousin, Rosemary." She paused to pull the back door. She led him to the sitting room. "Rosemary was warned to keep her distance from you if she didn't want to incur the displeasure of our family." She said in low tone, almost in a whisper.

"I understand perfectly well your family directive in that regard." Tom replied flatly. "I can see I will have to revise my opinions of your abilities too." She said admittedly. "Thanks for the compliments."

He responded politely as he divested himself of his jacket. And he sank into the sofa. "I'm glad to inform you that Rosemary admires your determination to get the relationship right and on sound footing. We're proud of our pedigree. We are of a royal family in my community. My father is a repository of family history," she paused as she watched her father walk majestically to the armchair. He sank into it. "Turn the music down," he said, making a gesture with his hand. "Go help your mother with the cooking of dinner. Get us some wine and wine glasses. I suppose Tom and I will have to sit up into the night," He said in a cultivated, pleasant voice.

Turning to face Tom, Chief Ote said, "You must place the demand of our family in their historical context. To understand and appreciate the significance of the Oso Festival, you need to go back into history. The local history of Abam is fascinating. Today Abam has earned her place in history books." He paused as he watched Arunma pour wine into the two wine glasses. Then he resumed his story.

"Abam people originally migrated from a place called Amiyi. When the Oba of Benin sought to extend his regal power over the kingdom of Amiyi, the ruling House of Akpo Uku refused to recognise the authority of the Benin Monarch. But the Oba went ahead and imposed his authority on Amiyi, regardless of the consequences. You know that the Oso Festival is traditionally held in November every year. Let me try and situate the events which led to the hurried and mass migration of the group in their historical context." He paused to catch his breath. Tom was getting excited. He noted with interest that Chief Ote made a simple story resonate with complex themes and emotions.

Just then Arunma and her mother came in to serve Chief Ote and Tom their meal. Tom acknowledged the presence of Mrs. Ote with a friendly nod. Conversation flowed freely throughout the meal. Chief Ote finished his meal, drank some water and waited for Tom to finish his too, before resuming the narrative.

"The House of Akpo Uku had renowned men of power and influence. They refused to accept or recognise the authority of the Oba of Benin over the Kingdom of Amiyi. In a show of power, the Oba ordered a punitive raiding expedition against the kingdom of Amiyi. It was a surprise raid which was carried out in the dead of the night. Many people were captured and carried away as prisoners of war. They were incarcerated in labour camps. This was a slap on the face of Amiyi. Quickly the Amiyi militia, consisting of powerful warriors was mobilized under the command of Atita Akpo, the King of Amiyi. In a lightening move, the warriors of Amiyi overran all the concentration camps, freed all the captives and took hostages of the soldiers of the Benin monarch. The Amiyi warriors killed fifteen Benin soldiers in reprisal for the assassination of three warriors of Amiyi.

This angered the Oba of Benin that he imposed economic sanctions on Amiyi. This posed a threat to agriculture and the food chain, and consequently to human health. He proceeded to impose a dusk to dawn curfew in Amiyi. When the army of the Oba sought to invade Amiyi the second time, the warriors of Amiyi put up a strong resistance. The House of Akpo Uku showed great courage in fighting against the oppressive regime of the Oba of Benin. There were hopes that the conflict could be resolved without further bloodshed.
Attempts to negotiate peace ended in stalemates and the armed struggle continued unabated.

By November of that year in the fifteenth century it became apparent to the House of Akpo Uku that the economic sanctions against Amiyi were taking their toll on the war efforts and economy of the kingdom. Akpo Uku summoned his warriors and told them that the House of Akpo Uku would never surrender to the Oba of Benin. "We will fight for as long as it takes." He told his warriors. In November of that year Akpo Uku and his warriors gathered in the community square and performed a war dance. They left Amiyi and took their journey eastwards towards the River Niger. Many people were forced by the economic sanctions to join the House of Akpo Uku and warriors to migrate from Amiyi." Chief Ote paused and looked at the wall clock. "It is getting on for midnight. Tom, let's get some sleep. We'll continue tomorrow. The guest room is to your immediate left. Goodnight." Chief Ote said, "Goodnight, Sir." Tom said rising from the sofa. He picked his jacket and went to the guest room.

After breakfast, Chief Ote relaxed in the armchair and watched Tom intently and said, "There are no dark secrets in our family. We'll go slowly to begin with."

"Dad, I would have loved to listen in, but I've got terrific amount of work to do on a Saturday like this," Arunma said. Her hair hung down her shoulders. She wore a flimsy cotton blouse and faded jeans. "Next time I'll repeat the story to you," her father replied. Arunma left the sitting room to do her domestic chores.

"Akpo Uku and his group wandered from the path into the woods. They got waylaid in the woods by the foot soldiers of the Benin Monarch. So they fought their way through the dense vegetation. Several soldiers were killed in the skirmish," Chief Ote said as he shifted his weight to one side of the armchair.

"When they got to the bank of the River Niger, they hired rowing boats and canoes and travelled down the river until they finally arrived at Andoni in the present day Rivers State of Nigeria. Remember that they mostly travelled under the cover of darkness. They wore charms and amulets as a protection against evil spirits.

They stayed a while in Andoni until trouble started. As warriors, their weapons consisted of machetes, spears, clubs, knives, cutlasses, bows and arrows. Their long journeys turned them into hunter- gatherers. One day a conspiracy was hatched and they were denounced in Andoni as spies. They were to be eliminated the next day. At dawn the warriors attacked the town. Several people were killed in the skirmishes. Again they left Adoni and took their journey through Opobo and Azunmi without further incidents until they came into Ngwaland. The group came under attack. The warriors quickly repelled the attack.

Remember, in those days there were feelings of hostility towards people from other backgrounds. The methods of communication during their journeys were primitive by today's standards. For their sustenance, they hunted for animals, birds and wild fruits for food." He paused, sipped from his glass.

"When they got to Ibeku they settled in Ubakala Ibeku. For a while they stayed with their hosts until they felt that they needed to dwell in their own homeland. They passed through Umuahia Ibeku and arrived at Ajata Ibeku. For a while they stayed at Ajata. Their hosts received them well. At last, the day came when they set out from Ajata amidst protests from their hosts who said that they should stay longer in their land.

It should be borne in mind that Atita Akpo had four sons. They were Onyerubi, Ezema, Egbebu and Obom. They were all warriors. When they got to Igwu River, they felled a big tree which fell across the river. All crossed over the Igwu River.

At a place called Amaelu, the wife of Onyerubi gave birth to a son. Onyerubi Atita exclaimed 'Abam', meaning, "I've settled." From there the rest of the group separated. Some settled with Onyerubi. Others like Ezema and Egbebu moved on. Ezema moved on to found the present Ohafia while Egbebu went on to found Edda in Ebonyi State. Obom settled with a woman and founded Ntalakwu.

But our ancestry is traced to Abam Onyerubi who later founded the present Abam. There are about twenty-five towns which make up Abam today.

Let me now dwell on the Oso Festival. Our family descended from the first son of Abam Onyerubi who founded our hometown Ozu Abam. We are the custodians of the customs and traditions of our community. Culturally, the Oso Festival commemorates the attainment of Eldership. It marks promotion into the decision making echelon of Elders. Not only are members achievers but they are also entrusted with day-to-day oversight of the community through collective decision making.

Let's look at the other limb of the attraction which the Oso Festival holds for young men like you. Participants are expected to run and encircle the entire circumference of our Community which may translate into traversing mountains, valleys, forests, rivers and what have you. Basically, it is aimed at testing courage, bravery, endurance, strength and resilience of young men. After lunch, I shall proceed to describe the nitty gritty of this aspect of the Oso Festival. Any young man who has not participated in the Oso Festival is not considered a man and cannot be entrusted with our daughter in marriage. Circumnavigating the length and breadth of our community is tasking and exacting. It tests the very limit of bravery, courage, resilience and strength of every young man. Do please remember that our ancestors arrived here as warriors who had to fight their way down to settle in the present Abam of our time." Chief Ote finished at last as he sipped from his glass. He beamed with self satisfaction.

"Thank you, Sir for throwing light on the historical significance of the Oso Festival," Tom said gratefully. Lunch was served. Arunma looked at Tom with animated smile playing across her face. "I'm bored by history, dates and all that stuff. But I'm always excited to hear about the heroic accounts of our ancestors. I always stand tall to announce anywhere that I'm a daughter of Abam. That's why I believe that any man who wants to marry me must first prove his courage, bravery, resilience and prowess by participating in the Oso Festival. I whole heartedly endorse the tradition of our family in this regard." She stated proudly and confidently. Chief Ote was proud of his daughter for her total support and endorsement of the family tradition.

It occurred to Tom that the Ote family did not place a premium on money or material things as had become commonplace nowadays. Within him, he was already longing for the month of November to draw near. He had to prove himself man enough to ask the hand of Rosemary in marriage. It was now beyond question that it was a task that must be done.

Chief Ote proceeded with his narrative after they had lunch. "Would you like to hear about the heroic battles Abam Onyerubi and his warriors fought or would you rather hear how Oso Festival is conducted?" Chief Ote asked, looking intently at Tom. "Well, I like to hear both segments of the story," Tom said enthusiastically.

"In that case, I'll begin by telling you about Ekenwofia, "the Python which owns the forest," Chief Ote offered. "But I suggest that we rest a while," Chief Ote advised rising from the armchair.

After they had rested, Tom turned to Chief Ote and said, "I hope you don't think I'm being too forward, Sir. But I want to know about what happened to Akpo Uku, Atita Akpo and Obom." "Wait till you hear this. It'll blow your mind," Chief Ote said in response to Tom's request.

Tom was dying to hear the fate which befell the Akpo clan. Chief Ote smiled knowingly as if he had divined Tom's thoughts. So he proceeded with the story.

"Long before they reached Amaelu, Akpo Uku had died. On the way, Atita Akpo had been taken seriously ill. The four sons of Atita Akpo: Onyerubi, Ezema, Egbebu and Obom were expected to provide leadership for the Atita Akpo clan. But a strange and unexpected thing happened," he paused for effect. Then he continued.

"Just before the party left Ajata Ibeku, Obom met a beautiful woman, by name, Mgbokwo. He was completely bewitched by her beauty. His heart was ensnared. So he got entangled with Mgbokwo. He was totally besotted with his new girlfriend. She thought that having his child would bind him to her forever. So it came to pass that Obom separated himself from his brothers and clan. He went and founded a town called Ntalakwu. From that moment his life became inextricably bound up with hers.

He turned his back on his brothers. He did not bother to visit their sick father. When his brothers sent for him, saying, "Come, quickly our father is at the point of his death," Obom refused to see his sick and dying father. The Atita Akpo brothers waited in the forlorn hope that Obom would one day come back to them. Atita Akpo, the great warrior, endured his illness with great fortitude. It was not clear if Obom wanted to make a clean break with the past.

Atita Akpo's breath came in convulsive gasps. His other three sons sent for Obom as they tried desperately to convey how urgent the situation was. Still Obom refused to come. What was going through Obom's mind was a matter for conjecture. Inevitably the Atita Akpo brothers came to conclude that Obom's case told of a classic conflict between love and duty. They agreed that Obom had behaved with great indignity. Atita Akpo's health deterioted rapidly and he died shortly afterwards.

Again, Obom was sent for. When he refused to honour the invitation, the Atita Akpo brothers dispatched warriors to bring Obom to them. The sun had disappeared behind the cloud by the time the warriors brought Obom to Amaizu to face the wrath of his warrior brothers. It was Onyerubi, the eldest son of Atita Akpo, who addressed Obom on behalf of the Atita Akpo Clan: 'Obom, when our father fell ill, we sent for you. When he was on his death bed, we sent for you. You didn't come. When our father died, we sent for you, yet you refused to come. What did we do to deserve this treatment from you? Today is the funeral ceremony of our father, the great warrior. Tell us why you have behaved so shamelessly.'

Obom displayed a belligerent attitude towards his brothers and clan. He was boiling with rage. He tried to blot out the image of Mgbokwo sad face. He behaved as if nothing had happened and wiped his hand across his mouth, and then belched loudly. A bemused expression spread across his face. The best thing to do would be to apologize, but not Obom. He was a warrior. He tried to walk away. It was then that one of the warriors moved to block his path. The path was no better than a sheep track.

Obom's conduct was a shattering blow to his brothers' pride. They were unanimous in their judgment: Obom had behaved with great indignity; he deserved to die. As a punishment, the Atita Akpo brothers ordered the warriors to behead Obom on the spot. They put his head in the grave of Atita Akpo and sealed the grave with sand." Chief Ote Paused and wiped his hand across his face.

"That was a tragic end for a warrior," Tom observed. "Quite tragic," Chief Ote agreed. "I'll like to hear the story of Ekenwofia," Tom requested. "I'll fill you in on what happened to him and his village," Chief Ote promised. He called Arunma to serve them some snacks and fruit juice.

"I'm getting forgetful in my old age. Let me quickly add that our story now centres on Abam Onyerubi and his descendants. The success of Abam clan depended on fortuitous circumstances. Uka Abam and his son, Dike Uka continued the conquest of the original settlers of the area now known as Ozu Abam. It's within this era we'll situate the troubles and irritations caused by Ekenwofia.

Ekenwofia manipulated people and tried to bend them to his will. Clashes often broke out between the Uka clan and other clans such as Ndia Chima, Ndia Orie Oma, Ngboro, Ndia Nkwo, Ndia Odo and Ofia Ukwu. Inevitably there were battles for supremacy in this region. Ekwenwofia belonged to the Ofia Ukwu clan. He was the absolute ruler. He was nine feet tall and weighed over 300 pounds. He was a dangerous, powerful, wicked and blood thirsty monster. It was widely believed that he was fortified with powerful juju. No one could challenge him. No one could harm him or hurt him with any weapon for that matter. Our present town, Ozu Abam was his hunting ground. At that time, a powerful medicine man called Ipia Nta Uma held sway over the section called Amaetiti.

It is on record that Ipia Nta Uma, Ekenwofia, Orie Oma, Chima, Nkwonta Odo and Ngboro were earlier settlers in the region we today call Ozu Abam, our hometown. As it might be expected, these powerful and dangerous men united in Confederacy to wage wars against Uka Abam and his clan. Remember, it was Uka Abam who founded the section of our town called Ndi Uka. Let me now return to the litany of troubles Ekenwofia inflicted upon my ancestors. His height gave him a clear advantage. There was a characteristic bounce to his steps which made people run for cover whenever he came to hunt in our territory.

The very name of Ekenwofia struck terror into the hearts of our people. There was a general feeling that things were getting out of hand unless the excesses of Ekenwofia were curbed. Few people dared to declare their opposition to the atrocities committed by him. For almost on daily basis, Ekenwofia would prowl the neighborhood of Ndi Uka clan defiling women without restraint. He had atavistic urge to defile any woman who caught his fancy. He would usually enter any hut, pick a woman he liked and carry her away. Ekenwofia had an invisible belief in his own abilities.

But the case of Mgbeke was the most pathetic in the clan. She had just given birth to a baby boy who was barely three months old. One fateful evening she heard a strange noise near her hut. She tensed, hearing the strange noise again. Tentacles of fear closed around her body. She cradled the baby in her arms. Ekenwofia's huge body stood over her as she lay on the mat. To her horror, Ekenwofia tore the baby from her and placed him in the far corner of the hut and raped her. She cried out in pain. Her husband rushed in to defend her. But Ekenwofia simply split the man's skull in two. Dike Uka was sent for. But just as he arrived, shrieks of fiendish laughter escaped from Ekenwofia as he devoured the new born baby. Dike Uka charged at him. But Ekenwofia escaped with only a broken arm. It was not beyond the bounds of possibility that Dike Uka and Ekenwofia would meet again one day. This dastardly act was the incendiary which aroused the entire Ndi Uka clan to rise as one man in calling for the total annihilation of the Ofia Ukwu clan.

Dike Uka, the great warlord of Ndi Uka clan, knew it would be sheer insanity to attempt the conquest of Ofia Ukwu without first destroying the evil confederates of Ekenwofia. It was a simple military tactical design which Dike Uka produced. The warriors of Ndi Uka would systematically decimate the male population of the clans which had formed evil confederacy with Ofia Ukwu clan. The objective was weakening the powers of Ekenwofia. Once that was achieved, Ofia Ukwu would be isolated and completely destroyed.

It was upon this resolution that Dike Uka mobilized the warriors of Ndi Uka to take on the clan of Ndia Orie Oma in a mortal clash," Chief Ote paused, stood up and stretched. He smiled down at Tom. The smile was acknowledged by Tom in equal measure. "I was waiting for the right moment to ask you; why did Dike Uka choose to levy war first on Ndia Orie Oma clan?" Tom asked. "I'll shortly come to that. Ndia Orie Oma clan as the closet neighbouring clan to Ndi Uka was the arrowhead of the evil confederates Ekenwofia had plotted to use in destroying Ndi Uka Clan." Chief Ote stated and quickly added, "Can you reach the light switch from where you're sitting?" "Sure," Tom replied in delight as he reached for the light switch.

Chief Ote resumed his position. "Tom, you know that our memory can atrophy through lack of use. Let me now proceed to describe the war my ancestors waged against Ndia Orie Oma. As the warriors of Ndi Uka clan gathered at Ebele - the place of the talking drum, Dike Uka the great warrior, addressed his warriors: 'We have enough weapons to annihilate the entire clan of Ndia Orie Oma,' he announced. This announcement of the verdict was accompanied by shouts and cheers. The warriors started talking animatedly. Dike Uka's face suddenly became animated. He took a step forward and did a war dance as the drummers eulogized his exploits as a warrior. There was no doubt about it; everyone agreed that Dike Uka, the son of Uka Abam, was a strong leader and a great warrior.

As the warlord of Ndi Uka clan, his personal ambitions had been subjugated to the needs of the clan. He slung his spear over his shoulder. He sheathed his machete and led the warriors of Ndi Uka towards the Osele Stream." Chief Ote paused, turned to Tom. "I'm proud to tell you I'm a descendent of Dike Uka, the son of Uka Abam. My ancestors were great warriors," he said, beaming with a smile of Self-satisfaction.

Chief Ote looked at Tom as if the young man would not be able to endure the ordeals of the Oso festival. "When the time comes for you to participate in the Oso Festival, your determination will carry you through the ordeals associated with the Oso festival. Now, let's continue with the rest of our story. Shortly before dusk the warriors of Ndi Uka Clan reached a fork and took the left hand track. The Osele Stream turned north at this point. A plank of wood bridged the Osele Stream. The path bent sharply to the right. The warriors took a right turn at the intersection. They kept on the right side of the narrow road and carried on until they got to the junction, and then turned left. They didn't reach the border of Ndia Orie Oma until after dark.

Fields and hills stretched out as far as they could see. At the other side of the valley was a steep ascent to the top of the hill. From here, the road continued as straight as an arrow. The two opposing armies of Ndi Uka clan and Ndia Orie Oma faced each other across the battlefield. Warriors of Ndia Orie Oma had fortified their area against attack. The war was carried into Ndia Orie Oma territory.

Dike Uka led the charge down the open field as he gave the battle cry. It was a clash of Titans. Incensed by the frequent guerrilla and arson attacks which Ndi Uka clan had suffered at the hands of warriors from Ndia Orie Oma in the recent past, the warriors under the command of Dike Uka seemed imbued with supernatural power. The warriors of Ndi Uka inflicted heavy casualties on Ndia Orie Oma on that Afor market day. All the warriors and men of Ndia orie Oma were massacred. The women and children were captured. The warriors of Ndi Uka clan divided up the spoils of war. Ndia Orie Oma suffered a crushing defeat. When the avenging warriors left, the entire village of Ndia Orie Oma had become a theatre of raging inferno.

On their return, the victorious warriors were given an enthusiastic welcome. Enyidiya, the wife of Dike Uka showed uncommon pleasure at the victorious return of her husband. She led other women to welcome the victorious warriors of Ndi Uka at the Ogo Ndi Uka - the village square.

The tragedy which befell the clan of Ndia Orie Oma was repeated in hushed tones in the clans of Ndia Nkwo Nta Odo, Ndia Chima, Ngboro and Ofia Ukwu. Fear gripped the hearts of the warriors in those clans. It was not long before the tragedy which befell Ndia Orie Oma clan was visited on Ndi Nkwo Nta Odo, Ngboro and Ndia Chima. Today these clans had ceased to exist. Those areas had become our farmlands.

Next, Dike Uka turned his attention to Ofia Ukwu. Guerrilla fighters from Ofia Ukwu clan usually attacked the people of Ndi Uka. It was widely believed that Ofia Ukwu was a clan of cannibals. Ofia Ukwu guerrillas also carried out arson attacks against Ndi Uka clan. Inevitably there was a serious deterioration in relations between the two clans. Ipia Nta Uma was generally regarded as a wizard who could make himself invisible. He was still in alliance with Ekenwofia and Ofia Ukwu clan. Naturally, there was a growing antipathy towards Ofia Ukwu, Ekenwofia and Ipia Nta Uma. The day of their reckoning was fast approaching. All Ndi Uka clan looked forward with great anticipation to that day of reckoning. They knew it would be a total showdown, not only of wits and muscles, but also of a clash of will and display of latent power. The result of such deadly encounter was predictable: total annihilation of Ofia Ukwu. Since Ipia Nta Uma's territory was a gateway to Ofia Ukwu Clan, it was only reasonable that Dike Uka should include the annexation of the gateway territory in his overall military strategy. Unexpectedly, Ofia Ukwu and Ndi Uka clans called a truce to avoid further bloodshed but Ekenwofia scoffed at the idea, believing he was invisible." Chief Ote paused, looked Tom straight in the eye. "We'll continue our narrative after dinner. I think dinner is ready. Let's move over to the dining area," he said. Tom nodded in agreement, as he shuffled towards the dining area where Arunma and her mother were already seated, waiting for them.

As Tom sat down, his eyes wandered towards the photographs on the wall. Chief Ote watched him from the corner of his eyes. "The photographs are the vestiges of our lives and times in England," he clarified. "I thought as much," Tom said. "You can see Rosemary holding her father's hand. To her left is her mother. You can see Edward and Arunma sitting on the floor. My wife and I are standing to the right of Dr Brown, my elder brother," Chief Ote explained. He then said the grace and they began to eat their dinner. "That reminds me now. I've reliably been informed that Rosemary goes about her job with a rare combination of youth and experience," Chief Ote observed. "She could yet surprise us all," Tom added. Conversation at the dinner table continued until they all finished their meal.

Back in the sitting room, Chief Ote resumed his seat. Suddenly he looked tired and there were deep furrows in his brow. He chose his words with precision. "This segment of the atrocities of Ekenwofia always repulses me each time I tell the story of our people," he confessed and proceeded with the story, nonetheless.

"To her horror, Mgbeke observed that she was pregnant as a result of the rape. She had spent the whole month wrestling with the problem. No one was left in doubt as to who was responsible for the pregnancy. Everyone in Ndi Uka Clan knew that Ekenwofia was responsible.

This caused no small stir in the entire clan. So she went to see Dike Uka to tell him about her predicament.

Mgbeke was mortified to realize that Ekenwofia had heard every word she had said to Dike Uka as her encounter with Ekenwofia that evening revealed. That evening she heard the characteristic bouncing steps of Ekenwofia towards her hut. Stooping, he entered her hut. "I've heard all about your ranting at me. I think you owe me an apology, woman," he said. His word wrenched a sob from her. You could imagine how mortifying it was for her to have to apologize. 'I'm carrying your child,' she said with a wry smile. He was furious to hear those words proceed from her mouth.

He kicked Mgbeke hard in the stomach, knocking the wind out of her. She was writhing around on the floor in agony. Her eyes widened in horror as she saw that he was now wielding a large knife. With it, he cut her stomach open. She stared at him with unblinking, dying eyes. She called up her last reserves of strength and placed a curse on him. She died as her neighbours were shouting themselves hoarse for help. Ekenwofia left the hut without a word.

The entire Ndi Uka Clan was outraged at the way Mgbeke had been treated and murdered. The people called on the warriors of Ndi Uka clan to avenge her death. It was time Ofia Ukwu and Ekenwofia were taught a lesson they would never forget in a hurry. A plan was formulated to capture Ekenwofia dead or alive. The crisis between Ndi Uka Clan and Ofia Ukwu was worsening. Dike Uka and Ogbuagu Ike, his second in command, were trying to prevent an even worse tragedy. Dike Uka and Ogbuagu Ike were determined to avenge themselves on the man who had murdered sleep in Ndi Uka clan.

Ekenwofia soon got a new woman in his life. Arodo was her name. She lived in the neighbouring clan of Ndi Oji. It was like Ndi Uka clan, a farming village. Even in those distant times, the clan of Ndi Oji offered many opportunities for wining and dining. Lately, Arodo's hut had become Ekenwofia's lair. With time, he became like a bird too tame to survive in the wilds. He had a wild and romantic love affair with Arodo. In return, she was totally wild about him.

Emissaries from Ndi Uka clan were sent to Arodo in Ndi Oji to let her in for the plan to capture Ekenwofia dead or alive. "Blood is thicker than water. On our farms the fox is considered vermin and treated as such. Ekenwofia is the wild animal that destroys our people. He must be contained," they informed her. She volunteered to help and then thought, "Oh, no, what have I let myself in for!"

"My people, what you've asked me to do could send me to my early grave. There is no one in living memory who does not know that Ekenwofia is an old bird that cannot be caught with mere chaff. Give me your word that you'll send the most powerful warriors in Ndi Uka clan to help me execute this plan," she pleaded. They gave her their word and departed.

Arodo knew that Ekenwofia was a loose cannon. So she gave her full cooperation in carrying out the plan. She was interested in him for purely mercenary reasons. The ties of kinship were stronger than the wild romance she had with him. After all, Ekenwofia's mercurial temperament made him difficult to live with. Arodo, therefore, followed the instructions about the capture of Ekenwofia religiously. With the plan a foot, she knew that Ekenwofia's life was placed at her mercy. She had also looked beyond the present to recognise the fact that she was exploiting the situation for her own ends. For, she reasoned that although the success of the plan was in the lap of the gods, her place in history was doubly assured. She gave the plan her wholehearted support and worked conscientiously towards its actualization.

She sent an invitation to Ekenwofia to visit her on the next Afor market day; she had a special treat of delicious meal and a keg of palm wine for him. Moreover, she hinted that her body would be his to ravish all night long. Ekenwofia sent his reply that he would honour the invitation but quickly reminded her that he was the python which owned the forest and that no matter how long a log stayed in the water, it would not become a crocodile. That invitation would turn out to be the kiss of death for Ekenwofia.

Feeling insecure, Ekenwofia sent a few of his warriors to resettle Arodo on a farm somewhere out in the wilds. They built a new hut on a hill on the outskirts of the village. He did not seem in the least concerned for her safety, rather it was concern for his security which informed his decision to relocate Arodo to the wilds. A path led up the hill where her new hut stood. The hut was built in the lee of the hill in the dense forest. There was also a path along the left side of the hut.

On that Afor market day, the more than twenty handpicked warriors of Ndi Uka clan left before daybreak under the command of Dike Uka. It was the D-Day. Their destination was the new hut on a hill on the outskirts of Ndi Oji clan. When they got there, they took positions behind the hut and were well concealed by the dense vegetation behind the hut.

Ekenwofia had a premonition of disaster. But he was too preoccupied with his own thoughts about his sizzling romance with Arodo to give in to his fears. Moreover, beliefs in his own invincibility emboldened him.

Ekenwofia set out on his visit by taking another route to get to Ndi Oji clan, a distance of twenty miles from Ofia Ukwu. His path took him through where the Osele stream widened and emptied into the Igwu River. The trees were swaying in the wind by the time he reached the outskirts of Ndi Oji clan. It was evening. At that moment Arodo felt the first twitch of anxiety. The atmosphere seemed to vibrate with tension. She seemed confident but in reality she felt extremely nervous. For, she was keenly aware that the success of the plan was now in the lap of the gods.

Later that evening there was a knock on the door, Arodo hastily opened the door and there was the towering figure of Ekenwofia. Immediately he was greeted by Arodo with hugs and kisses. The door swung shut with a bang as he entered the hut. His eyes
ranged the entire length and breadth of the hut. Satisfied that there was no danger, he sat down on a mat on the floor. Quickly, Arodo served him a bowl of meal and placed a big keg of fresh palm wine before him. Ekenwofia had a large appetite and in no time he had consumed the entire meal. He now began to gulp the palm wine from the keg.

Soon he began to feel drowsy. Arodo lay quietly enfolded in his arms. One by one he started to remove his charms and amulets and as he did so he explained what each was meant for. He kept them beside him and as he was fast falling into deep sleep, he told her what could destroy his charms and amulets. He charged her with the responsibility of taking care of them while he slept. Her face broke into a wide grin when he heard his characteristic heavy snoring. She disengaged from him.

She gave the pre-arranged sign by throwing an object through the only window in the hut. Quickly the warriors set to work. They bored holes through the mud wall of the hut. The big ropes they had were passed through the holes to Arodo. She tied loops of rope around his arms, ankles and neck. One of the warriors stood at the door to act as a look out. When she had performed her duties conscientiously, she gave another signal, got up, opened the door and disappeared into the night, fully convinced that she had played her role well. She took away with her all the charms and amulets.

When the warriors received the second signal, they started pulling the ropes from behind the hut. Quickly, the loops tightened around Ekenwofia's ankles, neck and arms. Drowsily, he woke up and sought to assert his power. He tried pulling his arms together and as he did so he was drawing the warriors on the other end closer to the wall. They pulled the ropes tightly again. Forth and back the tug of war went on for more than thirty minutes. As this tugging continued, Dike Uka took three warriors with him and entered the hut. At once they started hitting Ekenwofia with clubs. He was momentarily wounded by a blow to his stomach. He winced as a sharp pain shot through his left leg. At the same time those pulling the ropes, kept at it until his strength was spent. Standing over him, Dike Uka gave him a deep cut on the chest. He died from the wounds he had received to his chest. The warriors cut off his head and his body was buried in an unmarked grave in the forest. For Ekenwofia, death came as a merciful release.

6

News of the death of Ekenwofia spread like bush fire through all the neighbouring communities. Fighting immediately broke out on the outskirts of Ndi Uka community. The fight was started by a gang of youths from Ofia Ukwu when they heard about the ignoble death of Ekenwofia, their ruler and champion. Now there seemed to be little chance of rapprochement between the two warring clans.

Warriors from Ofia Ukwu were coming and going through Ipia Nta Uma's territory, but he turned a blind eye to them. Moreover, he asked his people to set up blockades on the paths leading out of Ndi Uka territory. The drums of war were beaten and the great warriors of Ndi Uka clan assembled at Ebele, the place of the talking drum. Dike Uka addressed them: "Ofia Ukwu people have dared to touch the tail of the tiger. Now the tiger must bare its fangs. Let us raze Ofia Ukwu to the ground! Let's give them a taste of their own medicine."

The warriors gave the gang of youths and a few warriors from Ofia Ukwu a chase and they beat a retreat. When the warriors of Ndi Uka Clan reached the territory of Ipia Nta Uma, they found to their chagrin that a large area of the land had become a big river with strong currents. There was no plausible explanation. It puzzled the warriors of Ndi Uka clan. Dike Uka was quickly notified about this inexplicable barrier.

With Ekenwofia's charms and amulets hanging around his neck Dike Uka looked left and right. He plucked a particular green leaf, squeezed out its greenish juice, rubbed it on his chest and waded into the raging river. Immediately, the river became dry land again.

Wild shouts escaped from the warriors. The warriors then beat a path through the undergrowth. The hills were hazy in the distance. The warriors gained access into Ipia Nta Uma's territory.

Suddenly the entire forest was swarming with huge pythons. Then the wind started blowing in gusts. The warriors watched fascinated, as the pythons began to move towards them. They stared in horrified fascination as the huge snakes approached. The situation looked dangerous but Dike Uka was urging caution. He urged the warriors to stay put. They all knew that this was a matter of some urgency. Dike Uka ran past the warriors and stood directly in the path of the huge pythons which were approaching them. He uttered a word of command, and immediately golden eagles appeared from nowhere and swooped down over the huge pythons and began to carry them away.

As the eagles continued their curious attacks, a tall figure suddenly materialized in front of Dike Uka. It was Ipia Nta Uma. He pleaded for his life and immediately surrendered. He was forced to sign a peace pact with Ndi Uka clan. In no uncertain terms he was told that his territory had been taken over by Ndi Uka clan. He was allowed to live with members of his family in his compound. That is the compound we call Ndi Ipia today. Their territory is now part of our farmlands.

The war raged on until Ndi Uka warriors had completely routed the warriors of Ofia Ukwu. Their village was razed to the ground. The women and the children were carried away as captives. All the men and warriors of Ofia Ukwu were massacred. Today, Ofia Ukwu village is no more. Their territory is now part and parcel of our farmlands. Amaizu which used to be a meeting place for warriors from Abam, Ohafia and Edda has become our farmland. When warriors from all the surrounding towns and villages decided to be meeting in Ebele, they referred to it as Ozuzu Abam - that is to say, 'a meeting place of Abam.' Thus our hometown came to be called Ozu Abam. Today, Ozu Abam occupies the territories formerly belonging to the villages of Ndia Orie Oma, Ndia Nkwo Nta Odo, Ngboro, Ndia Chima, Ofia Ukwu and Ndi Ipia Nta Uma.

Regretfully, our ancestors also carried back to our community the juju and shrines of all the conquered people. With time, Abam warriors became mercenaries who were hired to fight other people's wars. That's how our ancestors were nicknamed head hunters.

But today we are largely a Christian community. You should equally bear in mind that the distinction between right and wrong lies at the heart of questions of morality. We, the descendants of Abam Onyerubi, comprising twenty four towns and villages are cultured, civilized ad enlightened people. Our sons and daughters are occupying prominent positions home and abroad. Dignity and pride run deep in Abam. We are hospitable and we welcome strangers in our towns and villages.

The night is far spent. Let's get some sleep, tomorrow I shall endeavour to conclude the story by dwelling on the Oso Festival. You'll agree with me that there are no dark secrets in our family. Are there?" "No, I don't think so. Goodnight, sir," Tom said, rising to go to the guest room.

It was Sunday morning. A cool breeze from the Atlantic Ocean blew over Ikoyi, making the trees sway gently to the tune of the breeze. The whistling pines answered back with their melodious voices. Birds chirped their choruses from the overhanging branches. Inside the six-bedroom duplex on Robertson Street, the occupants were fully awake. Tom was still in the guest room. He was on the phone.

"Morning, dad," Arunma greeted her father. "Morning, my darling daughter. Where's Tom?" Chief Ote responded. "He's been on the phone to Rosemary for more than an hour," Arunma said as she sat next to the open window in the spacious sitting room. "That's what I call true love. That is to say, love is emotional tendencies resulting from excessive dosage of love," Chief Ote said jokingly. He sat on the armchair. "Dad, what's love?" Arunma asked with a wide grin across her face. "Love is to mistake an ordinary man for a prince charming and to regard an ordinary woman as a beautiful princess. It's the triumph of feelings over reason," Chief Ote asserted with a mischievous smile on his face.

"I don't think so, dad. Definition can create disagreement between us. Let's describe it, instead. Here comes Tom. Let's ask for his opinion," Arunma said beaming with smile. "Tom, Dad and I have been arguing about definitions or descriptions of love. How do you define or describe love?" Arunma asked. "Love is the good you feel in your heart for someone else. Love is not about you. It's about the other person with whom you are in love. It's on that person you lavish the treasures of your affection," Tom explained.

"Let's go eat our breakfast before it gets old. On a serious note, love is an action word. It's the doing of good to the other person, not expecting her to return your love, but simply to seek her happiness which is both to your joy and self satisfaction," Chief Ote pointed out.

"Dad, you always transform the most ordinary subject into the sublime," Arunma commended her father. "Thank you, my darling daughter. I think the gift comes with age," Chief Ote responded. They relapsed into silence.

Tom broke the silence: "In many societies women are subordinate to men. I'll never bring myself to think that Rosemary is my subordinate." He stated with emotion laden voice.

"Little wonder, these days Rosemary talks about Tom, morning, noon and night. "Even at that, my question is this; why are so many men scared to commit themselves to women who show open affections to them?" Arunma said with concern in her eyes.

"Despite our disagreements, we have been able to find some common ground," Chief Ote pointed out, carefully avoiding the question. For he knew that the question Arunma had asked was an open ended question. "Gentle men, breakfast will be served between 8 am and 8.30 a.m. We'll attend the morning service shortly after. Today is Sunday. It's the Lord's Day, remember," Arunma announced as she moved towards the kitchen.

"My darling daughter the point you made is perfectly valid. Sunday is the only day when I can relax. Tim, we'll continue our narrative when we return from Sunday Service," Chief Ote said as he rose from the armchair and moved towards the dining area.

Although the sun was radiant under a clear blue sky when they left the church building, a light rain began to fall by the time they got home. "What's for lunch? I'm absolutely ravenous," Chief Ote said as he stepped into the sitting room. "I'll just micro wave the lunch for three minutes, my dear," Mrs. Ote replied as she went to her room. True to her word, Mrs. Ote served lunch. When lunch was over, Chief Ote beckoned to Tom to take a seat. He sank into the sofa while Chief Ote sat on the armchair, relaxed.

"The Igba Oso is comparable to a long running race of about 50 kilometers which requires a lot of effort and patience to complete. It's open to able bodied young men under the age of 35. The race will take the competitors through hills, valleys, ravines, forests, thorns and thistles. The competitors may be exposed to wild animals and dangerous reptiles such as pythons and cobra. It's important to distinguish fact from fiction. I must admit that there is a strong sense of community in our town. The only way to conquer a fear is to face it. The Oso Festival, therefore, is a show case for young men to display their courage and bravery. Traditional values which reinforce these ideals must be reasserted. You know that Edward, my son is looking forward to participating in the Igba Oso Festival, to showcase all his talents," he paused, noticing slight furrows on Tom's face. "What's the matter, Tom? Do you want any point to be explained?" Chief Ote asked. "Is the Igba Oso a show biz?" Tom asked.

"No, it's not. It's a live event not usually open for rehearsal. There are elements of danger associated with the race; injuries cannot be ruled out. That's why it commemorates the heroic deeds of our ancestors. If two young men have a quarrel, they can settle it during the race. No one is allowed to settle them. If they are fighting, they will fight to their satisfaction without anyone separating or stopping them. In the distant times, young men could engage themselves in a mortal combat," Chief Ote explained and waited for Tom to ask another question. "What options are open to me?" he asked. "You have no options at all. That's why you should think twice before doing anything rash. You'll definitely explore the outer limits of human endurance and courage," Chief Ote pointed out. He watched Tom from the corner of his eye. "How much time is required to complete this marathon race?" Tom asked. "Time is of overriding importance everyone in our town will want to hear the news that the competing participants return safely," Chief Ote replied. They relapsed into silence. Chief Ote broke the silence.

"Let me now deal with some common misconceptions first timers or outsiders may have about the Oso festival. I'll simply do this by outlining the events on that Oso day. It's usually held in November on our Afor Market day. This is a brief outline of the day's events. All participants will assemble at Ogo Ndi Okorukwu near Ebele- the place of the talking drum. The leader of the Oso will bellow instructions to the crowd of participating young men and then he will proceed to admonish any faint-hearted man to return home. He will trot at the head of the crowd with the big Ogele. From time to time he will beat the big gong and shout: "Gbua rie o!" "Kill and eat!" The leader will repeat the phrase "Gbua rie o, Anyi ge gbu umu mba, rie O O-O-O!" which simply translated means; 'Yes, we'll kill strangers and eat them!'

All participants are expected to wear T-shirts and jeans or shorts. 'Nzu' also called white chalk is rubbed on the eyebrows. You may wear canvass shoes. In the distant times, you would go bare footed. As soon as the crowd clears the Amaetiti section of our town which previously belonged to Ipia Nta Uma – the leader will leave the road and enter the undergrowth of the forest. He must be able to trace the ancient path way of Oso or else all the crowd will get lost in the thick forest. By this time, the rest of the race will be through forest, hills, valleys and ravines. I need not say more now. You'll have to experience the thrills personally," Chief Ote finished at last and he stretched himself. Quickly he added: "I hope you have gained some insight into the historical context and significance of the Oso festival."

"I've been enlightened. I'm eager to participate in the Oso competition. How do I get to your hometown seeing that the festival is barley two months away?" Tom asked. Arunma, who had sat listening in, got up and took out a map and indicated the quickest route to their hometown. Tom took a mental note of the route especially from the Umuahia end. He knew he would take a flight from Abuja to Owerri. From Owerri he would travel by road to Umuahia.

7

Tom knew that his raw talents and determination would enable him scale the huddles of the Oso Festival. He radiated self-confidence and optimism. "Much as I would like to stay, I really must go home tomorrow," Tom said. "We would very much like to see you again, hopefully, in our hometown in November. The Oso is also meant to instill confidence and discipline in the participants," Chief Ote said, sprawling himself to watch TV.

Tom rose at dawn. He showered and got dressed. He took the morning flight to Abuja. Back in Abuja, he grew more anxious with every passing day. These days, he had an aversion to getting up early. Much as he disliked travelling to Ozu Abam, he knew he had to be there for the Oso Festival. A sense of fatality gripped him. He had weathered many contradictions in life at 35 and the Oso Festival would not make him to panic. He was not one to turn back after he had put his hand to the plough. He was proud of the fact that he was a self-made man. He was not someone who liked to wallow in self-pity. Although he was brought up by a cold and domineering father, he refused to allow any such character traits to define his personality. He chose to be kind, pleasant and caring.

At last, November finally arrived. He made preparations for his journey to Ozu Abam for the Oso Festival. He duly informed Rosemary about his travel arrangements. He did not arrive at the hotel he booked in Umuahia until very late. The next day he took a taxi and arrived at Ozu Abam and quickly checked into a Guest House on the outskirts of the town.

In the meantime, Chief Ote and his family were already in town. Mrs. Brown and her daughter had also arrived the day before yesterday. The whole town was in a festive mood. He observed that Oso Ozu was an occasion of great festivity. Tomorrow, he noted, was the Afor Market day on which the Oso Festival would hold. He was on ground fully prepared. He had upon his arrival put a call to his uncle to join him at the Guest House the next day.

The day was dull and overcast. The hills were covered in green vegetation. They were hazy in the distance. The pines bowed gently to the light wind. Modern houses dotted the entire landscape as far as Tom could see. It was a beautiful quiet town. There was a steady build-up of traffic in the afternoon of this Afor Market Day, particularly on the major road leading to Ebele, the town square; venue of the Oso Festival. There were signs everywhere urging motorists to reduce the speed limit in built –up areas. The carnival parade was a magnificent spectacle. The spectators consisting mainly of women, young boys and visitors from neighbouring towns lined the major road leading to Ebele - the town square.

As Tom joined the throng he recalled that the history of Abam stretched back to 1664. He could see that beyond the hills, the land fell away sharply towards the Igwu River. Tom felt invisible in the crowd. When he reached Ebele he noticed that four paths radiated from Ebele Square where the war dance drummers sat beating their drums. The leader of the Oso Competition, Kalunta, was in formidable form, attired in the warrior's costume. His teeth clinched a palm frond. In his hand was the big metal gong called Ogele. His machete was well sheathed. He painted his eyebrows with white chalk. A crowd of enthusiastic young men who were equally attired in the warriors' costumes milled around him as they waited for the kick off at Ogo Ndi Okorukwu, facing Ebele Square. Tom mixed with the crowd and waited too.

When the ruling elders of the community had poured libation, they implored God to lead the participants back in safety. After this brief ceremony the Oso Festival was declared open. All was now set. Suddenly Kalunta the leader of the Igba Oso Competition bellowed; "The Oso Competition is for men who have scrotum. If you don't have scrotum, go home now and stay with your mother and sisters. Gbua rie, O! Anyi Ge gbu umu Mba rie –O-O!!- 'Kill and Eat! We'll kill strangers and eat!"

When Edward who had joined the crowd heard the words his heart jumped inside his stomach. Cold sweat broke on his face. He had not had the opportunity of receiving first-hand information about the Igba Oso Festival. All his life he had lived a sheltered life in England. He rarely visited his hometown. In effect, he was like a stranger in his own hometown. Tom, on the other hand, appeared to be at home having been duly briefed about the Igba Oso Competition.

Kalunta walked slowly along the road. Suddenly he broke into a trot. The leader led the way and the crowd of young men trotted along behind him. As he went he kept bellowing, 'Gbua rie –O! O! Anyi ge gbu umu mba rie O,O-O!' The crowd repeated the refrain. The path Kalunta took continued beyond the town up into the hills. The land rose to the east, undulating and fertile. The path started to ascend more steeply as the race entered the critical phase which led through the crocodile pond.

The race was beyond the abilities of most of the participating young men. Some began to return home. The Igba Oso Competition had a strong practical bias. The Oso Competition was in reality an ordeal for those who had no physical stamina. Edward was not cut out for such rigorous exercise which the Igba Oso required. Driven by force of love, Tom committed himself body and soul to finishing the race.

The land sloped gently towards the crocodile pond. The Oso Competition path cut across the pond. Kalunta bellowed once more: "Gbua rie O,-O! Anyi ge gbu umu mba rie O-O! He waded through the pond as the crocodiles were ready for a fight. Terrified, many of the young men started jumping into the pond hoping to scare away the crocodiles. Edward's face was ashen and wet with sweat when tom accidentally marched on his toes as each participant tried to wade through the crocodile pond as quickly as possible. Edward was furious. "Are you blind asshole?" Edward blurted out angrily as the pain seared through his body. "I'm sorry, buddy." Tom pleaded. "Sorry for yourself; you good-for-nothing," Edward said. "Watch your tongue, boy," Tom cautioned as he tried to join the rest of the crowd. "Or else... What would you do asshole?" Edward pelted more abuse on Tom as he edged towards Tom menacingly. "I have said; I'm sorry. Do you want to fight me in this forest? Just go away, I don't want to fight you," Tom placated.

"It astonishes me that you could be so thoughtless, asshole," Edward said as he gave Tom a hard push on the Chest. "You had better be careful. Don't bring out the beast in me. Because if you do, you'll regret it," Tom warned. This further provoked Edward. He lost self-control as Tom was assailed with fierce blows to the head. Tom swiftly responded in kind. He knew Edward's assault on him was totally unjustified. Tom landed a blow on Edward's nose. Blood oozed out from his nostrils. As Tom and Edward were yelling at each other and exchanging blows, the crowd surged past them. Although several young men were passing, nobody offered to separate them. At last their anger subsided as they sobered up. By this time they had been outdistanced by the rest of the pack. So they wandered around in the thick forest for a while and landed up finally at Amaelu.

At Amaelu, the competitors had been halted by the strong men of the clan to negotiate for a passage as required by tradition. The Amaelu clan had put blockades on the path of the Oso Competitors to slow them down. As Edward and Tom, now looking haggard and tired, appeared on the scene, they overheard Chief Ukaike of Amaelu clan say: "If you think you're a man with scrotum like me, come and pass here. If you dare to pass this barricade without our permission, consider yourself dead, because I'll surely cut off your head. I therefore advise you to return peacefully to wherever you're coming from. There is no road here." A deafening silence descended upon the crowd. The first-timers and strangers were shaking to their bone marrow. Edward was pressed to quickly urinate by the roadside. Tom recalled that it was in Amaelu that the Onyerubi dynasty first landed. Amaelu therefore had a special role to play in the Oso Festival. By tradition, Amaelu clan was charged with the responsibility of delaying the progress of the Oso Competitors until a word was received from the elders of Ozu Abam to let them pass.

For more than three hours the Oso Competitors were detained by the strong men of Amaelu clan. At a pre-arranged signal after Amaelu clan had received word from the elders of Ozu Abam, Kalunta bellowed again, "Gbua rie-O; Gbua rie –O-O, Anyi ge gbu umu mba rie-O-O-O!!" He beat the heavy Ogele. All the young men got excited and stood at alert to cross quickly through the barrier. With the big Ogele, Kalunta cut asunder the barricade in a rush. Some people fell down and were trampled underfoot as the strong men of Amaelu began to flog the fleeing competitors. Edward and Tom were not spared as they rushed through the barricade.

Finally the competitors reached the "Barn of Skulls' and were forced to halt their race. Stern looking men of Ndia Nkwo clan prowled the entire place with their machetes drawn. Edward and Tom were visibly shaken when they saw the several human skulls neatly tied on sticks as if they were really yams in a barn. The crowd relapsed into silence. Suddenly a powerful, high pitched voice broke the silence. It was the voice of Chief Obidike, the leader of Ndia Nkwo clan who addressed the crowd: "Everyone should sit down. Don't move. Don't say a word until we tell you to go. If you disobey us, your skull will be hanging here as the ones you're seeing. Remember these skulls were once human beings like you. Our ancestors brought back the heads from the wars they fought. We, the descendants, have custody of the spoil of war." Chief Obidike finished at last.

The drums were beating loudly. The Ebele square was agog with excitement as the spectators anxiously awaited the return of the competitors. The warriors' dance at Ebele square appeared to most spectators to be the high point in the festival. Not long afterwards, Chief Obidike called on Kalunta to lead his troops to Ebele square as their arrival was awaited by the elders, the age-grade celebrants and spectators alike. Kalunta rose, beat the Ogele and bellowed once again, "Gbua rie –O-O, Anyi ge gbu umu mba rie-O-O!!" He rushed towards Ebele square in the final lap of the race.

At Ebele square the music and drumming rose to their crescendo. At once all the competitors became wild with excitement. They danced and flogged one another with sticks in a wild ecstasy of feigned aggression and hostility. A wild orgy of violence was released upon the dancers at Ebele. Tom and Edward were bewildered as nothing had prepared them for this aspect of the Oso Competition. Many people were trampled underfoot as the wild orgy of violence lasted up to five minutes.

Edward unable to endure the endless floggings ran headlong into a barricaded area where the war dance drummers sat beating their drums. Immediately one of the war dance drummers drew his machete to cut off Edward's head for daring to enter the barricaded area reserved only for those who had brought home human heads from wars. Edward was speechless as shouts rose from the crowd. Kalunta quickly intervened and pleaded for Edward's life to be spared. They questioned him to ascertain if he were a citizen of the town or a stranger. When he told them his father was Chief Ote, the man sheathed his machete and let him go. He let Edward go because his family was not only kingmakers but could also produce kings. The family was descendants of Dike Uka, the legendary warrior of Ndi Uka fame.

Without warning, someone rushed in and carried away one of the drums and rushed towards the Idogho Stream. Kalunta ran at the head of the Oso competitors towards the Idogho Stream. At Idogho stream the competitors jumped into the water and started bathing hurriedly for the stream was believed to possess healing power. Soaked and wet in their attires each participant returned home. The Igba Oso Competition had ended. Tom strolled along the road back to the Guest House. His uncle, Chief Ekelema was anxiously waiting for his return.

Tom and his uncle sat and talked deep into the night. Tom seemed confident about meeting Rosemary's family tomorrow but deep down he was quite insecure. It looked as if what he was doing was deep sea fishing. He believed that the difficultly of a problem was defined in terms of how long it took to complete. The first requirement he knew had been met, not without injuries and pains which still raked his body.

For him the defining moment had come to demonstrate how much he loved Rosemary. The next day as Tom stood outside the Guest House waiting for his uncle to join him, he looked towards the hill on which the town stood. It was sharply defined against the blue sky. Tom carried a shopping bag containing two large bottles of wine. In Abam as in any part of Africa he was aware of the fact that traditional beliefs still flourished alongside a modern urban lifestyle. At 35 he argued that no one should question the desirability of his getting married. For a moment, he felt a spark of hope that Rosemary's family would gratify his desire to marry their daughter.

Secured firmly in his convictions, he and his uncle set out to formally inform the family that there was a ripe Udara Fruit they had seen in the Ote's family. The Ote's family compound comprised of two units of identical five-bedroom storey house. One belonged to Chief Ote and the other was late Dr. Brown's. The roof of each story building was covered with slate. There was a porch. The front door was screened too. There was a picket fence. The balcony jutted over the street. Behind each house was a vegetable garden. The porch provided an excellent outdoor relaxation spot. The windows were a mixture of French and bay windows. On the roof was skylight window. The aerial antenna sat atop the Chimney.

With his uncle, Chief Ekelema in tow, Tom went to the front door and knocked. The door was opened by Edward. Immediately he recognized Tom. "What are you doing here?" he asked angrily and banged the door. Tom knocked again. Edward opened the door, held it slightly ajar and shouted, "Get lost now or I'll call the police!" At this, Chief Ote, Mrs. Ote, Rosemary, Arunma and Mrs. Brown all at once came crowding to the front door. Chief Ote threw the door wide open.

"Oh, it's you, Tom. Come inside," Chief Ote said as he moved to make way for Tom and his uncle. "Dad, you know this guy? This is the guy who fought me yesterday," Edward said angrily. As everyone took his seats, the spacious sitting room fell silent. "I'm glad to see you're back in the land of the living. We were worried about you. Now tell us what happened between you and Edward yesterday," Chief Ote urged Tom. Tom took a perfunctory glance around the room. For a fleeting moment his gaze fell on Rosemary. Their eyes met across the room. She met his gaze without flinching. He looked away. He was silenced by her unspoken rebuke.

Tom had amazing powers of recall. He gave the gist of the incident. He concluded by saying: "I didn't really want to fight but he insisted." Chief Ote turned to his son: "Tell me what really happened." Chief Ote said to Edward. It was apparent that Edward had taken an instant dislike to Tom. He did not reply. Instead he turned on his heel and left the room. As if he had a second thought on his behaviour, he returned to the sitting room. "Tom is no good for you, Rosemary. I can't support you to marry him," he said spitefully. Again, Edward left the sitting room. Rosemary groaned inwardly. Her thoughts turned inwards and her calm expression hid her panic. Certainly, her pride was hurt. She put her hand over her mouth to stop herself from screaming. Edward's cruel remarks cut her deeply. Looking Tom in the eye, she threatened, "If it's proved you're at fault, I'll call off the engagement." Tom did not say a word. Male pride forced him to suffer in silence. "You're too emotionally involved with the situation, Rosemary. Take as much time as you like to reflect on this situation. I know you're alarmed by your cousin's violent outburst. We shouldn't blame ourselves for what happened. Tom and Edward never met until yesterday when they met in very unusual and unfortunate circumstances," Chief Ote observed.

Arunma excused herself as she went to meet with her brother. Rosemary tried in vain to blink back tears from her eyes. Her mother noticed and excused herself and Rosemary. For want of what to do to contain the ugly situation, Chief Ote turned to Chief Ekelema. "How far back can you trace your family tree?" Chief Ote asked almost in a whisper. "I can trace my family tree to ten generations. I'm the custodian of our family history," Chief Ekelema responded. A mild smile lifted the corner of his mouth. Then he quickly added, "I think we should allow frayed nerves to calm down. We'll come back tomorrow." "I think you have a point there," Chief Ote said as he moved over to Tom. "My son, don't worry about it. We'll talk to Edward. I think he's overreacting. By tomorrow he'll be in a lighter mood." Chief Ote said as he put a protective arm around Tom's shoulders. Chief Ote and his wife saw them out.

Edward was in the garden facing away from the back door. He felt a hand on his shoulder. He hated talking about his feelings. He turned to face his sister. Arunma had a big smile on her face. "Can I speak with you for a minute?" Arunma asked. "What is it you want to see me about?" she smiled at him and he smiled back. " A strange thing happened yesterday. My mind keeps straying back to the fight between you and Tom at the Igba Oso Competition. It was unforeseen and unfortunate," she paused to look at him. Her obvious sincerity inclined him to trust her. "I was so furious I couldn't control myself and I hit him," he admitted, feeling like a complete idiot.

"How are you feeling today?" She asked with concern in her eyes. "Can you feel the bump on my head?" He responded as he directed her fingers to his head. "You'll feel better after a good night's sleep," she said beaming with smile. She recalled that there was a cheer when it was realized that everyone was safely back yesterday. Quickly, she asked, "Was there any incident you witnessed yesterday, apart from the fight?" "I almost lost my life at Ebele," he said almost in a whisper. "What happened?" She prodded him. "I mistakenly entered an enclosure reserved exclusively for former warriors who had brought human heads home," he stated. "Tell me more," she said. "Suddenly a fierce looking guy wanted to cut off my head, but for the quick intervention of the leader of the Oso, I would have been a dead man by now," he said as he felt cold shower run down his spine.

"God forbid. But you showed a reckless disregard for your own safety. Anyway, let's forget about that. Tom really likes you," she said as she touched his arm. "Who cares?" He said feigning indifference. When she heard her brother's words, something snapped inside her. "It's time to swallow your pride, Edward. What happened yesterday was purely accidental. Rosemary was deeply hurt by your careless remarks about Tom. She still speaks about him with great affection. Go mend fences with Tom," she advised him, turned and headed for the back door.

The house was strangely quiet. The weather had turned cool and windy. Arunma tried to call Rosemary but all she got was a busy signal when she dialed her number. She heard footsteps echo in the silence. And there was Rosemary coming towards her in the long corridor. There was a sparkle of excitement in their eyes. "Have you talked to Edward?" Rosemary asked, taking Arunma's hand. "I just finished talking to him. I think Tom is innocent. He didn't start the fight. Edward did. That much he confessed to me a moment ago," Arunma said, moving towards the sitting room with Rosemary. "Do you think he will patch up things with Tom now?" Rosemary asked with concern. She could feel herself blushing. She still had a lot of feeling for Tom. Soon   Edward joined them in the sitting room. The smells from the kitchen filled the sitting room. Arunma looked at Rosemary's hair. It was tied back in a neat bow. "I like the way you've done your hair," Arunma commended her. "Thanks. I want to look presentable when our kinsmen receive Tom and his uncle tomorrow," she replied.

Rosemary turned her attention to Edward. "Try and patch up your differences with Tom tomorrow OK?" She said, meeting his gaze without flinching. "I really resent the way he treated me," Edward complained. "I know the feeling. Tom is a really nice guy though," Rosemary said, beaming with smiles. "It doesn't matter. Can't you see he's taking advantage of you?" Edward said without any feeling. Rosemary didn't see the joke. "I'd better be going now. See you!" she said as she rose up, opened the front door and stepped outside, gently closing the door behind her.

The streets were silent and deserted. As Rosemary climbed the stairs to her room, she was lost in thought. She could not understand why several allusions were made by everyone in respect of her private affairs. Feelings were running high about her traditional engagement. Now she was beginning to feel as if she was a chattel and she resented this tag. She was aware that real hunters would only succeed if they hunted in their familiar terrain. She would seize the initiative and control the tempo of things pertaining to her private affairs. As she lay on her bed, sleep came to her in brief snatches.

Back in the Guest House Tom stood staring in the distance. A new twist had been introduced in the quest for Rosemary's hand in marriage. He realized that Edward had a definite strain of snobbery in him. Certainly, Edward was like a twisted mirror that distorted his shape. He, however, brushed aside his fears. Edward was incapable of stopping him in his quest even if he tried. As he got under the bed sheets, he recalled that he would not have reconciled with Rosemary if he hadn't gone to Esther's party. That party, it would appear was the elixir of their relationship. And now when he though the coast was clear; Edward had become another stumbling block. Life, he knew, was full of ups and downs.

Suddenly the lights in the Guest House went out because the system was overloaded. The room was plunged into total darkness. Outside, branches were tossing in the wind. He couldn't sleep but kept tossing and turning in bed all night. Only the snores of the sleepers in the adjacent rooms broke the silence of the house. It was anxiety that caused him to toss and turn in the bed. Just before dawn sleep mercifully snatched him.

8

Tom woke to a clear blue sky. He stared out of the window, lost in a day dream. It was a bright morning. By eight o'clock he had his bath. His uncle, Chief Ekelema was already having his breakfast when he entered the dining hall. "Sir, do you want breakfast?" the waiter asked Tom as he sat at table, facing his uncle. "Yes, bring me also a cup of tea," he responded. "Good Morning, Uncle," Tom greeted. "Morning, Tom. How are you?" Chief Ekelema responded. "I didn't sleep well," Tom said. "I understand. Anxiety can cause one not to sleep in the night. We should have seen it coming. There is no way you can keep going under all the pressure," Chief Ekelema observed. "I agree with you, uncle. We'll have to see how it goes today," Tom said drawing the tray to himself. His breakfast was served. He began eating his breakfast. Conversation flowed until they finished.

In the Ote's Family Compound, Rosemary threw the coffee dregs down the sink. "Hurry up and get dressed, Rosemary. Our kinsmen would soon gather here for the door knocking," Mrs. Brown called out as she went to her room. "I'm fully dressed, mum," she replied as she moved to the spacious sitting room to arrange the furniture. The sitting room was furnished with taste. Although she had very expensive tastes in clothes, she did not feel up to dressing for this occasion. Her mind was not in it. She was wearing a tight pair of jeans with a cotton blouse to match. Her hair was tied in a knot at the back of her head. She wore a chaste gold chain around her neck.

The kinsmen arrived sooner than expected. Chief Ote entered his late brother's house shortly after the kinsmen arrived. After Chief Ote and his kinsmen had exchanged the customary pleasantries, they got down to serious discussion. "Rosemary, get them some drinks while we are waiting for Tom and his uncle to join us," Chief Ote said, she was eager to please her kinsmen. Arunma soon joined her in the kitchen. She and Arunma served the drinks. Not long afterwards, Mrs. Brown fully dressed in blouse and wrapper with a headgear to match, came to welcome their guests.

"Sit where I can see you," Rosemary whispered to Arunma who nodded in silent agreement. Rosemary smiled her thanks as she took a seat beside her mother.

Outside, Tom and his uncle had arrived five minutes ago. Tom saw Edward moving slowly towards the next house. He walked up to him. "Can I speak with you for a minute?" he asked politely. "What do you want to speak about?" Edward restored angrily. "I want to apologize to you. I'm terribly sorry for what happened on the Oso day," Tom spoke in a low, strained voice. "That's ok. It's not for me to pass judgment on your behaviour. I'm not out for revenge," Edward replied without emotion. Thereafter he turned to go inside Dr. Brown's house. Tom and his uncle followed him into the house where the rest were waiting eagerly for them. Shortly after, Mrs. Ote entered too.

As soon as they entered the house, Rosemary, Arunma and Mrs. Brown knew intuitively that Edward and Tom had managed to patch up their differences. "Does Edward now speak with Tom?" Mrs. Brown asked her daughter. "I don't really know, but it seems to me they may be getting along well. Anyway, let's forget about that for the moment," Rosemary said. Her remarks passed without comment.

The sight of her son, Edward sitting with the kinsmen filled Mrs. Ote with pride. She felt that Edward was now a man. He could sit with elders and speak on issues affecting the extended family. After all, her son had participated in Oso competition required of all male citizens of the community. Suddenly her thoughts were interrupted as her husband cleared his throat and began to address the gathering. "My kinsmen, I greet you all for honouring our invitation. I sent for you to come and see what I'm seeing. Our people say that the snake one sees usually turns to python when one tells that story. Let me call on our guests, Tom and Chief Ekelema to tell us what brought them to our house," Chief Ote remarked as he beckoned to Chief Ekelema to state their mission.

"My fellow elders, I greet you. Tom is my nephew. My late brother, Chief Allison Ekelema, was until his death a top government functionary in the Federal Ministry of Mines, Power and Industry. We are from Edda. We are descendants of Ogbuagu Chima, the legendary son of Egbebu who was a brother to your ancestor, Onyerubi Atita," he paused as a murmur of agreement escaped from the elders. They nodded in agreement. His lip curved in a smile of thanks. "My nephew told me that he had seen a ripe Udara Fruit in your family. To indicate his seriousness in plucking the ripe Udara, he competed successfully in the Oso Competition last Afor Market Day. My fellow elders, we have only come to know the road so that we can return to tell our kinsmen. When the appropriate time comes, we shall return to fulfill our obligations as required by your customs and tradition. I salute you," he finished at last. Another murmur arose among the elders as each in turn shook hands with Chief Ekelema.

When Chief Ekelema mentioned the word 'ripe Udara Fruit', something snapped inside Rosemary. She raised her hand to ask for permission to speak. Immediately the elders saw her raised hand, a strained atmosphere took over the meeting. The faint smiles on their faces were immediately wiped off. A deafening silence descended that you could hear a pin drop. "As a child, I was surrounded by love and kindness. Right now, I feel as if I were a chattel to be shared by my kinsmen. I strongly believe I should have a say in my own affairs. Nowadays, women are considered as equal partners. If you feel otherwise, I may be forced to return to England. After all, I hold a British Passport," she spoke feelingly about her viewpoint.

"I call you to order, Rosemary! Let me put it more straight-forwardly. You're indeed, our asset. You're our pride. Your late father, our brother, bequeathed his entire estate to you, his only daughter and child. Your father is no more. Tradition demands that we should be actively involved in looking after the affairs of our late Kinsman. That's why we've gathered here today to ensure that our tradition is followed," Chief Obidike said, his voice throbbing with emotion.

"Honestly, I don't see how mere participation in a race entitles a man to exercise lordship over my heart without my full consent. In England, this would not be allowed to happen," her voice shook with emotion. Tears had smudged her mascara. The room was strangely quiet.

It was Chief Ote who broke the silence. "My daughter, we are Africans. Civilization started here in Africa. Besides, here is not England. I'm aware that emotional or mental problems can arise from a physical cause. Your main argument is a moral one, namely: your inalienable right to have a say in your own affairs. Whether it is right for us to infringe upon that right is a question of morality which in all good conscience I am not competent to comment on it. Let other elders state their views. You'll feel differently about it when the time comes," Chief Ote remarked in a pleasant, cultivated voice.

"I'm aware uncle that some strange customs have survived from earlier times. Treating women as a chattel is a survival strategy from Pre-Christian Times. I'll humbly ask you all not to discuss the matter further in my presence," she pleaded. Her face was taut and pale. She could divine what Tom was thinking just by looking at him. A tide of rage surged through her. He mother noticed it.

Quickly she stood up without waiting for permission to address the gathering. "Dear elders, please allow me to present my apologies. Most fathers wish to be present at the engagement ceremony of their daughters. At 32 Rosemary though a woman, is still a child – your child. I'll skip the usual preliminaries and come straight to the point. My people, times have changed. And we must change with the times. We must learn to consult with our children on matters which concern and affect them; listen to your daughter, Rosemary. She needs time to consider this second marriage although she wants to call the shots. It's her life. It's her private affairs. It's the affairs of the heart. Don't dismiss my suggestion out of hand. My elders, I salute you," she spoke forcefully. As she sat down, the room fell into silence again.

This time around, it was Chief Okonta who broke the silence. "Our wife, we hear what you're saying, but you're wrong. You're a woman. By our tradition you're to be seen and not to be heard. Ask your late husband's brother, Chief Ote to instruct you in the ways of our land. You think it's time we did away with our customs. You're greatly mistaken, you and your daughter. Our customs and norms define our corporate personality. They define our sense of community. They reinforce our pride and dignity. You and your daughter may excuse us. We want to confer among ourselves," he spoke with a note of finality and a hint of rebuke.

There was a distant look in her eye; her mind was obviously on something. All of them were painfully aware of the gradual disintegration of traditional values. In any case, their reaction dismayed her. Respectfully, Mrs. Brown bowed gently to them and beckoned to her daughter to follow her as she left the gathering. Tom looked tired and dispirited. Chief Ote took the floor again.

"I think we can dispense with the formalities. We must admit that times are changing. History does not only tell us about our past, but more importantly, it tells us that we have the capacities and inner resources to adapt to changes. Remember, it's neither the strongest nor the most intelligent of the species that survive, but the ones which adapt easily to changes, but then I'm prejudiced – after all, Rosemary is my niece," he summed up the situation.

"I know we cannot clap with one hand. Chief Ote, you're a man of good character and integrity. But then wine brought for door – knocking cannot return full. Let our guests present the wine they brought for door-knocking. We'll receive them next time. After all they've only come to know the way to our compound," Chief Obidike finished and smiled broadly. They nodded in silent agreement. "Here is the wine. Truly, we only came to know the road. We have also seen the ripe Udara in your family. In due season, we shall return to you and fulfill our obligations to this great and noble family," Chief Ekelema said as he offered two bottles of wine. Chief Ogbu collected the two bottles of wine and placed them on the centre table.

"We can see the side effects of technology on our traditional culture. Abam is a beautiful community full of culture and history. As Chief Ote had said, we must adapt in order to survive. Let's drink and make merry. After all, the Dane gun which fails to fire merely preserves the hunter's gunpowder," Chief Ogbu said as he gave a short, derisive laugh. All laughed merrily. Chief Okonta beckoned to Edward to bring in Mrs. Brown and her daughter. When they came in, they resumed their sitting positions and listened to Chief Okonta's summary of the decision.

"We've carefully considered all the sentiments expressed here today. We can see both sides of the argument. There is an obvious contrast between the cultures of England and Abam. Your late husband and I were contemporaries at College. His hatred of discrimination against women was equaled by his loathing for self-serving politicians. He believed in equality between men and women. Let Rosemary take as much time as she likes on this delicate matter of the heart. When she is convinced that the man in her life has proved himself worthy of her, you'll send for us and we'll gather again to dine and wine as our tradition demands. Our daughter is not a fowl to be disposed of so easily. Ogori says, 'If the road is good, he will pass through it twice,' I've finished." He said, laughing heartily and shaking hands with his fellow elders.

"Our elders, I thank you for your kind words. The essential character of our town is our deep sense of community. The locust says when legs are joined together the clay pot can be broken.' Once again, I salute you. Permit us to return to the kitchen. We're preparing lunch for all of you," Mrs. Brown responded, smiling with relief. She and Rosemary stood up, genuflected and retreated to the kitchen. Mrs. Brown, it would appear, had learned to shut out her angry feelings.

When everyone had gone, Tom waited behind to see Rosemary. "I'll wait outside until your meeting with Rosemary is over," Chief Ekelema said as he moved towards the front door. Tom nodded silently in agreement. Promptly he walked over to the kitchen and signaled Rosemary to meet him in the sitting room. Rosemary was busy washing off the plates and glasses in the kitchen. "I can hardly wait to see Tom alone," Rosemary enthused as she faced a volley of angry questions from her mother. "Dear daughter, why does Tom want to see you alone? Don't you think that this second meeting is coming too soon?" Mrs. Brown asked. As Rosemary moved to the sitting room, her mother cautioned, "Darling, be careful." "I will, Mum," she said. But she sounded more confident than she felt.

Tom sat on the sofa. He stretched and yawned lazily as Rosemary walked into the sitting room. She sat on the armchair, facing him. She smiled at him and he smiled back. "What is it you want to see me about? I can only see you for a few minutes. I have chores to do in the kitchen," she said. "I don't want to tie myself down to coming back to your family on a particular date," Tom began. "That's a terrible thing to say. I hate to see you unhappy," she said. "Did you see what happened?" he asked. "You tell me," she retorted. "You'll feel differently about it when the time comes." His voice was throbbing with emotion. "I don't know about that," she replied, shrugging her shoulders. "What we have here is a crisis situation. All my efforts have become futile. I felt like a complete idiot all through the meeting," he said, his voice rising.

"If you expect to fail, you will fail. It's a self-fulfilling prophecy. I know you're upset, but when all's said and done, it isn't exactly a disaster," she said, and gave a strained laugh. Her eyes were full of mischief.

"You acted selfishly in calling off the engagement. You were thoughtless," he spoke in a low, strained voice. When she heard the accusation, she couldn't help herself as a muffled laugh escaped her lips.

"You know why I'm laughing? You amuse me. Tom, I was almost on my knees begging you to take my heart just for the asking. But what did you do? You gave me a cold shoulder. If I may ask you, when did you start having feelings for me? If you truly love me, prove it," she said as she smiled a smile of dry amusement.

Tom got up from the sofa and went over to where Rosemary sat. She quickly got up too. His body was solid and taut. She could smell alcohol in his breath. "I can see through your little game," he said as he put his arm around her shoulders. "Let go of me," she said fiercely. She just tossed her head and walked away. Embarrassed, he staggered outside, and there was Edward standing on the drive way. He had a self-satisfied smirk on his face. "I've told my cousin not to speak to strangers. You're a stranger to this family," Edward said mischievously. Tom shrugged and said nothing. He joined his uncle and they strolled towards the Guest House to pick their things. It was time to depart.

After Tom returned to Abuja, events took a dramatic turn in the weeks that followed. Although this year's Oso festival attracted a record turnout, he felt betrayed. He didn't have any strong feelings about the festival itself one way or the other, except what it was; a stepping stone to his quest to win Rosemary's hand in marriage. As he sat down on the sofa, he felt something crawl up his arm. A wasp had flown in through the window. He slapped the wasp on his arm out of proportion.

Lately he had grown quite fond of Rosemary. Strangely she had grown elusive to reach. He got up, opened the front door and gently closed the door behind him. He turned the key in the lock. Turning up the collar of his coat he hurried out into the dark night. He turned into a narrow street. The weather had turned cold and windy when he got to Angela's Restaurant. No sooner had he sat down at a table in a corner of the restaurant than his cell phone rang. It was Akon. He had gone to his house and didn't see him. "Take the first turning on the right. Meet me at Angela's," he directed Akon.

In no time Akon arrived at Angela's Restaurant. He sat down facing Tom. They ordered for food and drinks. A fly was buzzing against the window. The pale walls provided a perfect foil for the brightly coloured furniture. Abuja was covered in a thick blanket of fog. With his back turned to the wall, Tom gazed into vacancy.

"The nights are getting longer," Akon paused when he noticed Tom was not listening. "It's about Rosemary?" Akon asked as his voice fell to a whisper. He thumped the table slightly to draw Tom's attention. "We arranged to meet at 7:30, but she never turned up. I think she's something up her sleeve. I'm afraid our relationship is under great strain at the moment," Tom said as he watched the waiter place a bowl of fried rice before him. "I hate to see you unhappy, my good friend. I'd like to take up the point you raised earlier. You're fooling yourself if you think none of this will affect you. If you fool about with matches, you'll end up getting burnt," Akon smiled faintly as he sat up to receive his bowl of pasta. "I feel like a fool. Imagine how I made a complete fool of myself in front of everyone in Ozu Abam!" Tom said regretfully.

"This tastes good. I've never tasted anything like it. Now back to Rosemary. I think she's just a vain, foolish woman," Akon said as he pushed some pasta into his mouth. "Foolishly, I allowed myself to be persuaded to enter the Oso Contest. I got the feeling that Edward, her cousin, didn't like me much," Tom said with mouthful of rice. "This drink tastes like apple," Akon commented as he sipped from his glass. He gave a wry smile. "I saw through her from the start. Poor me, I've always been a sucker for women with expensive tastes," Tom said. He looked pale and sullen.

"The way I see it, you have three main problems. First, try to see things from her point of view. Second, observe her body language. Third, find her G-string. By that I mean you should find out what turns her on," Akon advised as he sipped from his glass. "I get so annoyed with Rosemary! She drives me crazy," Tom said, pushing away the empty plate. He sipped from his glass. "Tell me about it. But you must learn to control your temper. Monkeys do not have any kind of protective armour. They use their brains," he said with the barest hint of a smile.

"Rosemary talks a lot of nonsense. Her unilateral decision in calling off the engagement is, I feel, a huge mistake. What does she take me for?" Tom said with angry snarl. His mind kept straying back to the events he experienced at Ozu Abam during the Oso Festival.

"You should follow up your earlier phone call with another one or e-mail," Akon advised, rising from his seat. "It's getting late. Let's go." Tom said as he rose, beckoned to the waiter and settled the bill. They left Angela's and then turned into the narrow street.

Last month, Julia resigned as Tom's secretary after ten years. She married John, her heartthrob. They travelled to Paris for their honeymoon. Tom had trouble getting a new secretary. He was also having trouble coping with the stresses and strains of his office. He was afraid that with the resignation of Julia as secretary, new secretaries would now come and go with monotonous regularity. Thus preoccupied with thoughts, he turned back to his work as he sat turning pages of a project proposal.

At the end of a busy day like today, he returned home showered and then sank thankfully into the sofa. While he was in that position he talked on the phone for over an hour. Rosemary was at the other end. "Don't phone me at work – people will talk," Rosemary said. Tom staggered under the impact of the words. "You should stop worrying about it. I'm sorry," he said, calling up his reserves of self-control. "Did you have a good day?" she asked in a pleasant voice. "It's been a long day," he answered. Quickly he added, "I'd like to take you out to dinner tonight; at Angela's Restaurant." "I don't think I'll make it, but let me try anyway. I'll be late if I'm able to make it. Let me have the direction, in any case," Rosemary said. "Here's the direction to Angela's in Wuse 2. From your Maitama end, the road turns to the left after Transcorp Hotel. Follow Adetokunbo Crescent until you turn right into a narrow street immediately after Ami Supermarket. The road turns right, follow it and you'll get to Angela's Restaurant. See you later! "Tom finished as he jumped up with broad smile on his face.

Rosemary arrived late, looking hot and flustered. Her sleek black hair was tied in a knot at the back of her head. She wore a tight pair of jeans and a blue cotton blouse with a pair of stiletto to match. She clutched her handbag. As she sat down, her heavy gold chain dangled round her neck. They sat at table for two. "Hello, Rosemary, you look great," Tom said, with a smile. She smiled her thanks as she tweaked his ear playfully.

They ordered for food and drinks. "This year's Oso Festival attracted a record turnout. Thank you for participating. Now that proves you're a man," Rosemary complimented Tom. "There's no need to thank me – I enjoyed doing it," Tom responded, his voice vibrant. "Did you notice that the nights are getting longer these days?" she asked. "Sure, that's part of the climate change. Everything seems to be unusual these days," Tom responded. There followed a short silence as the waiter served their food and drink. They began to eat their dinner with more conversation flowing. "Why don't you have a taste of special meal of the day?" Tom asked. "No, thanks," she replied.

"This dish has an unusual combination of tastes and textures. It's a tasty dish," Tom said. "I've never tasted anything like it. You can taste the garlic on this stew," Rosemary observed. She fluttered her eyelashes at him. "Haven't you heard? Julia my secretary had resigned. She got married," Tom said. "So I've heard," she replied. "How time flies!" he remarked. "When are you going to get a proper job?" she asked as she sipped from her glass. "I'm a property developer," Tom said flatly. He sipped from his glass. "How much money is there in your account to show for all your struggles?" she teased. "There is money to be made from property development," Tom asserted. "There are a lot of empty properties in this Wuse 2 Area, even in Maitama District; Asokoro District ditto. Prices of properties in all these locations have recently gone up enormously," Rosemary observed. At that Tom went into a long monologue about the property market in Abuja. He spoke with a seriousness that was unusual in him.

Suddenly he placed his hand on her hand, looked her straight in the eyes. "Rosemary, how long will you limp between two opinions? How long does it take you to make up your mind? Or are you suggesting that you're incapable of making a decision?" Tom asked. She looked into his troubled face. Her lips twitched with amusement. "Don't turn your anger on me. I don't know what you're talking about. Spill it out, Tom," she said, gently withdrawing her hand. She kept her hands folded in her lap. He focused his brown eyes on her. "Why don't you want to marry me?" he asked with seriousness etched on his face. "I don't want to rush into a second marriage unprepared. I'll turn 32 next week. I need time to know you better. Besides, you don't really know how to turn on the charm. I want a man who can turn me on, Tom," she stated. Her voice shook with emotion.

"You're a highly volatile personality. It's tempting to speculate about what might have happened to you in recent times. You're driving me crazy, Rosemary. You say awful things when you're in a temper. You think I'm after your money? No!" he spoke in a monotone drawl as he fluttered his hands around wildly.

"I suppose you're right!" she said resignedly. No sooner had she said it than she burst into tears. "Sorry, I don't follow you. I don't see how that follows from what I've just said," Tom said in a pleasant voice. "I need time to make up my mind. I've got a lot on my mind. I've been promoted the Sunday Editor of my paper. Only yesterday I received a call from my cousin, Arunma, informing me that my Uncle's health had taken a turn for the worse. Please bear with me if it seems I'm slow in reaching a decision. I admit that men admire me a lot. That's to be expected. After all, I'm young, beautiful and rich. I do hereby extend an invitation to you to attend my birthday party next weekend," she finished at last as she rose to her feet. She took her handbag. Tom stood up uncertain whether or not to say anything more.

"I feel as if I'd been led into a blind alley by you. If I may ask; why were you making overtures to me a couple of years back?" Tom asked perplexed. "Oh, that. I was suffering from post traumatic stress disorder. You can see I no longer drink. I see things differently now," she said as she tried to move away from the table. Tom beckoned to the waiter and settled the bill. As he turned to face Rosemary, he remarked, "You are seeing someone." Her face twisted in anger. She slapped his face hard. "It's none of your business," she replied. She thrust past him angrily and left.

He crept silently out of the restaurant and headed home. The narrow street he turned into was silent and deserted. When he got home, the house was strangely quiet. He went upstairs, showered and dressed in his pajamas and went downstairs and sank into the sofa. His mind kept straying back to their last talk together. He concluded that Rosemary had a definite strain of snobbery in her. No wonder he felt that their current relationship was under great strain. The food and wine made him sleepy. Soon he was fast asleep on the sofa.

9

The following morning dawned bright and warm. Dry season in Abuja was usually hot; with daily averages above 30° C. Tom had just eaten his breakfast. He felt heavy and tired. He had just drifted off to sleep when the phone rang. He answered it. It was Susan. She told him she wanted to see him. It was urgent. Thirty minutes later, there was a ring at the door. The door opened and Susan walked in. "What a nice surprise! Please make yourself comfortable while I get some coffee," Tom said as he retreated to the kitchen.

Susan shifted into a comfortable position on the armchair. Her eyes roamed the room. "Do you take sugar in your coffee?" Tom asked handing her a cup of coffee on a saucer. "Oh, thanks," she beamed with smiles. "Imagine my surprise when you walked into this sitting room," Tom remarked as he sat down, facing her. "You shouldn't be surprised to see me in your house. Can you lend me some money until tomorrow?" She asked in a soft voice. "Sure, how much do you want to borrow?" Tom asked. She hesitated before replying; "Two hundred thousand Naira." she said. "That's a lot of money. But I don't have that much cash on me now. I'll make out a cheque for the amount," he said as he went to fetch his cheque book. Soon he returned to the sitting room. "Here, this is the cheque for two hundred thousand naira. Aside, I'm wondering why your friend, Rosemary didn't lend you the money," Tom said as he gave her the cheque.

"Thanks. Talk about mean! Rosemary didn't even buy me a birthday card last week," she said as she collected the cheque. She sipped her coffee. He watched her carefully. "Did she tell you anything about our dinner outing last night?" Tom asked with curiosity. "Don't mind me – I'll just sit here quietly. I was scared, I don't mind telling you! I think she's seeing someone else. Mind where you're treading!" She said in a low tone, almost in a whisper. "I'd like to ask you a few questions, if you don't mind. Who told you about it? Who's this new guy in her life? Are they going steady?" Tom asked with concern.

"Have you minded how I found out? – It's true. Are you busy next Saturday? Are you invited to Rosemary's party? We'll meet on Saturday then," she said as she gave a small twisted smile. "How could she turn round and stab me on the back, after all I've done for her? Although I accepted the invitation thankfully, well, I'm not going, and that's that," Tom said fuming. "I should be going now. Please don't say I told you about her double game. All the same I met her new boyfriend last week. More surprises await you at her birthday party," she revealed as she got up and made for the door. Once again, she murmured her thanks. She turned the door knob, and stepped outside, quietly closing the door behind her.

He felt betrayed. His head felt as if it would burst. He wouldn't have minded so much if Rosemary had told him the truth. Lack of money and social class were the main problems as he saw it. He felt she had no excuse for mindlessly destroying their budding relationship. He knew that he had to confront his fears. At the moment he was dead to all feelings of self-pity. Worse still, he couldn't make out what she really wanted. And he was determined to find out. So he decided to attend her birthday party next Saturday.

The sprawling mansion perched precariously on a steep hillside in Maitama District of Abuja. Bars of sunlight slanted down from the tall narrow windows. Music blared from the open windows. The mansion had a barbed wire fence. Adjacent to the flower garden the sun shone on the swimming pool and the water danced and sparkled. This beautiful mansion was the venue of Rosemary's Birthday Party. It was her home. Preparation for the party started early this Saturday morning. She decorated the sitting room with flowers and balloons. The walls of the ballroom were splashed with patches of blue and purple. Early guests were having fun in the swimming pool, swimming or just splashing around. Inside the ballroom a live band was playing.

There were thirty-two coming to the party, all told. The telephone rang and Rosemary answered. It was Tom. He called to say he might be late. Edward and his friend colonel Peter flew down to Abuja. They perched on a couple of high stools at the bar, sipping red wine from their glasses. Soon the ballroom was filled to the brim as guests took their seats. Rosemary made her entrance after all other guests had arrived. Her entry attracted thunderous applause. She wore a simple band of gold on her finger. Around her neck was a heavy gold chain. She wore turquoise dress with a pair of stiletto to match. Her hair was twisted into a knot on top of her head. She was wearing bright red lipstick.

Food and drinks were lavishly provided for the guests. As they were dining and wining, Tom entered the ballroom. He wore black suit with a bow tie and a pair of black Italian shoes which gave him a rather dignified look.

As his eyes ranged the spacious ballroom he saw Rosemary chatting with a tall handsome man in his late thirties. Edward was hovering around them. Susan quickly edged towards Tom. "Hello, Tom, you're here at last. Look at that tall man over there, chatting with Rosemary. That's Colonel Peter. It wouldn't surprise me if they got married soon. Talking of Rosemary, that's the new boyfriend. I met him last week. Set yourself targets that you can reasonably hope to achieve. Tell me, have you had lunch yet? Should I get some food and drink for you?" she ranted on. Tom nodded in silent agreement. Just then   Rosemary turned. Her heart gave a flutter when she saw him. Her eyes followed him everywhere. He looked at her fondly and gave a shy smile and a little twist of his head. In return she gave a small twisted smile. She noticed the bunch of flowers he was holding. Slowly she made her way towards him. He gave her the bunch of flowers. She murmured her thanks. Impulsively, he tried to kiss her but she quickly pulled away. Immediately Susan took Tom's arm and pulled him along. "Follow me please. I'll show you the way. I've served your food." she said leading him towards the sitting room.

As Tom settled himself on the sofa, a tray of food and drink was placed on a side stool. In silence he began to eat. Susan perched on the edge of the sofa. A smile lifted the corner of her mouth. "I don't want you to make a fool of yourself tonight. Rosemary is a vain woman. She gets turned on by men in uniform," she hinted and gave a wry smile. "Are you telling the truth?" Tom asked curiously. "Yes. Promise you won't tell. Don't let her monopolize you like she did at Esther's Birthday Party," she advised as she made for the ballroom. Tonight he would act decisively. He was determined to steal the show.

When he returned to the ballroom the band had finished with a few slow dances. Suddenly Edward called the audience to attention. "Ladies and gentlemen, may I have your attention please? I'd like to propose a toast to the celebrant. Rosemary is 32 today and has also been appointed the Sunday Editor of her paper. By all standards, my cousin is a millionaire. Let's toast to her success and health," Edward remarked. Quickly he added; let's sing 'Happy Birthday,' to the celebrant." The guests took up the refrain and sang merrily. She was toasted in champagne. With this they entered into the spirit of the occasion. The next dance was a waltz. Tom moved over to Rosemary's side. "Let's have a dance," he requested. "Sure," she said as she took his outstretched arm. As they danced, their conversation flowed freely. "I fondly imagined that you cared for me. Over the years I have grown quite fond of you now. I have the feeling that you don't really love me after all," Tom said looking into her eyes. "Your personal feelings shouldn't enter into details at this stage," she replied and gave a smile of dry amusement.

Tom was not yet done. He hit the hammer on the nail to drive home his point. "I'm ready to take the bull by the horn. A new dimension in the form of Colonel Peter has been introduced into the ring. This possibility never entered into my calculations," Tom said with the barest hint of a smile. About the same time the band finished the waltz. By now every eye was focused on Rosemary and Tom as they gently disengaged from their close-up. It had silently percolated through to the guests that something interesting was about to happen.

Suddenly Tom went down on one knee. "Will you marry me, Rosemary?" He asked with high expectation. There followed a short silence. She hesitated before replying. "No, I won't," she responded. "Why not?" Tom probed. "I'm not ready yet. Besides, it's a woman's prerogative to change her mind!" She said in a monotone drawl with a note of defiance in her voice. A deafening silence descended upon the audience that you could hear a pin drop.

Nothing had presaged the dreadful fate that befell Tom. Thoughts of failure now preoccupied him. He had a premonition that he had lost her to his rival in uniform. Although he took care at the moment not to prejudge her decision, he felt that her decision to turn down his proposal was based on ignorance and prejudice. Inwardly, he suffered the painful feelings of rejection. With effort of will, he kept his emotions tightly reined in. He was aware that his heart won't stand the emotional strain much longer. For his male pride had been deeply hurt. Without speaking, he stood up and went out. He headed home.

Rosemary tried to remain cool, calm and collected. Against the backdrop of what had just happened, she knew that relations between them had definitely cooled. Tom had got her in a corner, and there wasn't much she could do about it. Out of the corner of her eye, she saw Edward drawing closer to her. He led her to where Colonel Peter sat. She cast a furtive glance over her shoulder. Edward paused, turned and gaily announced that the band was going to give a special number. The audience went totally gaga over the band as the music blared loudly.

"Come here, my dear," Colonel Peter said pleasantly. She went and sat beside him. "Would you like a drink, dear?" He asked crisply and signaled Edward to get her a glass of wine. Colonel Peter was dazzled by the warmth of her smile. Indeed, she was dazzlingly beautiful on this occasion of her birthday celebration. He looked at her fondly. She knew that he was looking at her, sizing her up. As Edward handed her a glass of wine, she murmured her thanks.

"What's wrong with that airhead you call Tom?" Edward asked as he sat down beside her. "There's nothing wrong with him," she said airily. She shifted uneasily in her chair. Her breathing was uneven. "Tom kicks up a fuss every time I even suggest slowing things a bit. He is a great talent, though," she said as she sipped from her glass. "He tends to thrust himself at all. That's why I can't see any future in this relationship. It's never worked from day one," Edward said in a flat monotone. "I think I should warn that guy to leave you alone," Colonel Peter volunteered. "Don't fuss, Colonel, everything is all right," she pleaded tracing the contours of his face with her forefinger. He gave a shy smile and a little twist of his head.

"I think Tom owes you an apology for embarrassing you before your guests," Edward suggested. "Tom? Apologize? That'll be the day!" She said, smiling broadly. "Anyway, don't let anyone spoil your day," Edward cautioned. "Susan, get me some apple, please." "Sure," she said as she went to fetch the apple.

Rosemary crunched her apple noisily. She admired the firm set of Colonel Peter's jaw. When she looked out of the window she saw that two birds had settled on the barbed wire fence. A hawk flew slowly past. She saw butterflies flutter from flower to flower. She was lost in her daydream as the band played cool music.

Susan sneaked out of the room quietly to make a phone call to Tom. She was yet to repay the money she borrowed from him. She was afraid Tom might ask for his money soon. "Hello, Tom. This is Susan. I commend your boldness. You acted perfectly and properly in proposing to Rosemary on this occasion of her birthday party. Take my advice though, leave her alone. She doesn't deserve you," she finished at last. Taking a sip from his glass, Colonel Peter said, "He who is afraid of doing too much always does too little." At this they laughed heartily. He became positively garrulous after a few glasses of wine. "We've got a spare bedroom, if you'd like to stay," Edward said as he watched Colonel Peter down his drink. "No, thanks, I don't want to put you to a lot of trouble. I'll pass the night at the Army Guest House," he said, springing into action. "OK. I'll see you out," Edward said as he staggered towards the door with Colonel Peter in tow.

That night Tom tried to sleep but he couldn't sleep. His mind was in turmoil. He found himself snared in a web of intrigue. He felt he could not live with the shame of other people knowing the truth. He sprawled in the sofa watching television to relieve the suffocating disappointment he suffered at the hand of Rosemary. At every turn he met with disappointment. What he did not know was that wealth and position were not important to Rosemary. She couldn't stand his jealousy and possessiveness. Once she had a hint to this trait in him she peremptorily rejected his proposal. Colonel Peter as the new man in her life had not yet entered into her calculations. She felt that it was the game of being chased by the male species that excited most female species. On his part, Edward felt he was already succeeding in his scheme to keep Tom at bay. As the night grew longer, Tom fell asleep on the sofa.

It happened on the weekend of 24 and 25 of April. Rosemary sounded very cold and distant on the phone. Tom had been pestering her with phone calls for over a week. "Tom, you think you can call me at all hours of the day and night. I work well into the small hours as an editor. I'll appreciate it if you could be a little more sensitive," Rosemary said. "I asked you to marry me. You refused. I'm sure your mother would have a fit if she knew you'd been dating Colonel Peter. By the way, what did you see in him?" Tom responded. "He loves me more than you do. He allows me to be myself. He brings out the best in me. Besides, he knows how to turn on the charm. Above all, he's an officer and a gentleman," Rosemary revealed. "So, that's it? A gentle man? An Officer?" Tom was still ranting when the line cut. He looked pale, with deep shadows under his eyes.

His phone rang and he answered it. Susan was on the line. "Hope you've not forgotten you promised to take me out for dinner tonight. I'll be ready in an hour's time. You remember where you'll meet me?" "Yes, I remember." Tom responded as the phone went dead at the other end. Just then there was a ring at the door. The door opened and Akon walked in, smiling radiantly. "Hello, Akon," he said, with a smile. "How are you, Tom?" He asked, shaking hands with Tom. "I see you're dressed for an evening outing. Who are you going out with tonight?" Akon asked with interest. "Promise you won't tell," Tom said. "I won't. Cross my heart," Akon pledged. "It's Susan." Tom confided. "You'll do no such thing. Are you out of your mind? What's come over you?"Akon asked visibly surprised. "It's not what you think. She's been pestering my life ever since Rosemary rejected my proposal. I don't want her to wear me out. My mind is not in it. It's just a harmless dinner. Don't read meaning into it, Akon," Tom said defensively.

"I'm only thinking aloud. Just be careful, my friend. That girl is an opportunist. Tread softly," Akon said, shifting comfortably in the armchair. There followed a short silence as Tom offered him a drink. He murmured his thanks and sipped his wine. He had a self-satisfied smirk on his face. "Esther and I are getting married," Akon announced cheerfully. "So I've heard. I'm happy for you, my friend. Have you fixed a date for the wedding yet?" Tom asked pleasantly. "In a couple of weekends our wedding will take place in July hopefully," Akon replied. "I'm afraid I don't have much time to spend with you, Akon. Bear with me. By the way, congratulations in advance," Tom said rising from the sofa. Akon got up as he finished his drink. "Be careful, Tom. Susan has been heard to make threats to her former lover." I will, Akon. Thanks for your concern," Tom said as he opened the door for Akon. He checked to see if all the doors were locked before he left to keep his date with Susan.

As they alighted from the taxi, Susan sidled up to Tom and whispered something in his ear. He looked sideways at her. "I feel silly in these clothes," she whined. Tom said nothing. "Do you have any brothers or sisters?" she asked as she took his arm. "Nope, I'm man alone," Tom answered without emotion. "So am I. Rosemary has been like a sister to me. But I can't say that of her lately. She's always been very close with her money," she said. Tom gave a shrug. "It doesn't matter," he said as he walked up the driveway to Angela's. The waiter came to take their order as they sat at table for two. "Why not have the dishes of the day?" Tom suggested. "Perfect," she said excitedly. She also took up his offer of a drink. Their order for food and drink was served. There followed a short silence as they ate their dinner. "How did you get entangled with Rosemary?" Susan asked.

"Rosemary and her late husband, Steve, returned from the States and came to settle in Abuja. They have nowhere to stay so I couldn't turn them away. Rosemary had nobody she could turn to as her in-laws didn't like her at all. Unknown to me, she has romantic designs on me but I kept her at bay and didn't encourage her overtures to me," Tom explained and gave a wry smile. "Men are all the same. You don't value what you have until you lose it. There's no need to cry over spilled milk. You've been depressed for weeks. In any case, I should be glad to help," she said with emotion. Within her she knew she was scheming. Her one thought was to ensnare a rich husband. Tom was no fool. He sized up the situation very quickly. The main course was preceded by fresh fruit.

"Would you like some more?" He asked. "No, thanks," she responded. "Would you like more drink?" He further probed. "Oh, yes. Thanks," she replied. Quickly she added, "Don't let Rosemary ruin your life. And don't play the second fiddle in her life. She travels around the world as if money is no object," she remarked with a hint of resentment in her voice. "Let's hurry up. It's getting late," Tom said as he beckoned to the waiter. He settled the bill. "Can you wait a second while I make a call?" Susan asked as she took her cell phone from her handbag. A smile touched the corners of his mouth. As soon as she finished making the phone call, she took Tom's arm and pulled him along. He looked sideways at her. She held him close and pressed her cheek to his.

"Let's take a taxi," Tom suggested. "Sure," Susan said cheerfully. "I'm not going home. I'm staying in your place this weekend," she announced. Surprisingly, he agreed straight away. Inside his sitting room, he flung off his coat and collapsed on the sofa. Mellow music and lighting helped to create the right atmosphere. "I'll shower and then run you a bath," Susan said as she went to the bedroom opposite Tom's. She was still tingling with excitement when she got into the shower cubicle. When she returned to the sitting room, Tom had drifted off to sleep. A gentle touch of her hand on his shoulder made him jump. "I've run you a bath. Please go have your bath," Susan said. She looked incredibly sexy in a cream evening dress. "Please see that all the doors are locked. Turn off the TV before you sleep," Tom instructed.

As soon as he finished having his bath, he lay down sprawled on his bed and was just dozing off when Susan crept into the room. She sat on the edge of the bed silently admiring his handsome face. Alcohol seemed to have scrambled her brain. She roused him with a gentle nudge. Deftly, she touched his face and moved her hand gently over his body. Slowly Tom opened his eyes. She reached over and flipped off the light. Tom held her hand as she resumed caressing his body. "Stop it! Let's not start what we can't finish," he said as he sat bolt upright.

She rumpled his hair playfully. The food and wine began to make him feel sexy. "Please return to your room. Let's not create a scandal. Scarcely a week goes by without some new scandal in the newspapers," he said as he watched her from the corner of his eye. "I'm frightened of sleeping alone," she admitted as she traced the contours of his face, smiling seductively. "Why are you frightened?" he probed. "At night, danger lurks in these streets," she said, twirling her full sensuous lips. As she tried to lie on his bosom, Tom gently pushed her away. "Stop it now, the joke has gone far enough!" he said. Rage bubbled just below the surface of his mind. "Tom, if you keep thinking about Rosemary while I'm here, then, I'll say you're selfish." There was a touch of sarcasm in her voice. "Do you think I'm being selfish by not letting her go? Any affair between us here and now will be driven by pure lust. Don't lust after me. I'm not available. I'm convinced more than ever before that your interest in me is purely sexual," Tom remarked. "Yes, I find you sexually attractive. Make me feel like a woman tonight," she said with emotion. She could feel herself blushing.

"Ssh! Keep your voice down. Don't talk such rot. What happened to your banker boyfriend?" Tom said, trying to manage the situation. "We had a brief fling but it's over now. He was determined to have one last fling before retiring. So, I threatened him. I hear he's shacked up with some woman in Lagos," she confessed without blushing. "I wish you'd take me seriously. What Rosemary and I have is not a fling. We deeply love each other. If there are obstacles on our way to marital bliss, we'll find a way to skirt around the obstacles. Please return to your room; we'll talk more tomorrow," Tom persuaded her. Reluctantly she rose from the bed and quietly left the room. Soon she surrendered herself to sleep. Tom dozed off soon after.

10

It was thundering all night but there was no rain. The roseate glow of dawn announced the birth of a new day. The hills were still shrouded in mist. Tom lay awake in his room reflecting on the seductive maneuvers of Susan last night. Doubts that had been submerged in his mind suddenly resurfaced. It was almost eight O' Clock. He wanted to put the record straight. "Wake up! It's eight O' clock. What time do you usually wake up in the morning?" Tom said, trying to rouse Susan. Slowly she opened her eyes, yawned lazily and sat bolt upright on the bed. Her room was bathed in the morning sunshine. A tide of shame surged through her as she took in the towering figure of Tom.

"About last night, I don't regret a thing. I'm a realist. If you put sugar in my mouth, I won't spit it out, though I'm overwhelmed by painful feelings of rejection," she said, struggling to regain some dignity. Tom shook his head regretfully. "I flatly refuse to discuss the matter. There are other things we can discuss. I have nothing further to say in this regard," he said as he dismissed her with a regal gesture. "I'd like to take my argument a stage further. Let me quickly shower, fix my hair and then we'll talk more. These are issues that touch us all," Susan said as Tom retreated to the kitchen to fix breakfast for two.

When Tom returned to Susan's room to tell her that breakfast was ready, he found her busy touching up her make-up in the mirror. Her hair was scraped back from her face in a ponytail. "I've been thinking, Tom, that your idea of life is a mirage. Rosemary could scarcely complain; could she?" she said, pursing her lips. "We live in troubled times. I didn't mean to hurt your feelings. Let me set the record straight. This situation can't go on. I'm not prepared to start a romantic relationship with you," Tom pointed out. "Let's be friends, then. That's all I'm asking from you," she said as her face lit up with hope. "We're friends already," Tom said flatly as he turned to leave the room. At the threshold, he turned briefly and added, "Breakfast is ready. Come with me to the dining room." He walked briskly towards the dining room. Immediately Susan followed him like a submissive child.

Tom scanned through the newspaper over breakfast. There followed a short silence. Suddenly Susan broke the silence. "I'm cash-strapped. Can I ask you a favour?" she said with expectancy. "Go on, ask me. But I don't want you to run away with the impression that all I do is sign cheques. How are you fixed for cash? Tom asked in a low tone. "I have only ₦1, 000 to see me through the week," she said as she tactfully skirted around the subject of money. Tom however felt she was exploiting the current situation for her own ends. At the end of the day, he would still have to make his own decision whether or not to bail her out. He was aware that he would come to a sticky financial end one of these days if he carried on like this.

"We don't have an endless supply of money, you know. Although there are endless opportunities for making money; it's important we control our cash outflow," he explained. Her expectation had now almost completely evaporated. He knew from past experience that Susan would not give up easily. "The payments I get barely cover my expenses," she whined. "I suggest that you keep an Expense Account. In addition, practise percentage budgeting every month," Tom advised. "You've said nothing regarding my request," she reminded him. "I've only ₦50, 000 cash in this house. I'll give it to you to tide you over until you get paid," Tom promised. "You're a darling, Tom. Last week I had a long talk with my boss about my career prospects. I'm sure I'll soon get a pay rise. Have you heard?" she quickly introduced a new item to the matter under discussion.

"Heard about what? Now, let's not spend the rest of the morning in mutual recrimination. So, what's new?" Tom asked pointedly. "Rosemary is relocating to Lagos to take charge of the family business. Both Edward and Arunma are not willing and prepared to run the business. The uncle's health as you know has taken a turn for the worse I learnt that Arunma got a new juicy job with NNPC. I'm afraid the setting is now ripe for a full blown romance between Rosemary and Colonel Peter in Lagos. I find Colonel Peter's devotion to Rosemary rather disturbing. When I found out that he was a Casanova, I took an instant dislike to him. Shine your eyes, Tom. If I may ask, what's your next plan?" She summed up at last.

"I think it's in the interest of everyone concerned that I should be out of circulation for a while. I'll relocate to Kaduna. I'll sell this house and put the proceeds of the sale in a fixed deposit account," Tom explained. He watched her facial expression. Her face registered disapproval. "I might never see you again," she moaned. "There's nothing to worry about. We'll keep in touch. After all, friendship should be kept in constant repairs," he said as he retired to the sitting room. That evening Susan tried to talk him out of leaving.

"Could you turn the TV up? Whose turn is it to cook?" Tom asked, trying to change the subject. "I'll cook for us while I'm here. How do you want the meat to be done?" Susan asked as she took the remote on the centre table. "Brown the meat on one side, then turn it over and brown the other side," he directed. He noticed that Susan turned her toes out as she went to the kitchen to prepare dinner. The smells from the kitchen filled the room. Out of curiosity Tom joined Susan in the kitchen. "Taste it and see if you think there's enough salt in it," she said. "Add a little salt and pepper to taste. The soup has very little taste. Spice it with Maggi or Knorr cubes," he advised. "You know Rosemary doesn't cook well. I don't know what you see in her. I can't see her changing overnight," she said with a hint of resentment. "You shouldn't have said such things in my hearing. You're resentful towards Rosemary," he said, leaving the kitchen. Later they ate dinner and turned in for the night.

For several years, Rosemary and Susan heard nothing about Tom. He disappeared and was never heard of for years. After disposing of his house in Abuja, Tom went into the army. He received his short service training at the Command and Staff College, Jaji near Kaduna. In the process of time he became a Commissioned Officer and was posted 321 Reece Regiment in Kakuri, Kaduna. He was appointed the Staff Officer at the operational headquarters. By this time he had been promoted to a major in the Nigerian Army.

Intelligence reports indicated that the Boko Haram insurgents had been sighted in the surrounding farming settlements scattered on the Kaduna-Abuja Expressway. Army Patrols were sent to reconnoiter the incursion of the insurgents into the North Central Area including Abuja. Troops patrolled the Kaduna-Abuja Expressway day and night. The troops were commanded by Major Tom. It was a sunny Friday afternoon. A jeep was sighted in the distance approaching from the Kaduna end of the expressway apparently heading towards Abuja. The soldiers flagged the Range Rover Sports down. The car squealed to a halt. A beautiful woman sat at the wheel. She wore gold rimmed sunglasses. From where he stood, Major Tom squinted his eyes to identify the Jeep; he could just make out a black Range Rover Sports in the distance. One of the soldiers at the Military check point approached the black Range Rover Sports and signaled the driver to wind down the driver's window.

The woman sat motionless but merely squinted through the tinted glass. Then she made a rude gesture at the driver of one of the Army Patrol cars nearest to her car. "Madam, get down from the car. We need to search your car," the sergeant ordered, slightly thumping the glass. Quickly, she wound down her window. "I'm running late. I need to get back to Abuja. I'm just coming from my construction site, officers," she responded. "Madam, we're on patrol duty. Get down now and submit yourself to a search, or else I might be forced to manhandle you," the sergeant threatened, trying to force the door. "You'll do no such thing," she said, climbing down from the Range Rover Sports. The Sergeant quickly grabbed her by the arm. "Get off me! That hurts. Nobody gets away with insulting me like this!" she screamed angrily. "Turn around. Raise your hands above your head!" the Sergeant ordered.

By this time Major Tom had found his way down to the scene. He watched with fascination. "Serge, let her go," Major Tom ordered. "Yes Sir," the Sergeant stood to attention. Quickly the Sergeant added, "Thank our commander, he rescued you or else I'd have dealt ruthlessly with you today." The lady with her face on the bonnet heaved a sigh of relief. She felt a light tap on her shoulder. Major Tom had recognized her. "What a coincidence! There you are, Rosemary," he said. She managed to get out a few words of thanks. As soon as she turned and saw the commander, her face was ghastly white. She immediately recognized him. "Tom," she said almost in a whisper. They embraced. "What are you doing here? Are you in the Army now?" she asked with self-satisfaction. He nodded in silent agreement.

She was giddy with happiness. There was a soft light in her eyes as she looked at him. She smiled at him and he smiled back. "We would like to apologize for delaying you. We're on patrol to checkmate movements of the Boko Haram insurgents," Major Tom apologized. "It's Ok. Don't look at me like that, Officer Tom. Or is it Commander Tom?" She said playfully.

"I'm now addressed as Major Tom," he corrected. "If you like, we could go out this evening, Major Tom. I'll be returning to Lagos, first thing tomorrow morning," she said with a self-satisfied smirk on her face. "I'd like to think it over. At weekends I like to sleep late," Major Tom said evasively. "You're now an officer and a gentleman, Major Tom. It didn't turn out like I had intended. I mean with Colonel Peter – I hear he's now a Brigadier General somewhere at the Brigade headquarters in Nyanya near Abuja. Darling Tom, I'll be expecting your call. We've got a lot to talk about. Here is my card," she said as she climbed into her Range Rover Sports. "Ok. I'll call you. Bye for now," Major Tom said as he helped to close her door. He saluted as the Range Rover Sports gave a gentle lurch. "She's nice. I like her." One of the soldiers said to Major Tom. "She's my girlfriend. We plan to get married someday," Major Tom said, walking back to his patrol car.

The sun was setting as Rosemary lay listening to the moan of the wind in the trees behind her sprawling mansion in Maitama District of Abuja. She had talked on the phone for over an hour. She felt a heavy burden lifted from her shoulders. She had cleared a lot of things with Major Tom. She had scarcely put the phone down when the door bell rang. The door opened and Brigadier Peter walked in with three soldiers in tow.

"Hello, darling," Brigadier Peter enthused. "Oh, hello sir," she said with a smug expression. "You're not looking bright, my dear. What's seems to be the matter, sweetheart?" he enquired as he tried to pull her closer. She pulled away and gestured towards the armchairs and sofa. The Brigadier and his men sat down. He observed her face. It was taut and pale.

"May I have a word with you, sir? Privately?" Rosemary said rising smartly from the sofa. They stood in the lobby. "You called to tell me that you're in town and that you wanted me to cook dinner for you. Now I see you have three other guests. I'm sorry sir, I didn't make provision for four. You'll have to play straight with me, sir," Rosemary said as a surge of anger passed through her. She was annoyed at having three extra guests suddenly thrust on her. "Watch your language, young woman! You're not afraid of the Brigade Commander of 45 Artillery Brigade," he said with mischievous wink. "I think you've overstayed your welcome. Please leave," she said. "I don't want a scene," she added. "You'll regret this Rosemary," he said as he grabbed her arm. "Let go of me," she said fiercely. She just tossed her head and was about to walk off when he grabbed her two arms. "Get off me; you're hurting me! Now leave my place," she said angrily. "I thought you loved me," he said with a hint of mockery in his voice.

With brutal honesty Rosemary told Brigadier General Peter she did not love him. She felt a pang of retrospective affection for Major Tom. Bored with the mutual recrimination, she retreated to her bedroom. The General felt humiliated and vowed to get even. Rejoining his boys in the sitting room, he shouted, "Boys, let's get out of this place!" It took a few moments for her eyes to focus in the dark as the front door was banged. She reached for the light switch and flipped it on. She looked pale, with deep shadows under her eyes. Apparently she couldn't grasp the full significance of what Brigadier Peter had meant when he said she would regret her action. It was scarcely an occasion for laughter. She, however, knew in her heart of hearts that she was making the right decision in discouraging Brigadier Peter from carrying on his amorous advances. The silence and emptiness of the house did not scare her. Soon she was fast asleep.

A week later, Major Tom finally plucked up the courage to ask Rosemary for a date. Surprisingly, she agreed straight away. He flew down to Lagos. The airport taxi took him to the six – bedroom duplex on Robertson Street, Ikoyi. The wind was moaning through the tree when he arrived. Her eyes nearly popped out of her head when she saw him. She had to pinch herself to make sure she was not dreaming. Her hair flopped over her eyes. A smile flitted across his face. "Hello Tom", she said with a smile. They embraced. He gave her a peck on the cheek. She closed her eyes tightly in a vain attempt to hold back the tears. It was tears of joy. "I missed you, Rosemary. And I don't want to miss you again," Major Tom said as he reluctantly disengaged from the embrace. "I've missed you, sweetheart all these years. I'm not going to let you slip out of my fingers this time around. Welcome. Come with me. I've prepared your room," she said dragging him along as they entered the house. She led him to the guest room. He flung himself onto the bed. She smiled a knowing smile.

"I'll run you a bath, darling," she said as she crossed into the bathroom. A few minutes later she came out and cheerfully announced, "Go have your bath while I fix dinner," she felt a rush of blood to her cheeks. When he heard her retreating steps in the lobby, he got up and rummaged around in his travelling bag for the gifts he bought for her. After he had his bath he wore a T-shirt and jeans. In the sitting room he sat on the sofa, turned on the TV and relaxed to watch a programme. A moment later Rosemary announced; "Dinner's ready." "Good – I'm starving", he responded as he briskly walked to the dining room.

"Where's everybody?" he asked, pulling out a chair. "Uncle is in the hospital recovering. Aunty Maggie is looking after him. They'll come back tomorrow. Arunma landed a juicy job with NNPC, Abuja. I'm expecting her tomorrow. Edward is on call but he'll be there tomorrow evening. Incidentally, my mum is flying down to Lagos tomorrow. She has visa interview at the US Consulate on Monday," she explained as she finished dishing out the evening meal. As she was about to sit down, Major Tom quickly stoop up, moved over to her and pulled a chair for her. She smiled and murmured her thanks. "You're truly an officer and gentleman, Tom," she said, sitting comfortably on the chair while Major Tom stood behind the chair until she sat down. Then he returned to his chair and sat down.

Al last the wind dropped. Insects chirped outside. It was a cloudless night sky. "Tell me all the latest gossip!" Major Tom said as he looked into her face. "We've got plenty of time; there's no need to rush," she said and smiled with relief. There followed a short silence. Outside, the streets were silent and deserted. There were fine wrinkles around her eyes. Something unspoken hung in the air between them. Major Tom knew he had become the unwilling object of her attention. His mind was cluttered with questions. But it would be unwise to comment on the situation without knowing all the facts. In any case, she had the sense that he was worried about something. She decided it was time to clear up her affairs with Brigadier Peter.

"Don't believe all the gossip you hear. I don't like Brigadier Peter, and it would be dishonest of me to pretend otherwise. He has a wife and children in Port Harcourt. I couldn't stand his jealousy and possessiveness," she paused as her gaze drifted around the dining room. Major Tom said nothing. So, she continued. "After his wife left there was a gaping hole in his life. That's what he told me. When he found out that I was not an easy lay he became hostile and possessive. Last time he came to my place in Abuja he had a foul mouth on him! Trust me. I wasted no time in showing him and his three soldiers the door. Be that as it may, I freely admit that I made a mistake in encouraging his romantic designs on me. Nothing is between us, really." She summed up and looked Major Tom in the eyes.

"Well, I was disgusted at the thought that he has touched you. I believe you. Give me a wine with a delicate fruit flavour," he said as a smile flitted across his face. She was all smiles. Quickly she fetched a bottle of wine and two glasses. "Each time he asked me to sleep with him, I always told him a flat no," she said as she sat down again. Major Tom drew the Cork but, poured wine into the two glasses and offered a glass to Rosemary. She murmured her thanks. They each sipped their wine. When they were done with dinner, Major Tom quickly offered, "You wash the dishes and I'll dry." A great sense of relief flooded over her.

In the kitchen, Rosemary looked sideways at him, edged closer to him and whispered something into his ear. He nodded in silent agreement. She was all smiles. "It was very good of you to come. I'm very happy," she confessed. The conversation drifted onto religion and politics.

"Is religion always a force for good?" He asked with amusement in his eyes. "I don't think so. Available evidence suggests otherwise. Nigerians are very religious people. Yet corruption is endemic. Why? She asked as she fluttered her hand around wildly. "I suppose the disconnection between praxis and theory about religion is the heart of the matter. They rarely live religiously. If we must see reformation in our country men and women we must practise the tenets of our faith," he explained at length. "Yes, that's a good point. Do you subscribe to the theory that there are two opposite principles in everything, for example good and evil? She asked. "That is self-evident. We need not belabour the point." He said as he retreated to the sitting room to watch the Network News of NTA at Nine.

She soon joined him in the sitting room. "Thank you for helping me with the dishes," she said as she sat beside him on the sofa. "Not at all, it was a pleasure," he said in a pleasant, cultivated voice. She was all smiles. "The Boko Haram insurgency is an albatross around the president's neck. It's a national challenge. The Nigerian Armed Forces are equal to the task," he said as he put a protective arm around her shoulders. "I still hold that the government economic policies are mistaken. The NTA had to field more than 200 phone calls after last night's programme on the Boko Haram insurgency. The debate about the remote and immediate causes of the Boko Haram insurgency in North-East Nigeria seems to have lost much of its initial impetus," she argued forcefully.

"Even at that there has been a call for amnesty to be granted to the terrorists. I can only feel disgust for these terrorists whose stock in trade is wanton destruction of lives and property. At any rate, I'm afraid this conversation is in danger of wandering into forbidden territory," he reasoned. "Let's talk about us. The gossip was that you had lost a fortune on the Abuja Stock Exchange. Susan has been gossiping about you," she said trying to navigate the discussion to safe course. "My brief and unsuccessful flirtation with property market in Abuja opened my eyes to plot my financial diagram with diligence. The idea of leaving Abuja was one of my wilder flights of fancy. Tell me about your business," he said holding her closer. A smile flitted across her face as she cast a sideways glance at him.

"Few businesses are flourishing in the present economic climate," she paused as there was breaking news on the NTA News at nine. "Reports reaching us indicate that Boko Haram insurgents are holding more than two hundred school girls in Borno State hostage. According to the commander of the Military Task Force in Maiduguri, North –East Nigeria, the release of the hostages would not be achieved without the use of force. In the meantime the US Military High Command has pledged to train Nigerian Armed Forces on Counter-terrorism measures. Just before we go, the headlines once again ..." Rosemary turned down the volume. There followed a short silence.

Suddenly Major Tom broke the silence, "Let's go to the movies tomorrow," he suggested. "Perfect, the movie *'Think like a man, Act like a Lady'* is showing tomorrow at the Silver bird Cinema, Victoria Island," she enthused. "What's the movie all about?" He asked. "It's the latest movie on the 90 day test for people in romantic relationships; I won't tell you more than this for now. You'll enjoy it; I'd put my money on it". She said excitedly. "I bought some gifts for you. Here, take these". He said as he shoved the item on her lap. "Oh my gosh! Diamond bracelets? These must cost a fortune. Thank you, Tom, my darling." She moaned in pure ecstasy. Quickly she gave him a peck on the cheek as she examined the diamond bracelets. He was alive with happiness. "I'd like to go to sleep," he said, rising from the Sofa. "Kiss me goodnight," she demanded with smiles on her face. Bending slightly he gave her a peck as he murmured "Goodnight."

The following afternoon saw Rosemary and Major Tom at the Silver Bird Cinema on Ahmadu Bello Way, Victoria Island. "There are still a good few empty seats," she said as they walked into theatre number two. The movie lived up to its billing. Rosemary and Major Tom thoroughly enjoyed it. The evening rush was just starting. Major Tom stuck the black Range Rover Sports in first and revved. At the Bonny Camp Military Cantonment they turned into Ozumba Mbadiwe Avenue. They continued until they took the right turn at the Law School intersection and joined the Bridge across the canal. They turned off right at Awolowo Road end of the Bridge until they took left turn and connected Robertson Street, Ikoyi. Once they were in the car returning home, Rosemary told Major Tom all her hopes, dreams and fears. In that instant he knew she was the right woman for him. He could easily identify with her yearnings and aspirations. Although she had niggling doubts about their relationship, she knew that the country had suddenly become alien and dangerous Major Tom was her only security.

As they entered the sitting room they noticed everybody was quietly seated. Chief Ote was looking much better. Arunma and Edward were each sitting beside their father. Mrs. Brown and Mrs. Ote were serving refreshments. Rosemary went and hugged her uncle. "I'm glad to see you hale and hearty, uncle," she said. She nodded to Edward and Arunma. Then she went to embrace her mother. "Welcome, Mum. Did you have a smooth flight?" She asked as she looked her mother in the face. Taking a cue Major Tom went up to Chief Ote and shook hands with him. "I hear that you're now a major in the Nigerian Army. That's lovely. The Nigerian Army is the pride of the nation." Chief Ote commented, radiating with happiness and self-satisfaction. Turning to Edward, Major Tom simply said, "Let's bury the hatchet. Let bygone be bygone." He gave a stiff smile.

"To be honest with you, the memory of that Oso day still haunts me. You were great. I didn't know you had it in you. Rosemary hardly talks to me these days. I have to admit that the idea of marriage scars me. I need to have it out with Rosemary once and for all," Edward confessed. Looking intently at Rosemary, he quickly added, "Try not to get into a hassle with this guy – he's now an officer and a gentleman." At this everyone laughed heartily. Major Tom seemed to gaze into vacancy. His thoughts were elsewhere. He was afraid that if he proposed the second time, Rosemary might refuse. Suddenly he went down on one knee looking up at Rosemary, "Will you marry me, Rosemary?" The sitting room was enveloped in a thick cloud of silence.

Rosemary gasped and her hand flew to her mouth. She felt her heart flip. For an instant the world stood still as all waited with bated breath. There seemed to be a conspiracy of silence about what was happening. She scanned the faces in the sitting room. "Yes, I'll marry you, Tom." She responded at last to the relief of everyone. Spontaneously there erupted thunderous ovation in the sitting room. There wasn't a dry eye in the house when they announced their engagement. She closed her eyes tightly in vain attempt to hold back tears. Major Tom got up, opened his arms wide to embrace her. She threw her arms around his neck. Her heart overflowed with love. He kissed her on both cheeks. "I love you, Rosemary I'll always love you," Major Tom said. His eyes showed open admiration as he looked at her. "You are a darling, Tom. I love you very dearly," she confessed. They left the sitting room and stood in the lobby whispering endearments to each other.

11

Edward did not envisage the announcement of the engagement between Rosemary and Major Tom. When it happened he was taken aback. "Why does she want to marry him? She must have taken leave of her senses," he complained bitterly to his father who was still in the sitting room. Arunma and her mother had gone to the kitchen to prepare dinner. Mrs. Brown had gone to take a shower. Edward stared at his father to say something in support of his disapproval of the engagement of Rosemary. His father smiled weakly in a forlorn attempt to reassure him that everything was all right. "They have only decided to formalize their relationship by getting married. There's no crime in that. I commend them," Chief Ote stated in a cool, pleasant voice. "But they shouldn't count on me for support," Edward said as he made for his room. In the lobby, Rosemary contrived to spend a couple of hours with Major Tom every Sunday evening in Kaduna or wherever he might be serving. She poked him in the ribs with her elbow. A smile flitted across his face. He was alive with happiness. Just before he left her to go to his room, she cheerfully said, "Kiss me goodnight." He kissed her on both cheeks "Night! Sleep well," Major Tom said as he took leave of her and made for his room.

Major Tom was vaguely aware of footsteps behind him. He turned sharply. It was Edward. "My cousin doesn't have to commit to you now; you should let her think about it. But if you decide to proceed with your plans to get married, don't count on my support," Edward said. "Don't worry about that, Edward," Major Tom said stiffly as he entered the guest room. He showered and went to sleep. The weekend seemed to be over in a flash. A month later both the traditional marriage and white wedding of Rosemary and Major Tom took place at Ozu Abam, the hometown of Rosemary. The kinsmen on both sides were present at the occasions. Rosemary and Major Tom broke with tradition and got married in a rural setting. That Saturday morning the local Church was filled to capacity. The local priest who was officiating in the marriage ceremony paused and asked, "Does anyone know of any impediment to stop this wedding from proceeding?" There followed a short silence. From the last pew, a tall man in his early forties rose up and indicated that he had something to say. Rosemary and Major Tom immediately recognized him, Brigadier Peter. The tension in the Church hall was palpable, almost tangible. "Rosemary has child for me," Brigadier Peter lied. Rosemary gasped and her hand flew to her mouth. A murmur of disgust escaped from the wedding guests.

The local priest gestured for silence. "Where is the child of whom you alluded to?" The Priest asked Brigadier Peter. "I didn't bring the child," he responded with a shamefaced smile. "In that case, this wedding shall proceed as planned." The priest announced solemnly. Thunderous ovation rose from the guests. "Do you Rosemary take Major Tom Allison as your lawfully wedded husband?" "Yes, I do." "Do you Major Tom take Rosemary Brown as your lawfully wedded wife"? "Yes, I do." "Where are the wedding rings?" the priest asked. The Best man gave them to the priest. He blessed the rings and asked the couple to exchange the marriage vow: "With this ring I wed you; with my body I honour you and all my worldly goods I share with you in the name of God-the Father, Son, and Holy Spirit, Amen." The couple exchanged vows with the refrain as they slipped in the gold rings into each other's fingers.

The bride and groom were showered with flowers as they left the Church. Their wedding turned out to be quite an occasion. Rosemary looked beautiful on this wedding day. The wedding reception was held at the Ote's family compound. Food and drink were provided. Guests ate and drank to their fill. The newly-wed couple greeted all guests with a fixed smile on their faces. Soon the reception was over. As guests began to leave the reception ground, the couple said goodbye and thanked their guests for coming. Hand in hand, Susan ad her Senator boyfriend came along too. Those who knew Susan felt she was openly flaunting her affair with the Senator. As the Senator excused himself to answer a call on his cell phone, Susan walked up to Rosemary.

"I've got a feeling that Major Tom likes me, but that might just be a wishful thinking," she said mischievously. Her hair was straggling over her eyes. "It's no use wishing for the impossible. Girl friend, you're openly flaunting your affair with your Senator boyfriend. A little discretion is recommended." Rosemary advised. "I don't care! It's none of your business, you slut," Susan said rebelliously. "What did you just say? You shameless prostitute! Is this how you repay me for all that I've done for you," Rosemary retorted angrily. Through clenched teeth she told Susan to leave.

Susan felt insulted. She slapped Rosemary hard across the face. Something snapped in her and immediately she gave Susan a hard push on the chest, almost shouting, "Leave me alone; just go away!" Susan staggered backwards and tripped over some wedding presents on the ground. She fell to the ground in a dead faint as her head hit a sewing machine. Pandemonium broke out when Susan fainted. Brigadier Peter watched, fascinated, as the ladies confronted each other. Dr. Edward who stood beside Brigadier Peter swung into action immediately as he administered first aid. An ambulance was called. Susan was taken to a hospital where she was diagnosed with a concussion. Senator Adibe approached Rosemary. "Are you pleased with the outcome? With all her faults I still love her. My wife is even aware of our relationship. Pray that nothing happens to her or else you'll taste my bitter pill," he threatened as he went to his car. Major Tom was now holding Rosemary close to him. "I find it astonishing that she should be so rude to you," he said consolingly.

Edward shamelessly admitted his part in the blackmail. He muttered a few words of apology and with that he left. Rosemary shut her eyes and wished for Susan to get better. "Please God, don't let her die," she whispered prayerfully. Inside the house, she expressed a wish to be alone. Fear showed in her eyes. Her husband smiled reassuringly. There followed a short silence as members of her family gathered around her in solidarity. "Can I use your phone?" she said as she broke the silence. "Feel free," Major Tom said as he gave her the phone. When she finished making the call, she murmured her thanks as she handed back the phone to her husband.

Major Tom looked at her with hurt expression. She blushed with embarrassment. He behaved with great dignity as he tried to be objective in his assessment of the situation. "Susan was teasing you. It was jealousy and resentment which motivated her to assault you. You should know better than to behave like that," he said, looking her straight in the eye. "You saw when she slapped me hard across the face. It took only a few seconds for me to fully realize what was amiss," she said admittedly. "Let's leave that for now. I'll be going to the Federal Medical Centre, Umuahia, to see Susan," Major Tom said to his wife. "Have you got any money on you?" she asked with concern. He felt in his pockets for some money. "Sure, I've got some money," he responded in a conversational tone.

"I've got a tight feeling in my stomach," she said, looking up to him. "I know the feeling. I'll use your car," he said. "Mum! I feel sick," Rosemary said with pleading eyes. "There's no need to exhaust yourself, clearing up; we'll do it," Mrs. Ote said reassuringly. "Excuse me, Tom. I'll like to go to my room and rest a while. Drive carefully, sweetheart," she said as she made for her room. Once in her room, she groaned at the memory, suffering all over again the excruciating embarrassment of those moments. The doubt was still there, in the deep recesses of her mind. It was apparent she was suffering from nervous exhaustion. Her face was grey with exhaustion. When Brigadier Peter tried to get into the house to console Rosemary, he found himself pushed without ceremony out of the house and the door slammed in his face. It was obvious he had consumed a large quantity of alcohol. Edward gave him a contemptuous look. He took him back to the Guest House that evening.

The trip to Umuahia took Major Tom less than three hours. It was about 8 p.m. when he slammed on the brakes and the black Range Rover shuddered to a halt. He quickly climbed down and moved languidly across the compound. By the time he entered the tastefully furnished sitting room, Rosemary had fallen asleep on the sofa. He gently nudged her to rouse her. She opened her eyes, stood up and threw her arms around his neck. "Welcome, my darling husband. How's she?" she asked with worried look. "All we can do now is wait, pray, and hope. She's still unconscious," he told her. "I must have made a mistake today," she said lamely as she went to lock the front door.

"Don't blame yourself. You couldn't have possibly foreseen this," he said as he followed her upstairs. Mrs. Brown had already gone to bed. "I'll be with you in a jiffy. Let me run you a bath, and then I'll get you something to eat", she said as she entered the bathroom. A moment later she came out. "Go have your bath. I'll get some food for you," she said retreating to the kitchen downstairs. He truly needed a bath and a good food. He got up, went into the bathroom and had his bath. Then he changed into his pajamas and sat on an armchair in the room. She perched on the arm of his chair and watched him eat. She was sublimely aware of the trouble she had caused. For her, love-making was an act of giving of herself, soul, body and spirit to her husband. She was worried that she was not in the right frame of mind tonight. And she did not know how her husband might react. For, most men would become irrational, if they were enjoined to control their sexual urge on a night like this.

She was looking beautiful tonight. Of course, Tom observed and even noticed that her nails were varnished a brilliant shade of red. As he closely gazed at his wife, he did not miss noticing that her hair fell over her shoulders in a mass of curls. Her lingerie was seductive. Unconsciously he allowed his imagination to run wild. He was jolted to reality when she suddenly remarked, "I almost forgot. Darling, a dispatch rider brought a letter for you. He said it was urgent. It is on my dressing table drawer." She reached out and took the letter. Across the letter was printed the words OFFICIAL AND CONFIDENTIAL. "Here it is," she said thrusting the letter to him. He felt her heart flip. It was from the Defense Headquarters, Abuja.

When he opened it, he saw that it was judiciously worded in a terse military style. He began to read. "Please report to National War College, Abuja immediately on arrival on the 25th instant at 1400 hours. You are proceeding to join other selected field officers for a course on Counter-terrorism measures. The Course is being facilitated jointly by Military Experts from the US Army and the Defence Headquarters of the Nigerian Armed Forces. The 3 week course is intended to equip field officers on the use of Counter-terrorism measures. Consequently, your leave has been cancelled forthwith. Signed by the Chief of Army Staff (COAS) and copied to GOC, 1st Mechanized Division, Nigerian Army, Kaduna." He folded the letter and let it drop on the floor. "I've been recalled to Military duty," he said flatly. "I'm going to miss you, dear," she said, looking into his worried face. "The feeling is mutual," he said, worried as he got up and lay on the bed. She joined him. She reached out her hand to touch him. He turned to face her. "My darling husband, believe me, when I say I do feel for you. I'm sorry for being unable to consummate our marriage tonight," Her apology seemed to assuage him. "Before I leave tomorrow morning, please remind me to give you my new contact number while I'm away," he said. He brushed her lips with his.

"I can't contemplate what it would be like to be alone," she moaned. Her husband contemplated her in silence. "It began as just an ordinary Saturday, but soon became a day 1 would never forget. I have looked forward to living together with you in wedded bless," she said regretfully. "Don't worry. Things will soon return to normal," he said reassuringly. "Sexual abstinence for six years is complicated enough in normal circumstances, but this unfolding situation is even worse than a nightmare," she said ruefully. "I've been celibate for the past ten years. So I can still control my sexual desire tonight. What's important in this relationship should be companionship and affection. Love is patient. I'll wait till you're ready, my darling wife". He said in a cool calm, voice.

"Your devotion and understanding are touching. I need you to stand by me no matter what tomorrow may bring," she urged him pleadingly. "That's precisely the vow I made to you today. Don't worry. I know you're not in the mood tonight. A gentle man who can't exercise self-control over sexual matters is not worthy of the appellation. Night! Sleep well, my darling. I'll keep on my side of the bed," he said as he reached to switch off the light. "Thank you, my dear husband. You're truly an officer and a gentleman. Sleep well. I love you," she said as she heaved a sigh of relief. Soon they were fast asleep.

Major Tom had a smooth flight to Abuja. All through the flight his mind kept straying back to their last talk together. Although he couldn't grasp the full significance of what he had said, he felt that he had propped his wife emotionally to wade through the maze of twisted maze which awaited her in the days ahead. He felt satisfied with himself and he was more than prepared to defend his wife anywhere, anytime.

The sky suddenly went dark and it started to rain. It rained for a couple of hours. The sun broke through at last in the afternoon. The weather was usually warm for this time of the year in Abuja. Major Tom arrived the National War College, Abuja around three o'clock. As he walked along the driveway rehearsing his excuse for being late, he observed how beautiful the place was. The sunflowers stretched tall and proud to the sun. They were spaced regularly about 60 cm apart. The National War College, Abuja, had buildings with 21st Century architectural designs. The trees threw long shadows across the lawn. He knew he would spend most of his waking hours here for the next three weeks.

From day one, Major Tom threw himself into the Counter-terrorism Course. Course participants were drawn from the Nigerian Army, Nigerian Navy and the Nigerian Air Force. It was arduous course with intelligence and fieldwork bias. All the course participants were trained to defend the civil populace against terrorist attacks. Major Tom kept in constant touch with his wife through daily phone calls. That was how he learnt that Susan had been transferred to the Lagos University Teaching Hospital (LUTH). He was glad to hear that. LUTH had a commitment to provide the best possible medical care. The Teaching Hospital was blazing a trail in the field of laser surgery. He hoped that Susan would soon recover.

As part of the fieldwork, the course participants were sent to Borno State, North-East Nigeria to enable them gain firsthand experience about the Boko Haram insurgents.

One day while on patrol, they came under terrorist attack from all sides. Quickly Major Tom assumed command of the troops. He had two hundred men under his command. "Begin to repel the attack when I give the command. All channels of communication should be kept open," he said in a tone of command. An assault on the Boko Haram insurgents was launched to repel the attack. The insurgents retreated immediately after they suffered heavy losses. Thereafter Major Tom ordered Army Patrol in the area to reconnoiter the stronghold of the insurgents. The commander of the Military Task Force was duly notified of the skirmishes. He wrote a report to the Army Headquarters with good commendation for the bravery of Major Tom. The course participants soon returned to Abuja.

Inside the large auditorium of the National War College, the course participants were hosted to a farewell dinner. Major Tom got an award for excellence. A row of medals was pinned to the breast of his coat. This was the proudest moment of his life. He would later send the photograph of this memorable day to his wife. The Nigerian Army was equally proud of him for coming top of the class. Even his course mates held him in high esteem for his brilliance and bravery. The farewell dinner was almost ended when a loud noise was heard. The noise came at two-minute interval. The report which filtered in indicated that there had been bomb blast around the AYC-Nyanya junction in Abuja. Over two hundred people reportedly lost their lives. The Boko Haram terrorists claimed responsibility and threatened to blow up the National Assembly Complex.

The Defence Headquarters was incensed. A strategic meeting of service chiefs was immediately convened. At an agreed signal the course participants left the auditorium. A distress signal for everyone to leave the building was given. Just then, as they stood outside the auditorium Major Tom received Army Signal requesting him to proceed to the scene of the bomb blast. An Army Jeep took him to the bomb site on AYC-Nyanya junction.

When he got there he met a gory sight as mangled bodies lay everywhere. He met Brigadier Peter at the scene of the bomb blast. "So, you're the new intelligence officer posted to the Brigade Headquarters?" Brigadier Peter asked in a tone of command. "Yes, Sir," Major Tom responded as he stood to attention. "Major, what conclusions did you draw from the incident? Definitely, we can draw some lessons for the future from this incident," Brigadier Peter said, moving towards his staff car. "The 45 Artillery Brigade Headquarters need to mobilize the intelligence Officers to set up patrol network day and night. Suspected terrorists should be detained. The new legislation provides for the detention of suspected terrorists for up to one month. Counter-terrorism measures should be speedily implemented," Major Tom explained, as he followed the Brigade Commander.

"It's up to the Army General Headquarters to put the counter-terrorism measures into effect. I'm afraid the matter is outside my province, Major," he said as he leaned on his staff car. His Orderlies were standing around the car with their Army issued sub-machine guns. "The country is now at war with terrorists, sir," Major Tom pointed out. "I don't know about that. All I know is that conflicts among the various Boko Haram factions do not augur well for the future of the peace talk," Brigadier Peter said. "Sir, the president said he wouldn't be blackmailed into agreeing to the terrorists' demands. I'll further suggest, sir, that 45 Artillery Brigade should spend quality time on reconnaissance. Time spent on reconnaissance is seldom wasted," Major Tom said as he still stood to attention. "Come and see me in my office at 1 p.m tomorrow. You'll be staying at the Army Guest House in the meantime. Oil does not blend with water. You'll do well to remember this, Major," Brigadier Peter remarked as he signaled his orderlies to take him to the Brigade Headquarters. "I'll keep this in mind while I'm here, sir," Major Tom said as he saluted stiffly. He watched the staff car drive away. There was suspicion and even downright hatred between them. The overall mood of the meeting was downbeat. All the while they were discussing, aircraft passed overhead with monotonous regularity. The Army Jeep took him to the Army Guest House.

That night, alerted by a noise downstairs, Major Tom sat up and tuned on the light. Nearby fire had started in an office building. His mind raced as he tried to work out what was happening. It took awhile for his eyes to adjust to the brightness. He sensed something was amiss as he raced down the stairs. He learnt that a man was seen prowling around outside the office building before the fire started. Major Tom had his service pistol in his hand. He immediately observed that there was no security patrol in the vicinity of the office building. Quickly he called the Police and the Fire Brigade. By the time the Fire Service men arrived on the scene, it was all over. The building was completely gutted. He felt there was security lapse. Consequent upon this security breach, he decided he would bring it to the attention of the Brigade Commander at the meeting later in the day.

Suddenly, sporadic shots rang out from the back of the gutted building. Spontaneously Major Tom fired four shots in rapid succession as the fleeing terrorists fired into the crowd at random. Some people were injured. The injured people were raced to the hospital. A light rain began to fall as he raced up the stairs to his room.

The sun had disappeared behind the cloud when Major Tom got to the office of the Brigade Commander. The principal staff secretary ushered the Major into the office. Brigadier Peter sat at his desk shoveling cornflakes into his mouth. Some digestive biscuits were in a saucer. A cup of coffee stood near the saucer. None of these things escaped the observation of the intelligence officer as he saluted and sat on a chair, facing the commander. After several digressions, Brigadier Peter got to the point. "Major, I'm glad you came along. Can you tell me how the fire incident and the subsequent shooting came about?" The Brigade Commander said, staring at Major Tom coldly. "I learnt a man was seen prowling around outside the office building before the fire started, sir," he said stiffly.

"Tell me the main points now; leave the details till later," Brigadier Peter probed further. Major Tom gave a graphic description of the incident. "What's your observation about the incident?" Brigadier Peter asked. "Speaking as intelligence Officer, I'm very concerned about counter-terrorism measures in this area," Major Tom said candidly. "Speak for yourself! Do you have an alternative solution, Major? By the way, who had the final say around here?" He asked in a tone of command as he rapped the table with his pen. The tension in the office was almost tangible.

"Major, do observe the following rules while you're here. One: Smoking is not allowed in the officers' mess. Two: You are not to stay out late. Three: Obey all lawful Orders without complaining. Four: You are not permitted to entertain any female visitor in the Guest House. Five: You are to do security patrol duty around the living quarters of the Brigade Commander. Six: You are not to travel outside Abuja without official permission granted by me." "When do the new rules come into force, sir?" Major Tom asked. "The new rules are now in force, Major. I doubt the feasibility of the counter-terrorism plan you outlined," he said coldly as he sipped his warm coffee. Major Tom felt alternatively hot and cold with anxiety. "Sir, the Nigerian Army stresses that we should not allow our private interest to predominate over public safety. Counter-terrorism measures are to be put in place in all Brigade formations, sir," Major Tom said stiffly.

"The Brigade Headquarters will make logistics arrangements for you. Alternatively, you can organize your own logistics," Brigadier Peter replied in a dry tone. "Sir, you must understand the ambiguity of my position," Major Tom confessed. I'm award that participating in the counter-terrorism course has given you real life in the Army. I'm sure I'll be able to amuse myself for a few moments. I have a chilling tale that will make your hair stand. Major, I call the shots here. Learn to behave as an officer here. That reminds me; Rosemary behaved very badly towards her guests on her wedding day. I was also a victim of her unruly behaviour. I demand an apology on her behalf," he said in a flat monotone. "Why should I say sorry when it's neither my fault nor hers?" Major Tom retorted with subdued anger.

"Your wife doesn't know how to behave in public. It may interest you to note that Edward phoned to tell me Susan's health is still in critical condition. She was put on a life support machine in intensive care. Doctors are fighting a desperate battle to save her life," he said as he again rapped the table with his pen. He silently contemplated the Major sitting across his desk. "It was most unfortunate incident which left a deep dent on our wedding day. But then Susan's behaviour that day was completely out of character. My wife is a woman of good character and integrity," Major Tom replied in defence of his wife. "Believe it or not, Rosemary asked me to marry her!" He said mischievously. "I don't believe it, sir!" Major Tom said stoutly. He had a sudden urge to hit Brigadier Peter. But he controlled himself by sheer force of will. Brigadier Peter silently contemplated him once again. It was obvious he was amusing himself. He sat back and gave a loud belch.

"So, there's nothing 45 Artillery Brigade can do about putting in place adequate security network and intelligence gathering, sir?" Major Tom asked as he sought to bring back the discussion on track. "Absolutely nothing, Major," he said flatly as he thumped angrily on his desk. "I'm here to help you, sir. The Boko Haram insurgency is an albatross around the president's neck. It's a national challenge. Major Tom said with patriotic fervour.

"I believe the government will achieve much more by persuasion than by brute force. The recent ultimatum issued by the government contained the threat of military force. The insurgents have agreed to desist from the bombing campaign. A ceasefire is an essential pre-condition for negotiation with the Boko Haram insurgents," Brigadier Peter stated non-challantly. "Sir, may I advise that you be careful you don't leave yourself open to charges of security breach," Major Tom advised. "There is a general belief that things will soon get better. Dissatisfaction with the government has grown beyond belief. What do those clowns in government think they are doing?" Brigadier Peter said as he thumped angrily on his desk. "Sir, I'm afraid this discussion is in danger of wandering into forbidden territory. We are agents of the State," Major Tom cautioned in a sharp tone. The Brigade Commander did not like the tone of the Major.

"I want you to behave yourself while you're here. I'll brook no nonsense from you, Major," he warned. The tone of his voice brooked no argument. "Yes, sir," Major Tom said stiffly as he sat bolt upright. "Lack of time preludes any further discussion. In the animal kingdom, some animas have no natural predators and conversely, some animals have natural predators. Don't expect to have any preferential treatment. One more thing, Major; remember no heroics here, just do your duty. I call the shots around here. Don't forget to lock the door when you leave, Major. The meeting is over," Brigadier Peter admonished with a hint of hostility in his voice. "Yes Sir. Thank you. Permission to fall out sir," Major Tom said as he stood up and saluted smartly. He stiffly walked out of the office, and gently closed the door behind him.

In spite of his military training and travels Brigadier Peter had remained very provincial. Major Tom had made a mental observation of this character flaw of the Brigade Commander. His opinion about the commander was that he kept himself aloof from officers and men under him. All through the meeting, Major Tom kept telling himself to be calm. As far as he was concerned there was a root of bitterness growing inside Brigadier Peter. He was prepared to lodge a complaint against the Brigade Commander with the Provost Marshal of the Nigerian Army if and when it became imperative. For now, barring any unforeseen circumstances, he had to tread softly. With this in mind, Major Tom comforted himself in the knowledge that he was conversant with the provisions of the Nigerian Army Act as well as the rubric of martial law. If he found out certain orders were illegal he would not obey them. It was only natural that he should get on the phone to his wife and keep her abreast of events in his new posting.

12

Susan managed to cling on to life for another couple of months before she died. The news of her death plunged Rosemary into deep depression. The day she heard the sad news she uttered wordless cry of despair. Immediately, she got on the phone to her husband. When Major Tom heard the news his heart plunged. "Do something!" he heard the voice of his wife cry at the other end of the line. "Stay calm. I'm flying down to Lagos to see you. You know I'll always be there for you," he said reassuringly. "You're coming? I'm so pleased," she said. "We commend her soul to God," Major Tom said. His voice wavered with emotion. The death of Susan cast blight on the couple.

Her death left Senator Adibe with a terrible sense of desolation. With everyday that passed the distinguished Senator became ever more despairing. As a deep sense of despair overwhelmed him, he vowed to avenge her death. In furtherance of his vow, he wrote a letter of complaint to the Assistant Inspector General of Police in charge of Zone 2 of the Nigeria Police. He alleged that Rosemary had caused the death of Susan. A warrant was issued for her arrest.

Rosemary got on the phone to her husband two days before her arrest. "Darling can you come at 9.30 tomorrow?" she asked as she held her cell phone to her left ear. "That's cool," Major Tom responded. "I'll make arrangements for you to be met at the airport," she informed him. She was visibly shaken as she finished her call. Major Tom was, however, detained in a meeting so he missed his flight. Eventually he took the last fight and arrived late. As soon as he saw his wife he embraced her. "I'm sorry I'm late," he murmured apologetically. She detached herself from his embrace. Immediately he noticed that she wore a sad smile. When her husband sought to know how she had been coping while he was away, Rosemary struggled to articulate her thoughts. All he could hear were loud sobs, but no articulate words. She felt calmer and more in control when her tears had run their course.

"Would you like a cup of tea?" Major Tom asked. "Yes, please. Thanks," she replied. As he went to get a cup of tea, she sank into the sofa and curled her legs up under her. Soon he returned with a cup of tea. She drank the whole cup. "Tomorrow we'll go and see Chief Ebele Agu. He is a Senior Advocate of Nigeria. I've already contacted him. We need the services of a good lawyer like chief Agu," Major Tom said reassuringly. "My darling husband, thank you very much. But I'm so afraid. I don't want anything to come between us," Rosemary said anxiously. "Nothing is going to come between us. This is a testing time for us all. Everybody knows you're innocent," he comforted his wife. "There must be a way around this problem," Rosemary said pleadingly. "You must stand on the threshold of your convictions. In the end, what really move us are our personal convictions," he said in emotional tone.

Although her husband was very loving and understanding, she felt smothered. Every aspect of their private lives would be laid bare from now. She pulled him gently towards her. "I love you, Tom. I'm sorry for all the troubles," she whispered. "We are in this together my dear wife," he said as he kissed her on both cheeks. Reluctantly he detached himself as he went to shower. Major Tom was aware his wife was deeply disturbed and depressed by the turn of events. Her mind was in turmoil. There was a distant look in her eyes; her mind was obviously on something else.

He returned to the sitting room to find her staring blankly into vacancy. "Can I fix a drink for you? I'll fix supper," he said crisply. He stood yawning, his pajama jacket gaping open. "I'm not hungry, sweetheart. Just a moment, please. Come over here," she said almost in a whisper. Quickly he moved over to where she was sitting. In her hand she was clutching her cheque book. She vouchsafed to him certain family secrets. His eyes lingered on the diamond ring on her finger. Nervously she twisted it. "I don't want to belabour the point but it's vital you understand how important this is. I'm unaware of the fate that may befall me. True marriage requires us to show trust and loyalty. Can I count on you loyalty?" she finally asked as she clenched her fists to stop herself trembling.

"If you put your trust in me, I will not let you down. After all, marriage is like stumbling along in the dark, trusting to luck for you to find the right door. Honesty is the bedrock of any healthy relationship," he replied, his eyes suddenly intent. She silently contemplated her husband. She looked at him intently. She knew she was taking a gamble but decided it was worth it. "I'm going to write a cheque for ₦35 million. How to spend the money is for you to decide. I'll also give you this large diamond ring which glitters on my finger for safe custody. It holds the key to a numbered Swiss account in Zurich," she said in a flat monotone as her husband listened respectfully. Her eyes roamed the sitting room. She was rocking backwards and forwards in her seat. For a moment she remained calm and collected as she made out a cheque. She gave it to her husband. Pulling out the large diamond ring on her finger she presented it to him reverentially.

Major Tom was bereft of word as he received the objects of trust, both the cheque of ₦35 million and the large diamond ring. "You're one person I can trust. I'm aware that any business venture contains an element of risk. Lodge the cheque tomorrow and have the money transferred to your account. Please turn the TV off before you go to bed. It's late I think I'll turn in. Night! Sleep well," she said rising from the sofa. Her husband stood up, held her two hands in his and looked into her troubled face. "We live in troubled times. I'll stand by you through thick and thin, although I don't feel ready to take on new responsibility; I'll prove myself worthy of your trust," he said as his mouth quivered in the suspicion of a smile. They vowed eternal friendship. He let her go upstairs. He knew it was true love between them. It was also true that he could do the job, but would he fit in with the rest of the team – employees and family members? He trusted her judgment. She had fallen asleep on the bed when he joined her upstairs.

At the reception area of the law firm of Messrs Ebele Agu & Co., Chief Agu, SAN, beckoned Major Tom and Rosemary into his spacious office with a wave. "Please sit down, Mr. and Mrs. Allison," Chief Agu offered as he looked at them over the rim of his glasses. As they sat down, Rosemary stared at the heap of files on the desk of Chief Agu. He took a file from the heap, opened it and poised to take notes. "Would you like some tea?" he asked the couple. "No, thanks," they answered in chorus. "Mrs. Allison, cheer up. In this country, you are innocent until proved guilty. I'll see that you get a fair trial if the case goes to court. Now tell me exactly what happened on your wedding day. I want to take your statement," Chief Agu began the interview. She chose her words with precision as she narrated the genesis of the quarrel she had with Susan. Chief Agu made notes while Rosemary gave a graphic narration of what led to the quarrel. When she finished, Chief Agu looked up, gave a cry smile. "I don't see any causal relationship between her death and murder. The essential elements required to establish a case of murder are absent. Don't worry, I'll ensure that the charges are quashed. I understand the Police have arrest warrant ready. In case they come to arrest you tomorrow, call me immediately. I'll like to accompany you to the police station. I don't want any police officer to intimidate you. Of course when we get to court you'll plead not guilty," he explained. "Can I refuse to give testimony?" Major Tom asked Chief Agu.

"If you're subpoenaed to appear as a witness and you refuse, you will be convicted of contempt of court," Chief Agu explained "I'm sure there are several witnesses who will testify for Rosemary. I believe she is innocent," Major Tom asserted. "Major, there's no need to worry about that now. When we get to the bridge we'll know how to cross over it," Chief Agu advised. As the couple rose to leave, Chief Agu quickly added, "I'll send to you a bill for our professional fee. It's just ₦5 million. My secretary will see you out," Major Tom and his wife exchanged silent glances as their faces lit with knowing smiles. As soon as the couple left Chief Agu's office, he resumed his work as he went through the files.

The rain was clearing slowly when the door bell rang. Major Tom answered it. As he opened the door two men stood outside. Quickly they identified themselves and stated their mission. "I'm Inspector Ayo and my colleague is Sergeant Sunday. We are from Zone 2, Onikan Lagos. We have arrest warrant for Mrs Rosemary Allison. May we come in please?" "I'm Major Tom of the Nigerian Army. Please come in, officers," he said as he made way for them. As the officers stood in the sitting room their eyes ranged the room. Rosemary was dressed and was sitting on an armchair. She looked up. "Good day, Madam. We are from Zone 2, I'm Inspector Ayo and my colleague is Sergeant Sunday. Here's the warrant of arrest. You are under arrest on suspicion of murder of late Susan Tete," Inspector Ayo said professionally as he flashed the arrest warrant. "I should like to call my lawyer," Rosemary said, rising from the armchair. There followed a short silence as Rosemary put a call to Chief Agu.

"Madam, please come with us to the station. We have a police car waiting outside," the officer said politely. "Can I come, too?" Major Tom asked as he smartly jumped to his feet. "Of course, you can." Major Tom followed in the black Range Rover Sport. Mrs Brown had been informed of the development by her daughter. She was flying down to Lagos. Chief Ote suffered a relapse and had to be flown abroad. His wife was nursing him over there in the hospital. Edward had tactfully distanced himself from his cousin since the death of Susan. Arunma had shown concern for the health of her cousin from the day the sad incident happened.

At the police Station, Onikan, Lagos, Inspector Ayo asked Rosemary to sit down. He gave her sheets of paper to write down her statement. "Madam, don't worry, you have nothing to fear from us. The police are your friends," Inspector Ayo said but his voice was frigid. Rosemary scanned the faces of two other officers in the room. She felt the frigid atmosphere in the room. As she started writing down her statement, Inspector Ayo was hovering over her. "Leave me alone," she said testily. Chief Agu and Major Tom sat at a respectful distance as they monitored events in the room. They had observed the Investigating Police Officer – inspector Ayo hovering over Rosemary. "What's that police officer up to? He should know that everyone is entitled to the presumption of innocence until they are proved to be guilty. Of course, the return of a verdict of guilt is the function of a competent court of law and not that of the police," Chief Agu remarked.

As Rosemary was being questioned she answered with an air of detachment. This did not go down well with the investigating police officer. He wanted her to stop being so cool, so detached, so confident. He eyed her suspiciously. After being questioned by the police, she was remanded in police custody, charged with the murder of Susan. She was, however, allowed to go outside to meet with her lawyer. So, she went outside seeking a few moments of repose. Chief Agu went to see the AIG in charge of Zone 2. Major Tom went to meet her under the shade of tree. In repose, his face was sad when he learnt that his wife would be taken into police custody till the next day.

There followed a short silence as the couple stood under the tree. The difficulties in her way merely strengthened her resolve. She resigned herself to fate as she did not allow herself to be lulled into a false sense of security. Chief Agu soon joined the couple under the tree. Rosemary complained of intimidation during the interrogation. Chief Agu promised to file a formal complaint as soon as he left the station. "I have a horrible suspicion that we've come to the wrong police station. I am convinced of her innocence," Major Tom said as he put a protective arm around his wife's shoulders. "You will appear in court tomorrow. Please remember to plead not guilty. Be strong. All will be well in the end," Chief Agu said to Rosemary as he patted her on the shoulder. As he turned to leave he shook hands with Major Tom and said, "I'll see you in court tomorrow. The case comes before Honourable Justice Adesina of Lagos High Court. I don't need to remind you, Major, that you should be courageous." He briskly walked to his car, opened the door, started the car and left Zone 2, Onikan, Lagos.

Major Tom watched Chief Agu drive away and then he swiveled around to look at his wife. She closed her eyes tightly in a vain attempt to hold back the tears. "Life is a teacher. I believe I have lessons in drawing from life. Above all, I wish I could bring Susan back to life," she said and heaved a sigh of regret. Her thumbs were hooked into the pockets of her jeans. "The fight for justice and liberty should never be compromised. Together we'll win this fight for justice and liberty. Go and sit down a while. Let me go get some snacks and soft drink some you," Major Tom said as he led her wife back to the interrogation room where Inspector Ayo and two police officers sat waiting. As her husband drove away, Rosemary followed the car with lidded gaze. She was aware that nobody could legislate against bad luck. Yet she could not conceal the deep resentment she felt at the way fate was treating her.

Just before Major Tom left his wife at the police station this evening, his wife dangled a company chairmanship in front of him. When he sought to know why she was dangling such an offer before him, she rhetorically answered, "Such decisions are normally the province of higher management. Now a providential wind of fate has carried the decisions to my lap. Our lives are inseparably linked. You are my alter ego. Sleep over it, my dear husband."

That evening as Major Tom sat nodding in front of the television, someone was tapping lightly at the door. When he opened the door, Mrs. Brown walked in with a suitcase. "Welcome Mama. How was your flight?" he asked as he took her suitcase and carried it to her room. "My son, I had a turbulent flight. But thank God, I'm here now. Where's your wife?" she asked, enquiring after the welfare of her daughter. "Mama, Rosemary was arrested by the police and held for questioning. The police have opened an investigating into the death of Susan. The police investigation is ongoing. At the moment she's been taken into police custody." he explained as he opened the door of the room and kept the suitcase in a corner. "What's her crime? If people can bribe police officers it makes a complete nonsense of the legal system," Mrs. Brown said, fuming. As Major Tom turned to leave the room, Mrs. Brown said, "Can I have something non-alcoholic?" "Sure. I'll be back in a jiffy," he responded as he went to fetch the drink. "Here it is," he said handing her a can of malt drink on a saucer with some digestive biscuits. She murmured her thanks.

"What options are open to us? I don't want my daughter to be messed up," she said as she sipped from the can. "Chief Agu will tell us tomorrow when we get to court. Rosemary will appear in court," he said. "You know, doctors are not infallible. Medical malpractice may not be ruled out," she hinted, pushing some biscuits into her mouth. "You have a point. I'm glad you came. I got a call from my Brigade Headquarters requesting me to return to base immediately. Meanwhile, dinner's ready," he announced as he moved toward the door. "Good – I'm starving. I'll join you after I've showered," she replied.

As Major Tom and his mother in-law sat at table, eating their dinner, she insisted upon being given every detail of the case. After an hour of insipid conversation, he said, "I hope you have gained some insight into the difficulties we face," "Life is hard as it is. There's no telling what will happen next," she said as she heaved a sigh of resignation. He nodded his head sympathetically. "There's no need to exhaust yourself clearing up; I'll do it. Good night, my son," she said in a flat tone. "Night, Mama. Sleep well." he intoned as he went to check if the doors were securely locked. He switched off the TV and headed for the bedroom he shared with his wife.

By 9 am they were already in court. Shortly after, Chief Agu entered the court room with two lawyers. They were fully robed in their wigs and black gowns. Chief Agu asked for the cause list from the court registrar. He perfunctorily glanced through the cause list. The case was not listed. Quickly he scanned the faces in the court room. He saw the prosecution counsel, a senior State counsel. Immediately, he beckoned to him with a wave. The prosecution counsel whispered something to his ear. He nodded approval. He walked out of the court room as the judge was not in court yet.

Outside the court room, Major Tom and Mrs. Brown met him with anxious looks on their faces. "Rosemary is not in court today. She will appear in court tomorrow. I understand that the First Information Report is yet to be filed. The police are waiting for the First Information Report from the office of the director of public prosecution on the case. As it stands now, there isn't enough evidence to bring the case to court. I called the investigating police officer to enquire after the welfare of Rosemary. He told me she was fine. There's no cause for alarm. I'll see you again tomorrow. Let me run along, I have a matter in the next court," he explained as he took leave of them.

Major Tom and Mrs. Brown drove home in silence. Mrs. Brown prepared lunch. On the way to the police station she spoke with feeling about the plight of her detained daughter. At the police station, they learnt the police officer who intimidated Rosemary during the interrogation had been suspended while the complaint was being investigated. As Rosemary was brought out to meet with them, they observed she was bright, tough and spunky. Major Tom embraced her. "How are you coping, darling?" he asked as he looked her up and down. I'm OK," she said. Her mother watched her daughter detach from her husband. She opened her arms wide and Rosemary ran into her arms. Mrs. Brown held her daughter tightly to her bosom. "Poor Child!" she moaned. "You look like you slept badly," she commented as she looked her daughter up and down. "Mum, don't worry about me. It'll be fine. I'm innocent," she said as she closed her eyes tight in a vain attempt to hold back the tears. "We brought you some food. Let's find a place to sit down," she said looking to find a place. The police woman on duty brought a small table and three plastic chairs for them to sit down. Mrs. Brown placed the warmer on the table. She brought out a spoon she kept wrapped in her handbag. "Here, take the spoon and eat. I cooked your favourite fried rice with roasted chicken," Mrs. Brown said as she gave wry smile. "Thanks Mum," she said as she began to shovel some rice into her mouth. Major Tom and Mrs. Brown watched her eat.

When rosemary finished eating, she drank some water straight from the bottle. Her mother also gave her some snacks including fried meat. She received them and murmured her thanks. "I brought you some clothes. You'll be in court tomorrow. You need to appear in court looking respectable," she said as she put a protective arm around her daughter's shoulders. "I'll return to my Brigade Headquarters the day after tomorrow. Trying to reason with Brigadier Peter only enrages him even more. We have to accept the inevitable," Major Tom said stiffly. "I can only imagine how difficult it must be for you working under such terrible conditions. You should be wise in your dealings with such a man. I trust it'll be fine," Rosemary said stoically. In spite of herself, she was nervous, her insides were like jelly. He observed her closely. "We all have our fears and insecurities. Nobody is going to hand you freedom and justice on a plate. You must fight for them," Major Tom encouraged his wife. She silently nodded her agreement. She insinuated her right hand under his arm.

"Madam, it's time to return to custody," the police woman politely announced. Rosemary got up, kissed her husband on both cheeks. She embraced her mother. Then she detached herself and said, "It'll be fine." The police woman promptly took her back to the custody. Major Tom and Mrs. Brown could see she bore her detention nobly. Nobody knew what to say. In silence they left the police station and returned home, trusting all would be well. All through the night Mrs. Brown kept thinking about the dramatic turn of events. Her daughter was always open with her. She wondered why Rosemary took the decisions to transfer so much money into her husband's account as well as practically handing him the chairmanship of Arunma Group of Companies. She hoped that her daughter had not taken a gamble. That night sleep came to her in snatches.

It was raining this morning. Major Tom and Mrs. Brown got to the Igbosere Chief Magistrate Court before 9 o'clock. Only last night did Chief Agu call to say that the police were bringing Rosemary to the Chief Magistrate Court instead of the Lagos High Court. Little knots of people had gathered at the entrance of the court. When the police led in Rosemary, she was asked to enter into the dock. Chief Agu and two of his junior lawyers were already in court. When the case was called, Chief Agu promptly stood up, and announced his appearance for the defendant. "Your Worship, with utmost respect to this court, I am Chief Ebele Agu, SAN, with me are Dan Okonta Esquire and Silas Etum Esquire. We appear for the defendant."

After he sat down, the prosecution counsel rose to his feet and announced his appearance. "Your Worship, I am Ayomide Olumide, Senior State Counsel, for the prosecution." Major Tom silently contemplated the lawyers. They were all wearing black suits and ties. He wondered why they did not appear in their wigs and gowns; he would ask Chief Agu about it after the court session.

Chief Agu quickly got on his feet again. "Your Worship, with utmost respect, this court lacks the jurisdiction to try this case. The charge stated that it is a case of murder," he pointed out. As soon as Chief Agu sat down, the prosecution Counsel rose to his feet again. "Your Worship, we are aware of this fact. The police brought the accused to the court because they cannot continue to detain the accused in their custody; they don't want to be slammed with Fundamental Rights Enforcement suit," he stated and sat down. "The learned silk is right in his observation. This court lacks the jurisdiction to entertain this case. Consequently I order the defendant to be remanded in Ikoyi Prison until the defendant be arraigned at a court of competent jurisdiction," the Chief Magistrate ruled. A chorus of, "As the court pleases," echoed in the hallowed chambers of the court. From the court the police drove Rosemary to the Ikoyi Prison.

Outside the court room, Mrs. Brown and Major Tom met Chief Agu. "I'm sorry; the police planted a legal landmine. They were in a fix. They are yet to receive the advice of the Director of Public Prosecution on the case file. The First Information does not disclose a case of murder. The police do not have enough evidence to bring the case to court. The police cannot detain Rosemary indefinitely," he explained. "Then they should discharge her," Mrs. Brown said, sadness etched on her face. "The point is that the Magistrate Court lacks the jurisdiction to even entertain the case. It has only holding charge. This possibility of bringing her to the Magistrate Court never entered into our calculations. In any case, I'll apply for a writ of Habeas Corpus," he said and headed for his car. Major Tom mentally noted that Chief Agu was non-committal about when his wife could regain her freedom. This greatly bothered him. Mrs. Brown was subdued, choosing to keep her fears and anxiety to herself.

When they got home Mrs. Brown stood in the doorway for a moment before going in. She looked tired and dispirited as she inserted the key in the lock, turned the handle and opened the door. They had hardly sat down on the armchairs, when the phone rang. Major Tom answered it. It was Akon. He said he was in the neighborhood. A few moments later, Mrs. Brown calmly remarked, "There's somebody at the door." Akon scarcely had time to ring the door bell before the door opened. He walked in, looking radiant. "Can I introduce my mother in-law? Akon, this is Mrs. Brown. Mama, this is Akon my friend," Major Tom said as he introduced them. "It's a pleasure meeting you, Ma," Akon said. "Nice to meet you, too," Mrs. Brown said, stretching her had for a hand shake. There followed a short silence as they all sat down.

As Akon looked at his friend, he could see he was wearing a sad face. He was dismayed at the change in his friend. "Give me the dope on Rosemary, Tom," Akon said as he broke the silence. "Rosemary was arraigned on a charge of murder. You may have heard about the quarrel between Rosemary and late Susan on our wedding day. Chief Agu, our lawyer, told us that there wasn't enough evidence to bring the case to court. That's why they have remanded her in Ikoyi Prison," Major Tom summed up the situation in a few words. "I don't think you'd be at home but I just called by on the off chance. We are faced with a difficult choice in this case. What did Chief Agu Propose to do in the circumstance?" Akon asked with seriousness etched on his face.

Mrs. Brown was now emotional. She did not wait for her son in-law to respond before she cut in. "Poor child. She is so meek and mild. My heart bleeds for her. Son, please get on the phone and call Chief Agu now, and ask him what he meant when he said something about writ of habeas corpus," she said pleadingly as she blinked back tears.

Major Tom promptly got on the phone to Chief Agu. "Hello, chief, it's Major Tom here. You mentioned in passing at the Magistrate Court today that you'd apply for writ of habeas corpus. What does that mean?" he asked as he scanned the faces in the sitting room. "Oh, that. Writ of habeas corpus is a principle of law that states that a person who has been arrested should not be kept in prison longer than a particular period of time unless a judge decided that it is right. Everyone has a right to be treated with respect. Proving Rosemary's innocence has become a matter of honour. These rights are enshrined in our constitution," Chief Agu explained at length. "A mistake could kill. You cannot erase injustice from the world. We should plan everything very carefully and leave nothing to chance," Akon said, shifting comfortably on the sofa.

Major Tom chose his words carefully. "We must strive to build a society where justice and equity prevail. If I had the choice, I would resign my commission tomorrow. Brigadier Peter does not like anyone challenging his authority. I'm deeply concerned about my wife in Ikoyi Prison awaiting trial. Yet I must return to my Brigade Headquarters tomorrow," he said with a sigh of regret. Mrs. Brown covered her face with her hands. "What is at issue, I think, is whether she could be held liable for the death of Susan. There could be other extenuating circumstances which may have occurred in the weeks that followed the quarrel," Akon observed.

13

Darkness fell and enveloped Ikoyi. Major Tom wore a sad countenance this evening. After his wife was driven away to Ikoyi Prison, he felt a gaping hole in his heart. Even now, in the company of others, he was bereft of words. At last he found his voice. "Will you be staying for dinner?" Major Tom asked Akon. "I'd like to stay if it's not too much of an imposition," Akon responded tactfully. Mrs. Brown looked up. Tears welled up in her eyes. "This case has been handled very badly. Certainly, proving her innocence has, indeed, become a matter of honour for me. How long my daughter will remain in Prison Custody is now a matter of mere conjecture. We can't predict the outcome of this trial. There are too many imponderables. I pray God should protect my dear child," she said emotionally as she got on her feet and made for the kitchen. She seemed to have lost interest in food.

Major Tom excused himself as he went to the kitchen. "Mama," he began. "Don't distress yourself. Rosemary is a very independent-minded young woman when it comes to standing on her convictions. She's innocent. She'll be fine," he consoled his mother-in law. "We lose our innocence as we grow older. Rosemary is my only child. I know her more than anyone does. She has lived a sheltered life up until now. There's no telling what will happen next," she said sadly as she set about preparing dinner. He nodded in silent agreement. "Is there anything you'll want me to do for you?" he asked with concern. "No, thanks I'll manage. Go keep your guest company. Dinner will soon be ready," she responded as a wry smile lifted the corner of her mouth.

As Major Tom returned to the sitting room he was deeply disturbed and depressed at the turn of events. Akon had not seen his friend for a long time, though they had kept in touch somehow. They had lost track of each other in the ensuing years. Watching his friend keenly, Akon knew his friend was deeply disturbed and felt he might be bleeding inside. "Time is a great healer, Tom. I'm in total agreement with your mother-in law when she said that this case had been handled very badly. It would appear we have no choice in the matter. But brace up as a man. After all, you're now an officer and a gentle man," Akon said consolingly. "There's a twist of irony at play. Our suspicions have hardened into certainty. Do me a favour, Akon. Can you get me a driver to help my-in law while I'm away?" he asked with concern.

"By the way, my uncle lives just down Robertson Street here; I'll talk to him about it. He runs a transport service company. I'm sure he'll get a good driver for you. I'm on a course at the Administrative Staff College of Nigeria, Badagry," Akon said. There followed a short silence as they glued their eyes to the television. Dinner was soon served. "Mama, you should spend more time out of doors in the fresh air. I beg you, from the bottom of my heart, to visit my wife regularly while I'm away. I'll come back as soon as the date for the trial is fixed. I've asked Akon to talk to his uncle to get you a good driver; his uncle lives just down the street. For me, the whole event has been like some hideous nightmare," Major Tom said as he shoveled some fried rice into his mouth.

"My son, don't worry about Rosemary I'll look after her. I'm her mother. She's my priority. That's why I'm here. Remember to give me the phone number of Chief Agu," she said as she picked her meal. Eyes downcast, she continued eating and did not speak again. "Thank you, Mrs. Brown, for a delicious meal like this. I must go now. It's getting late. I hope we'll meet again soon," Akon said as he rose from table. Major Tom got to his feet and saw him out. Mrs. Brown nodded her head in agreement. She looked tired and dispirited. Dutifully, she cleared and washed the dishes. Then she went to her room, showered and turned in for the night.

In the grey light of dawn, Major Tom awoke to prepare for his return to his Brigade Headquarters. Mrs. Brown also awoke early after a disturbed night. She made a cup of tea and prepared bacon for her son-in law. As he prepared to leave the house that morning, she was overwhelmed by emotion and entreated him not to go. He wore a dove-grey suit. "Mama, duty calls. I must go now – I have a flight to catch," he said as he put a protective arm around her shoulders. His response rather disconcerted her. As he left her, he was aware that she was trapped in a downward spiral of personal unhappiness. He was also keenly aware that Rosemary's destiny was entwined with his. Without doubt, he felt the proverbial wind of life had changed direction. He could feel a knot of fear in his throat. A taxi came along and he flagged it down. "MMA2, please," he said as he put his suitcase into the car. For once he knew that the struggle for justice and freedom had really begun.

When the airplane touched down at the Nnamdi Azikwe International airport, Abuja, Major Tom knew that he had to show good cause why he had travelled without permission of his Brigade Commander. Inside the arrival hall, a sergeant was waiting for him. As soon as the sergeant saw him he walked briskly to Major Tom, saluted stiffly and carried his suitcase to the army jeep waiting at the parking lot. Major Tom hopped in and the army sergeant revved the car as he headed for the city. It was then that Major Tom learnt there had been another bomb blast in Abuja. Army patrols were seen every two kilometers on the road. The Airport – Abuja motorway was busy. It was a wet and gloomy day. The various checkpoints held up traffic for several hours.

Major Tom dropped off his suitcase at the Army Guest House before going to meet the Brigade Commander in the office. At the office, the principal staff Secretary asked him to wait at the reception. He had the strong impression that someone was watching. The principal staff secretary was aware of what lay in wait for the intelligence officer whose heroics had been noised widely in the Nigerian Army. She cast a furtive glance over her shoulder. Quickly she gave him a piece of paper with a phone number scribbled on it. He tucked away the piece of paper in his pocket. Suddenly the phone rang and she answered it. "You may go in, Major," she said stiffly. He knocked two times and waited. "You may come in," Brigadier Peter said in a tone of command.

Major Tom pushed the door open and entered. He stood to attention and saluted. "Major, take a seat and let's get down to business," Brigadier Peter said testily. "Yes sir. Sorry I'm late. . There was a hold – up on the Airport – Abuja Motorway," Major Tom apologized as he drew a chair and sat down, facing Brigadier Peter. "Major, are you aware that you are in breach of rule number six, namely; 'You are not to travel outside Abuja without official permission granted by me?' Brigadier Peter asked, looking the intelligence officer straight in the face. "It was an emergency situation, Sir. Besides, I was detained in a meeting and by the time I came to your office, you were out," he responded tactfully. "May I enquire as to the nature of this emergency, officer?" Brigadier Peter probed further.

"My wife was arraigned on a charge of murder. Prior to this, she was arrested and detained on a suspicion of murder. I had to be there to give her my support," Major Tom tried to explain the extenuating circumstances under which he acted. "What a bunch of hokum!" Brigadier Peter exclaimed as he thumped angrily on the table. "What's that, Sir?" Major Tom asked, surprised. "I mean your argument is stupid. That's what I think, major. I have never in my entire life heard such nonsense! Do you honestly expect me to clap for you? My expectations from you have been met in full measure in the reverse," he blurted out angrily as he went to the window and peered out.

Major Tom made a half hearted attempt to justify himself. No doubt, he was painfully aware that he had got himself into a hole and it was going to be difficult to get out of it. He bravely held back his tears. Brigadier Peter sat down again. "Major, I hope, for your own good, you don't think about Rosemary everyday; because if you do, you'll have to choose between her and your commission," he looked at the Major intently. "Hardly a day goes by without my thinking of her. Even now I'm feeling very guilty – I've been meaning to enquire after her welfare, but still I haven't got around to it, Sir," Major Tom confessed unashamedly.

"You may think I'm hard hearted but in Military Service you have to harden your heart to pain and suffering. You have to learn how to handle yourself in the Military Service. Let me give you a friendly advice; high dosage of affection for a woman can cause you emotional hallucination. A word, they say, is enough for the wise. Are you ready to subordinate your domestic affairs to your official duty?" Brigadier Peter finished at last. After a moment's indecision, Major Tom said yes and quickly added, "Sir, I've been placed in an impossible position." "In any case, I am not satisfied with your explanations and intend to invoke my residual power to discipline any erring officer. Strict discipline is imposed on army officers under my command. I'll send for you tomorrow to let you know what disciplinary measures I've decided to mete out to you. Major, you may go now. This meeting is over," he said dismissively with a wave. As Major Tom went through the reception, the Principal Staff Secretary winked at him with a knowing smile.

Back at the Army Guest House he refreshed himself with a cool shower. He wore T-shirt and jeans. He took his mini tape recorder and safely tucked it away inside his jacket's pocket. One of the lessons he learnt as an intelligence officer was to be prepared for information gathering. Taking his cell phone he dialed the phone number scribbled on the piece of paper. "Hello, Annatu, this is Major Tom here." "Hi, Major. What's up?" "Let's meet at a place to relax and find refreshment for mind and body," Major Tom said. "How about the officers' mess?" she suggested. "Perfect. See you at 7," Major Tom replied.

The sky was dappled with fleecy clouds when Major Tom walked towards the rendezvous. He was not aware of Annatu's frequent visits to the Officers' mess until now. The bar had been completely remodeled. Annatu Usman, the principal staff secretary to Brigadier Peter was deep in meditation and did not see him come in. Major Tom smiled distantly. "You're early! I wasn't expecting you till seven," he said pleasantly. "Well, I'm at your disposal now," she enthused. As Major Tom sat across the table, she could see herself reflected in his eyes. They ordered for drinks and fish pepper soup. "I admire your personality, Major," she complimented him. "Everything you do or say is reflective of your personality. Your clothes are often a reflection of your personality, your status ditto," he elaborated. The waiter served them with two plates of steaming fish pepper soup and a bottle of red wine. Two glasses were placed on the table.

"It's refreshing to meet someone who is so dedicated to his work. I think the boss was green with envy when he received signal from Army Headquarters about your posting to 45 Brigade Headquarters. You know who I'm referring to?" she hinted as she sipped her wine reflectively. She always referred to Brigadier Peter as the boss. He nodded in silent agreement. The mini tape recorder was silently recording the discussion. They were enjoying the Fish Pepper Soup. "Does the boss have a record?" Major Tom asked tactfully. "Can you keep a secret, Major?" she asked rhetorically. "Yes. I'm an officer and a gentleman. I give you my word that your secret is safe with me, Annatu," he reassured her. Instinctively, she cast a furtive glance over her shoulder.

"What I know about his past gives me a hold over him. I hold him on the scrotum. No disrespect intended, sir; it was just a joke. Let me start from the very beginning. Please, refresh my glass," she said as she lit a stick of cigarette. He was alarmed. "Please refrain from smoking in this place," he urged as he refilled her glass. She let out a cloud of grey smoke. "Who says so?" Annatu asked, with amusement in her eyes. "The boss; It's one of the six rules he handed to me the first day I reported to him," Major Tom said, bemused. "Those rules were made for you only. The boss vowed to get even with you because you married his girlfriend. No such rules are obtainable here," Annatu said, smiling. Major Tom smiled as he stared morosely out of the window. He was now leaning non-challantly against the wall. He felt he had been screwed.

He could feel his face reddening with embarrassment. His face expressed his grief more eloquently than any words. "I knew quite early on that the boss wanted to marry Rosemary because he had ditched his girlfriend. And if he had, I would have been dead by now. Your wedding was front page news. By your marriage to Rosemary you saved my life indirectly," she paused as she blushed at her words. He laughed merrily. "You may laugh but I'm in deadly earnest," she pointed out. He could tell she spoke in earnest. Somewhere, distantly, he could hear the sound of music. "I'm a trained nurse. It's not always easy for nurses to distance themselves emotionally. Let me elucidate. I was working at the General Hospital Kaduna when the boss underwent an operation to remove a bullet that was embedded in his leg. That was when the boss entered my life," she paused to refill her glass. Soon she was reeling after several glasses of wine. She ranted about the dark past of the boss of which she had become an unwilling custodian. At last she began to sum up.

"The boss is stupendously wealthy. He wants to take early retirement. The idea of retiring to Paris is highly seductive. He plans to live a life of ease in Paris where he has a mansion. He wants me to go with him. Nothing on earth would persuade me to go with him. I never completely feel at ease with him," she paused to watch him. He did his best to remain calm, but there was a distinct edge to his voice. "How is it that you're his principal staff secretary?" he asked. He stared at her and she reddened. She observed that it was getting late. "I'm not just his principal staff secretary. I also double as his private secretary. Previously, I was his mistress. Each time he was posted to a new command, he was sure to bring me along. I'm the only person in living memory to know his dark side and how he made his money. Never fear, everything will be all right. I must go now – it's late," she said as she staggered to her feet. Major Tom beckoned to the waiter and settled the bill. She wanted to walk home but he wouldn't hear of her walking home alone in a state of drunken stupor. Not minding the probable scandal, he took her home.

At the Army Guest House he was extremely tired but sleep eluded him. So he decided to listen to the recorded discussion. After listening to the replay, he tried to sum up the gist of the story as he lay back on the bed. Finally, he remembered the tiny details that had eluded him the first time he had listened to the replay.

What she knew about Brigadier Peter's past gave her a hold over him. When she lost her job at the General Hospital, Kaduna, where she met the then Colonel Peter, he had promised to help rebuild her life completely. The opportunity came when he served in the ECOMOG contingent in Liberia. According to Annatu he got involved in gold and diamond racketeering while in Liberia. He needed someone to launder his ill-gotten wealth. In his visit to Liberia after cessation of hostilities, he took Annatu along with him. In Liberia, Colonel Peter, as he then was recruited other persons who helped recover his gold bars and diamond pellets. Everyone involved was sworn to secrecy. When they recognized that the task was not straightforward, they began to talk. All were summarily executed except Annatu. At first she had scruples about the business. With time, she overcame her moral scruples and began to think that the then Colonel Peter would marry her. But her passion for him was not reciprocated. She however recoiled from the idea of betraying her own mentor for so she had come to regard him.

To protect his secret, he helped Annatu get enlisted as a non-combatant soldier in the Nigerian Army. Left to her, she had no desire to rake over the past. Everything that happened that dark night in Liberia was obliterated from her memory. Now as the principal staff secretary, she was warned by Brigadier Peter to keep her distance from officers and men under his command. Indeed, she had become an albatross around his neck. Most of the numbered and Swiss Bank Accounts all over Europe and the Bahamas were opened in her name. It was a relief for her to be able to talk to someone about it as she had bottled in a lot of flooding vortex of emotions that sought to make her insane. She also knew that when Brigadier Peter went to Sandhurst Military Academy in England, he came into contact with a medical student called Edward. She used to send some coded instructions to him on the cocaine business he was coordinating. Brigadier Peter, she knew, had always been reckless with money. His expensive lifestyle did not help matters either. Their working relationship was more or less a marriage of convenience. Although she had not sought an escape from his iron grip on her life, she felt her time and opportunity would come one day. And when that day came, she would grab it with both hands. For now, it was enough for her to tag along. Major Tom heaved a sigh of relief as he turned over on the bed and willed himself to sleep.

It was a bright and sunny Thursday morning. Major Tom showered and got dressed. At the officers' mess he had his breakfast. As he entered the office of the Brigade Commander, Annatu flicked him a nervous glance. "The boss is expecting you. Just be careful, major," Annatu said as she gave him her sweetest smile. "It'll be fine," he replied, with a nonchalant shrug. The door was slightly ajar as he knocked and pushed the door wider. Brigadier Peter did not even as much look up from the file before him. Major Tom stood to attention and saluted. "Several telexes arrived this morning. The World Economic Forum would be officially declared open next week. So, you can see I'm very busy. Tell me why disciplinary action should not be taken against you, Major. Even dogs can be trained to obey orders. Last night you were seen with a female guest in the Army Guest House," Brigadier Peter alleged as he looked Major Tom up and down.

Major Tom saw his frown and hastened to explain. "Please give me a chance to explain. It's not the case that I had a female guest entertained at the Army Guest House. Two, the alleged guest happens to be a colleague serving in this Brigade headquarters. Three..." Major Tom was rudely interrupted. "Enough! Nobody pushed you into the Army, did they? I have zero tolerance for insubordination," Brigadier Peter said as he thumped angrily on the table. Quickly he pressed a button and his orderlies came rushing in. They stood to attention and saluted. "Take him and detain him in the cell. Don't give him food or water. Let him remain there until he learns I'm his commanding officer," Brigadier Peter ordered. "Yes, Sir!" they saluted again as they took Major Tom away. When Annatu saw the soldiers take away Major Tom, she covered her face with her hands. She felt the punishment was harsh and unfair. Indeed, she remained calm as she had the strong impression that someone was watching her. Of course, she knew that the boss lacked profundity and analytical precision.

Major Tom felt the Brigade Commander was witch hunting him. Nothing could purge the humiliation from his mind. The walls of the guardhouse were not white, but rather a sort of dirty grey. Three armed guards were posted outside the building. Annatu who worked as principal staff secretary or rather, a personal assistant was deep in meditation and did not see Brigadier Peter come into the reception area. Suddenly she felt a firm grasp on her arm. He dragged her behind him to his office. Annatu gaped at him, horrified. "Isn't it time you started to get organized? I'm sure you don't need me to organize you. Such meeting you had last night with Major Tom ought not to be allowed. Don't take his word as gospel. You should be more guarded in what you say to him. He's an intelligence officer," he cautioned her. "I live alone and often feel lonely," she reminded him. "Maybe you should place a lonely hearts ad in a newspaper," he teased her. "Can you look up the time of the next flight to Paris? You'll leave for Paris the day after tomorrow," he said, almost in a whisper. She looked at the safe at the corner of the office. He always locked her passport and hard currency notes in the safe. A look passed through them.

He lolled back in his chair by the window. It was not long before she had persuaded him to temper justice with mercy in punishing Major Tom. "Let me worry about that. There's a list of repairs as long as your arm. The roses in the garden have got greenfly. The gardener phoned in from Paris to tell me about it. Stay as long as you like in Paris until you've sorted out everything. That's enough for now- let's go on with it tomorrow," he finished at last. Ideas were beginning to gel in her mind as she returned to her desk. It was common gossip among officers and men of the Brigade that she and the commander were having an affair. No one knew the nature of the affair between them. The hall of the apartment building where Annatu lived was decorated with flowers and greenery. This warm evening she was casually dressed in mufti. She climbed onto her new Ford SUV and revved the car. Then she turned up the driveway, only to find her way blocked by an army jeep. A guard jumped down and saluted stiffly as he tucked a note into her hand and murmured his apology. She gave him a grateful smile. Immediately she opened the folded note and read it: "You've been a great help. I owe you a great debt of gratitude. Thanks a lot. Please keep me posted on unfolding events and news. You can always reach me on my email address or better still call me on my cell phone. Major Tom."

Two days later, Annatu flew down to Paris to sort out the private affairs of Brigadier Peter. An Army signal from Army Headquarters was received by Brigadier Peter. Immediately he ordered the guards to release Major Tom to him. Major Tom was seized by curiosity. In the end he had to walk or rather run- to the office of the Brigade Commander. "Several telexes arrived this morning. The matter was passed on to me, as your commanding officer. You should report immediately at the International Conference Centre- venue of the World Economic forum. Ensure adequate security measures are put in place." "Yes Sir," Major Tom said stiffly. As he turned to leave the office, Brigadier Peter suddenly asked, "How much do you know about my principal staff Secretary?" "I don't know her well. I've only met her once in a close-up. That was two days ago, Sir," he responded flatly. He was at the threshold of the door when he heard Brigadier Peter say, "If you want peace, prepare for war." "I entirely agree with you, Sir, except that one cannot choose freedom for oneself without choosing it for others," he retorted as he left the office.

14

The rain continued to pour down. Elsewhere, the weather today had been fairly sunny. Three months had passed and Major Tom had heard no news of the release of Rosemary. He grew more anxious with every passing day. He was in his chalet at the Army Guest House, sprawled on the armchair, watching the news on TV. Suddenly the phone rang and he answered it. It was Chief Agu. A writ of habeas corpus had been issued directing the Nigeria Police and the Nigeria Prisons Service to bring Rosemary to court the day after tomorrow. He was overjoyed at the news. Quickly, he put a call to his commanding officer and informed him about his plan to fly down to Lagos.

The next day he flew down to Lagos. He arrived at the six-bedroom duplex on Robertson Street, Ikoyi. He knocked three times and waited. The door opened and he walked in. Mrs. Brown warmly welcomed him. As he went to keep his suitcase in the guest room, Mrs. Brown sat down again on the sofa and resumed her knitting. When he returned to the sitting room, he could see Mrs. Brown was more radiant and hopeful. He felt it was not unconnected with the news of the imminent release of her daughter. Their conversation ranged over a number of topics. Then it turned to the arraignment of Rosemary. Much of the evening was spent by Mrs. Brown on her knitting. Major Tom closeted himself away in his room.

In the grey light of dawn Major Tom and his mother-in law were fully awake. They each showered and got dressed. Breakfast was soon ready and served.

The new driver, Dickson, came in about 7 o'clock. He cleaned the Range Rover Sports. Traffic was heavy and cars were closing up behind each other. From CMS Bus Stop the driver turned into Igbosere Road. The narrow Igbosere road was clogged with traffic as they drove to the Lagos High Court.

Inside the courtroom, Major Tom and Mrs. Brown sat close together on the litigants' pew. Chief Agu and his junior lawyers were already seated in court. By 9 o' clock when Honourable Justice Adesina took his seat, Rosemary still had not been brought to court. Mrs. Brown was every anxious to see her daughter, Major Tom ditto. The Black Maria arrived at that very moment, as if in answer to her prayer. It was 9.30 a.m. when Rosemary finally emerged from the Black Maria.

As she was led into the courtroom by a prison warder and an armed Police officer, Mrs. Brown gasped and her hand flew to her mouth. Rosemary was looking pale and fragile. Mrs. Brown could not help herself as tears poured down her cheeks. Major Tom patted her on the knee consolingly. He felt nervous and uncomfortable. But he mastered his emotion.

When the case was called, the prosecution counsel rose up and announced his appearance. "With humility my Lord, I am Ayomide Olumide, State counsel." He sat down as he adjusted his wig. Chief Agu sprang to his feet. "With utmost respect to this Honourable Court, my name is Chief Ebele Agu. Appearing with me are Dan Okonta and Silas Etum. We appear for the defendant. We are most obliged, my lord," he announced in his deep voice. The court registrar read the charge and concluded with the question: "Are you guilty or not guilty?" "Not guilty," she responded with a flat monotone. The judge cast a glance at the prosecution counsel. "Is the prosecution ready to open their case?" Justice Adesina asked. The prosecution counsel stood up. "My Lord, we have not concluded investigation into the case. We need more time to conclude our investigation. To avoid unnecessary interference while investigation is ongoing, we urge this Honorable Court to remand the defendant in Ikoyi Prison pending when we shall conclude our investigation," Barrister Ayomide Olumide submitted, adjusted his wig and sat down.

Surprised, the judge looked at Chief Agu, and then nodded his approval for him to make a reply. Hardly had the prosecution counsel sat down when Chief Agu jumped to his feet. He gave a wry smile as he adjusted his gown. He scanned the faces of the court registrars and the judge. Still smiling, he flung out his arms in a dramatic gesture. "My lord, what the prosecution is doing is like dribbling a ball all down the front of the defendant, to score a cheap goal. The law frowns on legal ambush. On a serious note, my lord, I feel strongly that the prayer of the prosecution is like the disjointed thoughts of a dying man. I would further contend that the thinking of the prosecution is flawed on this point. To further keep the defendant in prison custody without trial is an injustice and a direct assault on her right to freedom. It is trite criminal law that it is not for the accused to prove her guilt. My lord, to ask the defendant to prove her guilt as the prosecution seem to suggest is a perversion of justice .Justice according to law is the fulcrum of our legal system. As a minister in the temple of justice, I consider it my duty to urge this honourable court to discharge the defendant for want of evidence and diligent prosecution. May my lord be pleased: we are most obliged," Chief Agu submitted as he argued eloquently on the presumption of innocence of the accused. He sat down again.

The court waited in silence for the judge to give his ruling. In his ruling, Justice Adesina elucidated a point of law. "Basic human rights, including freedom of fair hearing, individual liberty, and presumption of innocence are now constitutionally guaranteed. The court as the last hope of the citizens, guards jealously against any encroachment upon these fundamental rights. Anarchy and chaos will hold sway if the law is slack or is twisted or manipulated at will. This court is a court of justice. It is also a court of law. It is a court of equity. I therefore discharge the defendant. If the Police have any evidence which they have discovered, the doors of this court are wide open. Until then, the defendant is hereby discharged. Let me also warn that any person who disregards this order will be in contempt of court. Such a person could be jailed for two years for contempt. I rise," the judge ruled as he rose for a short recess. "As the court pleases," both lawyers and litigants said in chorus as they rose up. The judge recessed into the judge's chambers.

"At last, I'm free!" Rosemary cried. As she stepped out of the dock, wave after wave of pent up emotion poured out. Major Tom held his wife in a warm embrace. Tears poured down her cheeks. He could see that the prison experience had left her emotionally drained. There were tears and embraces as friends and acquaintances circled her. Her mother shed tears of joy as she held her daughter in a warm embrace after Rosemary had detached herself from her husband. Major Tom patted his wife's hand consolingly. Together they walked outside towards the parking lot as the news reporters clicked away with their cameras. Dickson had positioned the black Range Rovers Sports near the entrance of the court room. Major Tom helped his wife climb up. Mrs. Brown sat beside her daughter as she put a protective arm around her shoulders. Major Tom climbed up and sat down in the front passenger's seat. Quickly he strapped his seat belt. Dickson revved the car as he headed home.

After the court session Chief Agu bantered with reporters and posed for photographers. Back home Rosemary saw a banner on the door. "Welcome home, Rosemary. We love you." As the door flew open, Arunma opened her arms and embraced her cousin. They exchanged hellos and forced smiles. Rosemary was barely able to stand. Immediately she sank into the sofa. Bars of sunlight slanted down from the tall windows. Tears blurred her eyes. "It's ok, my child, you're home at last," Mrs. Brown said consolingly. "My dear, the ordeal is behind you now, so try to forget it," Major Tom said as he patted his wife's hand consolingly. She held her husband close and pressed her cheek to his. "I need to change and clean up," she said, rising. Quickly, she added, "I'll like to cook dinner for my husband." In her room, she entered the bathroom and indulged herself with a long hot bath. Suddenly, the future did not look so gloomy after all. Nothing could, however, purge the ordeal from her mind. She tried to dissociate the two events in her mind.

In the kitchen, Mrs. Brown looked her daughter up and down. "You've got to try this recipe-it's delicious. Boil plenty of salted water, and then add the spaghetti," she suggested. "I'll boil the kettle and make some tea," Rosemary volunteered. "I'll boil vegetables and eggs. Then you can fry meat and fish," Mrs. Brown advised. Their conversation continued until they finished cooking dinner. Just as dinner was served, Major Tom received a phone call from Abuja. It was an order which came down from on high that all field officers who took part in the counter-terrorism course should report immediately to the defence headquarters, Abuja for security briefing. When Rosemary learnt about it, she hid her face in her hand for she felt sure the order had some hidden meaning. "I'm coming with you," she said in a tone of finality. "Why don't you rest tomorrow? You can come the day after tomorrow," he suggested. She nodded in silent agreement. In the light of her recent ordeal, he feared she would be more of a hindrance than a help. But unknown to him, she was determined to fly down to Abuja, come hell or high water. When she looked at him, she saw there was a haunted look in his eyes. Consequently she resolved to make passionate appeal to Brigadier Peter to let her husband be. For, she was aware that Brigadier Peter was insanely jealous.

She served him dinner. "I've got a cold. I don't want you to catch it," she told her husband. They ate in silence. As Arunma and Mrs. Brown cleared and washed dishes after the dinner, Rosemary snuggled close up to her husband. A news flash on the court session was shown on the television in the sitting room where she sat close to her husband. It was strange to see her own face in close up on the screen. A sigh of relief escaped from her as she looked at the time. "It's close on midnight. I've had it I'm going to bed. Sleep well, dear," she said as she got up and made for her room upstairs. "Night! Sleep well," he said. Soon Major Tom dozed off in front of the Television and slept on the sofa.

The next day he took the first flight to Abuja. On arrival he took a taxi at the airport and reported at the defense headquarters for security briefing. He read his emails on his cell phone. There was an email from Annatu Usman. He learnt that Annatu was now in Paris. Brigadier Peter had chosen the right bait to persuade her to go. She had no intention of returning to the Army as she had handed in her letter of resignation just before she flew down to Paris. She further hinted that she had her own game plan which she would soon unfold.

This same evening, in a bar at Elvis Gardens, somewhere in Asokoro district of Abuja, the trio of Brigadier Peter, Senator Adibe and Dr. Edward Ote were relaxing over a bottle of champagne and roasted Chicken. An eagle circled overhead, and glided with the warm evening breeze. Abuja was just a red glow on the horizon from their vantage point. Brigadier Peter rubbed his hands in glee as he thought of the wicked conspiracy he and Edward had designed for Major Tom and his wife. In the garden, he looked up and saw the eagle gliding high over head and thought within him that he would soon soar high in his primitive accumulation of wealth. His thoughts were interrupted.

"Is this one of your usual haunts, brigadier?" Senator Adibe threw the jibe at him. "Sure. I like to chill out here. You can see the fresh air has brought a healthy glow to my cheeks," Brigadier Peter responded. "As you are aware, Rosemary has been discharged by the court for want of evidence to ground conviction. Our plans will, like a boat, sink unless we bail out. That airhead husband of hers has been defying my authority ever since he was posted to my command. We must all get our pound of flesh for the varying degrees of insults and pains the couple had inflicted on each and every one of us here," he said, carefully laying the foundation for the conspiracy. "I entirely agree with you," Senator Adibe concurred. He sipped his wine. "What do you propose we do?" Edward asked with interest.

"Let's get a murder weapon-say a club, and give it to the IPO. Upon receipt of this club, we'll urge the IPO to have Rosemary rearrested," he explained the plan he had in mind. "That's splendid. We need to give a tip to the boys. I suggested ₦5 million," Senator Adibe suggested. "I'll have to call the Inspector handling the case right away. Once he collects the money he can arrange everything else," Brigadier Peter reassured them. "Good idea! We'll plan everything very carefully and leave nothing to chance. I expect you, senator, to play ball," Edward added his voice. "Senator, don't you think you should bankroll this project?" Brigadier Peter asked. There was a friendly bantering tone in his voice.

Senator Adibe was clearly caught off balance by the unexpected question. A barest hint of smile lifted the corner of his mouth. It was as if he was about to suffer double jeopardy in this case. Susan was no more, yet he was about to cough out the sum of five million Naira just to grease the palm of the police. It was expensive bait, yet he took the bait in order to massage his over bloated ego. Reluctantly, he nodded in silent agreement. There was a gleam of triumph in the eyes of Brigadier Peter. They became positively garrulous after a few glasses of wine. It was in an alcoholic haze they eventually left Elvis Gardens later in the night.

Early morning clouds covered Abuja. The sun peeped out from behind the clouds as it broke through at last in the afternoon. Rosemary drew back the curtains and let the sunlight in. she needed to break out of resting in her sprawling mansion and do something exciting while basking in the euphoria of her release. She got on the phone to Brigadier Peter. "Hello, it's me, Mrs. Allison. I'd like to talk to you about a personal matter. It's urgent. I'll see you in thirty minutes," she said tersely. "Ok see you then," Brigadier Peter said as he smiled coyly. The line went dead. He allowed his imagination to run wild.

In the broad daylight the events of the past three months seemed like a bad dream. She was casually dressed in jeans and T-shirt. Her hair was tied back in a neat bow. Closing the door gently behind her, she turned and securely locked it. She stood outside the gate of her sprawling mansion in Maitama district of Abuja. She hailed a cab and gave an address at Asokoro district. The cab drew up outside the house. It was an imposing mansion. Tree branches were overhanging it. She knocked three times and waited. The door was suddenly flung open. This was the moment she had been dreading. She looked hot and flustered. "Look, who's here! I miss you dreadfully, Rosemary," Brigadier Peter said as he opened his arms to embrace her. Her heart gave a flutter as she stood in the door for a moment before going in. She shrugged him away angrily as he attempted to grab her hand. He gave a wry smile. With much ado he ushered her into a spacious reading room. Her eyes alighted on a bundle of documents on the table as Brigadier Peter drew a chair for her. She sat down across the table. Her eyes ranged the reading room.

He offered her a glass of wine. She murmured her thanks. Quietly she sipped her wine. He looked at her fondly. "So far, the police investigation has drawn blank," she began with a smug expression on her face. "Your arraignment was fully reported in the media. Yet your husband couldn't help you," he teased her. "Don't drag my husband into this discussion," she retorted angrily. "I wonder what you see in him," he further teased her. "I've finally found the man of my dreams. Recall that I was only talking to you to make him jealous. I'm tired of your petty jealousies. Tonight, I'm going to make him drunk with my love," she boasted as she smiled a knowing smile. Quickly she drained the last of her wine. He stole a covert glance at her across the table. "I'm afraid there's been a dreadful mistake on your part in marrying him. I'm your dreams," he said and smiled coyly. "Where do you draw the line between genius and madness? Most of the stories about my husband are apocryphal. I'm proud of him, anywhere, anytime," she asserted confidently. "Believe me, he's not right for you." "I don't believe it. You're a man inflamed by jealousy. I love my husband very much. I admire his passionate belief in what he is doing. He means the whole world to me," she confessed unashamedly. In one gulp, he drained the glass. "What are you doing here? What's this meeting all about? Stop bugging me, woman! I'm anxious not to build up your false hopes," he said as his eyes bulged. His behaviour towards her was becoming more and more aggressive. "I feel called upon to warn you that you shouldn't meddle in our private affairs. Major Tom and I are legally married," she said seriously. His face glowed with embarrassment as he heard this warning. "I'm sick of your rudeness; I won't have it any longer! You've got balls, I'll say that for you," he remarked as he thumped angrily on the table. Something snapped inside her.

"Bugger off and leave us alone!" she said angrily. But her voice was surprisingly calm. Quickly, she got up and left the spacious reading room. The door banged shut behind her. She knew that whatever she decided, her husband was right behind her.

Outside, two police officers were barring her exit. "What's the meaning of this, officers?" she asked angrily. "We have orders to re-arrest you on a suspicion of murder. Here's the arrest warrant," Inspector Ayo with Sergeant Sunday flashed the warrant of arrest. Her mind was racing. "Let me call my husband. This must be some mistake," she said almost in a whisper. Quickly she called her husband. "Sweetheart, I've been rearrested by the police. I think they are taking me to the Nnamdi Azikiwe International Airport right away. Please call Chief Agu. Meet me in Lagos. I don't really know what's going on," she blurted out emotionally. Immediately, she was whisked away in a waiting police car. Brigadier Peter stood at the threshold of the front door, watching the drama. There was a gleam of triumph in his eyes. He burst out laughing as he gently closed the front door.

Major Tom was dozing in front of the television in his chalet at the Army Guest House when he received the call from his wife. Suddenly he found himself awake and fully alert. Quickly, he made a call on his cell phone. Chief Agu said there was nothing to worry about that incident. The case would come to court the day after tomorrow. Next, Major Tom got on the phone to Brigadier Peter. He told his commanding officer that he would fly down to Lagos the following day as his wife had been rearrested by the police. Brigadier Peter refused to grant him permission to travel outside Abuja.

When Major Tom enquired as to the reason for withholding of the permission, the Brigade Commander cited official duty. He informed Major Tom that he had been given guard duty for a whole week. Major Tom protested vehemently that as a field officer he was exempted from guard duty. In a tone of finality which brooked no further argument, Brigadier Peter threatened him with court-martial if he travelled without his permission.

This incident only hardened his resolve to resign his commission one of these days. He felt he had allowed Brigadier Peter far too much latitude to meddle in his private affairs. He was quick to remember that the first law of defence was to mount a surprise attack. Consequently, he resolved to forward a petition to the Provost-Marshal of the Nigerian Army against Brigadier Peter. At the Lagos High Court, Rosemary was arraigned on a two-court charge of murder. When the amended charge was read, Rosemary pleaded not guilty. Chief Agu made an application for bail. "My lord, we urge this honourable court to let us know the bail conditions so that when bail has been perfected, the accused is allowed to go free until the trial," he submitted. The prosecution opposed the bail application on the ground that murder was not a bailable offence. The judge refused bail as he aligned his position with that of the prosecution. Consequently, the judge ordered the accused to be remanded in prison custody. Chief Agu however informed the court that the prosecution counsel had been trying to prejudice public opinion against the accused. The judge was displeased with the conduct of the prosecution counsel and warned him to desist from such unprofessional conduct. The case was adjourned. When the judge asked both the prosecution and defence counsel to suggest a date for the prosecution to open their case, the two lawyers consulted their diaries and agreed on a date. The trial was then fixed for 25th of next month.

In a curious twist of irony, Major Tom was subpoenaed by the court on the application of the prosecution to appear as a witness for the prosecution. This worried him. He felt nervous and insecure. Mrs. Brown was aware that the legal challenge to free her daughter was unsuccessful. Ineluctably she began to sink into despair. She was deeply disturbed and depressed when she heard the sad news. Rosemary felt shocked and totally disoriented. By degrees, she found herself unwittingly trapped in a downward spiral of personal unhappiness. Major Tom on his return to the Brigade headquarters in Abuja was severely punished by the Brigade Commander for disobeying orders.

To keep away from the edge of emotional cliff, he disciplined himself to exercise at least three times a week. He was worried about testifying for the prosecution. This twist reinforced his natural dislike for the legal paraphernalia of court hearings, delays, adjournment and appeals. For days he was prostrated with grief. Although he felt the weight of his grief, he would not make any hasty decisions about resigning his commission in the Nigerian Army. In the meantime, he continued with his regimented life at 45 Artillery Brigade headquarters.

15

The Paris Fashion Show was an annual event. Fashion enthusiasts often filled the streets of Paris during the event. Edward had booked a flight to Paris several days before the fashion week opened. Brigadier Peter was completely unaware of the affair between Annatu and Edward. She had discretely hinted that she would want him to meet her in Paris during the fashion week to perfect their plans. Apart from that, she needed to unburden herself to somebody she could trust. She was still uncertain of his feelings for her. At first, Edward had obstinately refused to consider a future with her. He maintained that such a possibility did not enter into his calculations. For he prided himself on the notion that he was not in the habit of ogling ordinary women like Annatu. But he had an axe to grind with Brigadier Peter. He knew Brigadier Peter always cheated him out of his share of the profits from their sleaze. The problem had been gnawing at him for years. His immediate solution had been to arrange a marriage of convenience between Rosemary and Brigadier Peter. He had hoped that he would have a firm hold over Brigadier Peter through that arranged marriage.

But Major Tom had unceremoniously dashed his hopes by marrying Rosemary. He was embittered that Rosemary had contrived to spoil his happiness and so he resolved to pay her back in kind. His plots and actions to get a pound of flesh from the couple could only be understood in context. His public image was in direct contradiction to his personal lifestyle which was shrouded in secrecy. Early on, Annatu had emphasized that their plan would mean sacrifices and hard work. Ultimately, he convinced himself that to actualize his plans, a degree of critical emotional detachment was required. After all, he was a trained medical doctor, skilled in the art of emotional detachment. He was spurred on by a strong sense of greed and ambition. Although he still desired Annatu, and she him, he sought to rein in his emotions. At Charles de Gaul International Airport, Paris, there were over 150 arrivals and departures today. The train he boarded at the airport arrived at the station 20 minutes late.

Annatu was standing on the platform when the train arrived. He apologized for the late arrival of the train. She was there to welcome him. "It's a pleasure to welcome you to Paris, Edward," she said. There was a demure smile on her face. He held her in a warm embrace. Emeralds ring on her ring finger-caught his attention. She wore a black gown. They emerged into the evening sunlight of summer as they headed for the parking lot. Edward put his small suitcase into the boot of the Peugeot 607 car. Annatu was at the wheel. At the Elysees roundabout she took the third exit. "Paris is the fashion capital of the world," she said. "So I've heard," replied Edward pleasantly. "La Belle Mansion is on the outskirts of Paris," she said as she flicked him a nervous glance. He nodded in silent agreement. His face wrinkled in grin.

She was looking forward to this meeting enormously. She looked incredibly sexy in a black evening gown. Soon the Peugeot 607 came to a halt at the edge of a landscape with expansive skies. Edward looked out over flat expanses of open farmland. La Belle Mansion was in a beautiful position amid the lemon groves. The gardens were laid out with lawns, flower beds and fountains. The large gardens were bordered by a stream. "Welcome to La Belle Mansion," Annatu cheerfully announced as she alighted from the big car. She led the way to the front door. Inside the spacious sitting room, Edward flung off his coat and collapsed on the sofa. "I'll run you a bath," she said as she rumpled his hair playfully. Her full sensuous lips were inviting.

"You look beautiful and gorgeous, Annatu," he complimented. "Thanks. I'm flattered, though," she said coyly. She could feel herself blushing. A smile touched the corners of his mouth. When he had changed and cleaned up, he returned to the sitting room. Immediately he noticed something was bothering Annatu. "You look wretched- what's wrong?" he asked with concern. There was a faraway look in her eyes. "I don't know if I'm doing the right thing. I've never betrayed the confidences of the boss," she said uncertainly. He noted certain hesitancy in her voice. "As far as I can see, you've done nothing wrong. We've all got problems of one kind or another," he said reassuringly. His words wrenched a sob from her.

She had spent the whole weekend wrestling with the plan. "Do you mind if I put the television on?" Edward asked. "No, I don't," she responded. He gave a thin smile. The sitting room was flooded with evening light. "What do you think of the fashion show so far?" she asked as she saw the pictures on the screen. "Splendid," he responded. "Are you sure I'm doing the right thing? You're not angry then?" she asked seriously, watching his facial expression. "Far from it! I've never laughed so much in my life. The boss has always been quite crude, but this time he's gone too far. He's been spending money like it's going out of fashion," he said with a hint of distaste. She nodded in silent agreement. She was busy touching up her make-up in the mirror. "I know the feeling. It's mutual," she said in a monotone drawl.

"Maybe the pressure of the insurgency is weighing heavily on him. The insurgents attempted to wrest control of the border town in Borno State from government forces. Major Tom has been sufficiently stressed up. The boss has been at dagger drawn with the Major ever since Rosemary rejected his amorous advances," she revealed. "That serves them right. Look, the trial was a farce. We fixed it to punish Rosemary," he said mischievously. "Why would you do a thing like that? Don't treat her like that- she's a person, not a thing!" she said pleadingly. Her words wrenched at his heart. She really did not want to be involved in the whole family thing. "This discussion is leading us nowhere," he observed. "We have a lot to discuss but, first thing first, let's have a cup of coffee," she suggested, rising to go and make coffee. She ran her tongue over her lips. The sky was clear and studded with stars as Annatu looked out of the kitchen window.

There followed a long silence as she prepared two cups of coffee. Although she had a mild flirtation with Edward when they first met, they were not having a sexual relationship at the time. As she returned with two cups of coffee and a loaf of French bread, he gave a shy smile and a little twist of his head. She carefully placed the cup of coffee and saucer on a side-stool near him. The French bread on a tray was placed on the centre table. "Edward, you could at least listen to Major Tom. He's really a nice guy. He sees you differently," she said, hoping to draw attention to the difficult position in which Major Tom had been placed. "How others see me is the least of my worries. Wait till I get my hands on Major Tom or whatever he calls himself! He's a joy-killer," he said threateningly. She looked at him, surprised.

"The situation in the North-East of Nigeria is far worse than we had been led to believe. Major Tom ought to resign his commission to give full support to his wife at this trying period. Their marriage seems to lurch from one crisis to the next. I appeal to your sensibilities to refrain from punishing the couple," she pleaded. He was deeply troubled by the allegations. She looked into his troubled face. "You expect Major Tom to resign his commission? I don't think so. All he ever thinks about is money. Romance is one thing, marriage is quite another," he spoke in a monotone drawl. "It's one thing to tease your cousin, but it's another to destroy her. If I were you, Edward, I'd stay away from her! I'm convinced that she's innocent," she said seriously.

Her gaze settled on his face. "Can an act that causes death ever be lawful? Don't talk about innocence. Rosemary has been married two times, so she knows a thing or two about men. Don't worry about the couple, they are of no consequence. Let's talk about us and our future together," he said as he tried to lead the conversation back to the main issue. Edward was hoping to get laid tonight but the conversation had skidded off course. He looked at Annatu with an evil leer. Gently, he sipped his coffee and then he tore the long, narrow French bread into shreds, pushing them into his mouth. He listened respectfully as Annatu began to lay her plans. "The boss flirts outrageously with girls young enough to be his granddaughters. I'm sick and tired of being at his beck and call. I want out. I've been thinking over what you said in our last telephone conversation," she said as she gnawed at her fingernails. Self-doubt began to gnaw away at her confidence. "Will you have dinner with me tonight?" he asked, trying to divert her thoughts to something else. "It's cold tonight. I'll microwave the prepared dinner for three minutes," she replied. "I hope you're worried about our relationship. There's nothing improper about our relationship. Settling down as man and wife in the South of France is quite seductive. By the way, I like the position of this mansion," he said appreciatively. "The position of the house combines quietness and convenience. This house has all the modern conveniences. One more thing, I've been thinking seriously about the probable cause of death of Susan," she paused and watched his demeanor. He shifted uncomfortably. "What are you thinking?" he asked with concern. "A patient who is not fully conscious should never be left alone. I've been thinking that the doctor on duty that night she passed on should be questioned by a panel of the hospital," she pointed out. There was a pained look on his face. He knew that the proverbial wind has changed direction and common sense dictated that he should tread softly. He felt nervous and insecure. He was aware of the consequences if a coroner's inquest was ordered into the cause of death of Susan. Clearly he remembered that night. He was the doctor on duty and it would be within his knowledge to tell such panel of what he knew. And what he knew would be enough to nail him. It was not surprising that he sought to navigate the conversation to a safe course. "There's another thing I'd like to ask you. Will you marry me if the opportunity presents itself?" he suddenly asked as he moved over to where she sat. He put a protective arm around her shoulders. There followed a short silence. She ran her tongue over her lips. She wanted to tell him the whole truth but she checked herself- it was not the right moment. She hoped the plan she had hatched would checkmate Brigadier Peter. Unceremoniously she gnawed at her fingernails. Her face told its own story. Now she chose her words carefully. "It's difficult to define the border between love and friendship. The question is: do you love me? Or is it my song you love? I'll be ready with an answer for you if and when you give me an appropriate answer," she tactfully responded as her lips clamped tightly together. She gave him a chaste kiss on the cheek as she rose to go to the kitchen to fix dinner. The room became strangely quiet. In a way, he felt it was hard to draw clear lines of demarcation between business and romantic relationship. It seemed to him the two were mutually exclusive.

He, therefore, wondered why women often demanded leisure and money from their partners. The same women would want their spouses to spend more time with them and at the same time would ask for all the goodies that made life worth living. What he did not know, however, was that Annatu was a goldmine.

He contended, rightly or wrongly that there was no straightforward equivalence between economic progress and social well-being. It seemed to him an act of monumental folly to fly down to Paris without getting the proverbial Golden Fleece. He would try another approach. As soon as Annatu served him dinner, he stood up and tried to kiss her but she quickly pulled away. "Don't mistake lust for love. They won't blend, the same way, water and oil don't blend," she pointed out as she settled to eat her food. Her one thought was to snare a rich husband or given the opportunity she could create one given the resources available to her if she should convert them. "You need to think big. If you want to make money, you've got to think big. Marry me and I'll be your dreams. I'll take you to the ends of the earth," Edward intoned coyly as he sat down to eat his meal. "I think of this place as my home. But if you really love me, then, join forces with me and let's checkmate the boss," she stated nonchalantly. He gave a broad smile. "I'm with you all the way. Don't worry about him coming after you. I'll lay you any money you like that he won't come. Leave that to me," he said reassuringly. After this, they ate their dinner in silence, each lost in their thoughts and scheming. Suddenly, Annatu heaved a sigh of regret. "The boss thought he could fool me but I got wise to him. I'm older and wiser after ten years in the business," she said wistfully. "I can understand your wish for secrecy of our affairs. If only I had known you then," he said regretfully. She blushed with embarrassment. A bottle of chilled white wine sat on the table. He reached to it, drew out the cork and poured generously into their glasses.

It was not long before they found their tongues loosed. They began to talk about private matters. Surprisingly, they agreed to get married secretly in the South of France. That night they slept in different rooms. Annatu had a dream and was awake half the night worrying. In the grey of dawn, they were fully awake. Edward showered and got dressed. Annatu dressed and went downstairs to prepare breakfast. Over breakfast, she quickly reminded him, "I booked you on the ten O'clock flight. Do you know your check-in time?" "Just a moment, I'll go and check," he said as he rose and went to the room to fetch his flight ticket. When he returned, he said, "We check in at least an hour before departure." As Edward grabbed his suitcase to leave the mansion, he held Annatu in a warm embrace. "I love you, sweetheart. I'll soon return for you. Let me go back to Nigeria and arrange my affairs," he said pleasantly. "That's fine. I'll wait for you, honey," she responded as she slid him a sideways glance. In a flash she gave him a chaste kiss on the cheek. Then she managed to wrench herself free. She saw him off to the train station where he would take the Metro to Charles de Gaul International Airport. At the airport, he checked in his luggage and went through to the departure lounge. Over the Public Address System he heard that flight BA125 for Lagos was boarding at Gate 34.

The flight from Paris to Lagos was smooth except for a few minutes of turbulence over the Sahara desert. When the plane landed safely at the MMA1, he took a Cab home. Later he called Brigadier Peter's Office, and was reliably informed that the Brigade Commander was attending an important meeting at the Army General Headquarters.

The Army General Headquarters at Area 10 Garki, Abuja had an imposing auditorium and other smaller structures. There was a large garden behind the main auditorium. The garden was overshadowed by tall trees. Inside the conference hall of the main auditorium Brigadier Peter sat facing a panel of senior Army Officers. The Chairman of the panel was Lt. General Sanusi Abass, the provost-Marshal of the Nigerian Army. "Brigadier Peter, you know why you are appearing before this investigation panel?" Lt. General Abass asked. "Yes sir. It is in connection with petitions written against me," he responded. The other officers on the panel were busy taking notes. "What do you say about these petitions?" The Provost-Marshal further asked. "Why are the media persecuting me like this? The petitions were ethnically motivated. They lack merit in their entirety. My detractors are after me. They envy my success," he replied, looking sad. The panel members were perplexed by his response. Most of them stared at him in perplexity. "Give us an honest assessment of Major Tom as an intelligence officer under your command," Major General Garba asked him. Brigadier Peter wore a baleful look. "His role in the intelligence unit of the Brigade has been overplayed. In my opinion, Major Tom's work has been vastly overrated. Intelligence can be overvalued. Besides, he has a tendency to oversell himself," he replied non-challantly. The panel of senior army officers noted certain hesitancy in his voice. They could see a hint of resentment in the Brigade Commander's assessment. It was General Abass who voiced out the general feeling of the panel on the assessment.

"I know you don't like him but try not to make it so obvious," General Abass cautioned. "Recently the Nigerian Army suffered some reversals in North-East Nigeria on account of the armed insurgency. How do you assess the security challenges there?" Major General Ihejirika asked. "I don't profess to be an expert in counter-terrorism or counter-intelligence. It's easy to oversimplify the issues involved. We need to make an aerial reconnaissance of the entire area. A reconnaissance mission should be set up with dispatch. Accordingly, our first task is to set up a communications system," he answered brilliantly. "That will be all for now, Brigadier. We will like to recommend you to the Army High Command to consider you for the Military Task Force Commander for the North-East geographical area; you may earn yourself promotion to a Major General. We would recommend you to book your flight to Maiduguri early in case there is no military transport plane. For the other weighty matters contained in the petitions we may choose to sweep them under the carpet unless there are compelling reasons to dust them up," the Provost-Marshal summed up. Brigadier Peter stood up and saluted stiffly. He left the building feeling downcast. This twist of recommending him for posting to head the taskforce in the North-East did not enter into his calculations. It was too risky a venture to contemplate. He would resist it. The seductive appeal of becoming a two-star general might be tempting to resist, it was nevertheless too risky to contemplate. At the officers' mess, he sent for his deputy to join him over a bottle of wine. After several glasses Brigadier Peter became garrulous.

"Colonel Chris, you now I enjoy the occasional glass of wine. What the Provost-Marshal and his bunch of lay about said at the investigation panel, is a matter of complete indifference to me," he said as he shrugged indifferently. "My CO, I think you should not dismiss them out of hand," Colonel Chris advised his commanding officer. Brigadier Peter glared at him. "It is premature to talk about success at this stage in the fight against the armed insurgents in the North-East. Why should those pot bellied office administrators even thought of it? Posting me to fight bloody untrained area boys?" he asked rhetorically. As might be expected, he uttered a stream of profanities. Colonel Chris was alarmed to hear such profanities from the mouth of his commanding officer. The Brigade Commander was obviously drunk. Tactfully he helped his Commanding Officer as he called the Military Patrol to take Brigadier Peter home immediately. The next day a letter arrived from the Army General headquarters posting Brigadier Peter to assume command of the Military Taskforce in the North-East with immediate effect. The reasons for the decision were not immediately obvious. Even when he attempted to ignore the letter, he found himself opposed by his own deputy. Colonel Chris had been informed by the Army General Headquarters to stand by to step in as the acting Brigade Commander. Quickly, Brigadier Peter wrote and dispatched a reply to the Army General Headquarters politely rejecting the posting. He cited his lack of expertise on counter-terrorism and counter-intelligence as the ground of his refusal to accept the posting. The tone of his letter displeased the Army High Command. Immediately the Army headquarters responded by slamming suspension order on him. He was forced to relinquish his command of 45 Artillery Brigade. Swiftly he was arrested. The report of the investigation panel made out a strong case for court-martial should he reject the posting. Later he was court-martialed for desertion. At the trial it was held that rejecting or refusing military posting was desertion. The Army High Command stated that the Army was badly affected by desertions. Consequently, he was convicted at a court-martial.

This further led to his indictment on allegations of drug trafficking, money laundry and racketeering. But the court martial held that its jurisdiction did not cover such offences and recommended arraignment on these charges before a competent court of law. Brigadier Peter was equally indicted for cruelty, human rights abuse, and gross insubordination. He was subsequently dismissed from the Nigerian Army. He felt his dismissal was unfair and punitive. In a swift move, he decided that the time had come to retire to the South of France. Quickly he made his travel arrangements and booked a flight to France. When he got to the Nnamdi Azikiwe International Airport, Abuja, he was stopped as he went through passport control. His international passport was confiscated. The incident was eagerly seized upon by the local press. Two days later he received an invitation from the Economic and Financial Crimes Commission, otherwise known as EFCC. He was questioned and detained on allegations of money laundry and drug trafficking. The EFCC applied to the court to have his assets seized and his bank accounts which he operated frozen. Promptly, he was arraigned before a Federal High Court, sitting in Abuja on charges of money laundry and drug trafficking. The court found him guilty and sentenced him to ten years imprisonment.

Edward was secretly overjoyed at the news of the imprisonment. But Annatu in far away Paris was sad at the news. She reminded herself time and again that she would not wish such terrible fate even on her worst enemy. After all, he was her former boss and mentor.

Major Tom had been away on official duty in Borno State over the abduction of more than two hundred school girls of Government Secondary School, Chibok, by Boko Haram insurgents. On his return to base, he found to his dismay that he had been cited for contempt of court. The judge issued a contempt citation against him for violating a previous court order to testify for the prosecution. There was also attached a notice of court session slated for the day after tomorrow. It stated that it was the commencement of the trial. The prosecution would be expected to open their case. On the strength of this he was urged to arrive in Lagos on time to meet with the prosecution counsel. He decided he would arrive on time. But there was delay at the airport. The flight delay was occasioned by the need for further security check. While Major Tom was waiting at the departure lounge he took his Notebook PC out of a sparter bag. So many thoughts whirled around in his mind. It was up to the Army High Command to implement his recommendations on the armed insurgency in the North-East geographical area. At last, his resignation letter was ready. A thought crept into his mind and urged him to check out the lie of the land before he made a final decision to resign his commission. Swiftly, he silenced the thought.

Nothing would make him change his mind. Luckily for him the driver of the army jeep was still sitting behind the wheel, waiting for the plane to take off. Quickly, he called the soldier on his cell phone and asked him to see him at the departure lounge. The soldier walked briskly in and saluted stiffly. He asked the driver to wait and collect a letter. Major Tom then found a cybercafé nearby and printed a copy of the resignation letter. He handed it to the soldier and instructed him to deliver it by hand to Army headquarters on his way back to the Brigade headquarters. The soldier took the letter, saluted and left. The plane eventually took off an hour late.

He had planned to arrive in Lagos sometime after two. He did not arrive at Robertson Street, Ikoyi until about four in the evening.

16

They all sat close together: Arunma, Tom and Mrs. Brown- on the litigants' pew. The courtroom of the Lagos High Court was filled to its capacity. By 8.45 a.m. Rosemary was led into the dock by prison warders. At 9 O'clock on the dot, Justice Adesina's appearance was announced by the court clerk as he knocked two times on the door of the judge's Chambers and bellowed, "Court!" Everyone stood when the judge came in. After the judge had sat down on his seat, both litigants and lawyers took their seats. There was stiff silence inside the courtroom. The court clerk got up and announced: "LD/115/C/2014; Commissioner of Police Versus Rosemary Allison." Thereafter Justice Adesina called out, "Appearances!" "With respect to this honourable court, I am Ayomide Olumide, Senior State Counsel," he said as he stood and announced his appearance. Then he sat down. "With humility and greatest respect to this court, my lord, I am Chief Ebele Agu, SAN. With me are Dan Okonta, Esquire and Silas Etum Esquire; we appear for the defendant," he said as he stood and announced their appearance.

He sat down. The judge looked at the Prosecution Counsel and then asked, "Counsel, are you ready to open the case of the prosecution?" Barrister Ayomide Olumide stood up and answered, "Yes, my lord. The prosecution is ready to open their case. We only want to remind your lordship that contempt charges are still hanging on the neck of the prosecution witness 1, Major Tom. We will urge your lordship to proceed with the contempt charges," he said without emotion. Swiftly, Chief Agu rose up. "My lord, that indicates that the prosecution is not ready to open its case. In that case, I shall urge this court to discharge and acquit the accused for want of diligent prosecution," he said passionately, and sat down. "Counsel, I agree with you. There are contempt charges pending against Major Tom Allison. But a balance must be maintained between the two opinions; either to proceed with the contempt charges or to discharge and acquit the accused. But let me hear from Major Tom Allison why this court should not commit him to jail for contempt of court," Justice Adesina said as he sought to tread softly.

Major Tom smartly stood up. "My lord, I was away for several weeks when I was sent on military duty to Borno State to help find the over two hundred school girls abducted by the Boko Haram insurgents. I returned two days ago to my Brigade headquarters only to find contempt charges slammed on me," he answered honestly. The judge silently contemplated him. "The contempt charges are hereby dropped by reason of overriding national interest. The officer was on military duty and could not reasonably be expected to know about contempt charges," the Judge ruled. "As the court pleases," the audience said in chorus.

The prosecution counsel rose to his feet, adjusted his wig and said, "My lord, we wish to call Major Tom as prosecution witness, that is to say, PW1." There was a hint of malice in his voice. Major Tom's heart thudded madly against his ribs. As he took the stand as the first witness for the prosecution, he was faintly embarrassed. Rosemary seeing her husband takes the witness box, presumably to testify against her fell to the floor of the dock in a dead faint. The court was in a state of panic. Tom panicked as he saw his wife faint. Justice Adesina pushed the panic button near him. Pandemonium broke out in the courtroom. Soon the Lagos State paramedics arrived and administered first aid to revive her. When the paramedics revived her, they took her away to the General Hospital on the Lagos Island. The case was adjourned indefinitely. Tom with Arunma and Mrs. Brown went straight away to the General Hospital on Broad Street. When they got to the hospital she was under sedation. Plain clothes police officers were seen standing outside the hospital ward, closely watching Rosemary. Mrs. Brown waited for her daughter to wake up, dazed and frightened. Rosemary did not wake up until the next day. When Arunma left the hospital, Major Tom and Mrs. Brown kept a round-the-clock vigil at her bedside. They dozed fitfully until dawn when Rosemary opened her eyes. She smiled faintly.

Tom could see she was still weak. He was, however, dazzled by the warmth of her smile, faint and weak though it might be. He smiled with relief. "Where am I?" she asked suddenly. "You're in the hospital, dear." Her mother answered as she patted her daughter's hand consolingly. Rosemary was curious. She seemed to have suffered temporary loss of memory. Mrs. Brown held her daughter's hand and recounted what happened in court yesterday. Rosemary felt embarrassed and upset but quickly recovered herself. "How are you, dear?" Tom asked his wife. "Oh, I can't complain," she responded as she smiled weakly. Gently, she sat up on the bed. She looked him up and down and observed his hair was crew cut. Then she looked at the hospital loose dress she was wearing. "I feel silly in these clothes," she observed. "And I feel like a nerd in these shoes," Tom said. He laughed despite himself. Mrs. Brown smiled faintly. "Come here and give me a kiss!" Rosemary demanded. Tom lamely obeyed. Her lips pouted invitingly.   There was a pained look on his face. "What's the matter, dear?" Rosemary asked suddenly. "I'm feeling guilty- I've been meaning to tell you, but still haven't got around to it. I was never meant for the army. I resigned my commission. I want to be close to you, dear," he confessed emotionally. "Oh, Tom, you did that for me? I love you, dearly. Don't ever leave me alone," she whimpered. With effort of will, she reached up, held his face in her hands and kissed him on both cheeks.

"My son, I'm so glad you resigned your commission in order to have enough time for your wife. That's a sensible thing to do. We are so proud of you," Mrs. Brown enthused. Tom beamed with self-satisfaction. "Have an apple to keep you going till breakfast time," Mrs. Brown told her daughter as she beckoned to a woman hawking apples outside the ward. She bought some apples and gave one each to Rosemary and Tom. She took one and started eating it.

Just then, someone knocked at the door. A hush descended over them. "Just a second, please, I'll check," Tom announced calmly as he went to the door. "Oh, it's you, doctor. Please come in," Tom said as he made way for the doctor. A nurse carrying a tray with drugs and syringes and bottled water followed him into the private ward. "Hello, Rosemary, I can see you're awake. You've recovered from the shock," Dr. Stephen said. Turning to Tom and Mrs. Brown, he quickly added, "We are also treating her for malaria. Test conducted indicated traces of malaria parasites in her blood stream." "What caused Rosemary to faint yesterday?" Tom asked suddenly. "She's had ME for several months," Doctor Stephen answered. "Doctor, what's the meaning of ME?" Mrs. Brown asked with concern. "It's the abbreviation for Myalgic Encephalomyelitis. It's an illness that makes people feel extremely weak and tired," Dr. Stephen explained. "What about treatment?" Tom asked, worried. "The condition is usually treated with drugs and a strict diet. In any case, the recuperative power of relaxation and sleep cannot be overlooked. That means she's going to stay with us for a while. You'll have to excuse us. We want to check her temperature and give her drugs," the doctor expatiated. Mrs. Brown and Tom went outside the ward and stayed at the lobby.

Not long afterwards, Arunma and Edward walked down the corridor of the hospital. They met Tom and Mrs. Brown at the lobby. Edward nodded his greeting to Mrs. Brown and cast a casual glance at Tom. He asked to be taken to the ward to see Rosemary. He claimed that he was on call. They all went towards the ward as Arunma held Mrs. Brown's hand. Rosemary was receiving treatment when they entered the ward. Dr. Stephen looked up, surprised. "Hope all is well?" he asked no one in particular. "I'm Dr. Edward from LUTH. Rosemary is my cousin," he introduced himself. "Ok. Just give me a moment. I'll soon be through with the routine," Dr. Stephen was alarmed when he looked at Edward and saw his dark malevolent eyes. Of course, his malevolent thoughts and intentions were soon revealed to all in the ward as Edward showed his hand. "Sorry to inflict myself on you like this! Hope you're better now?" he greeted his cousin. Arunma went to hug Rosemary. Before Rosemary could reply, Edward jumped in with a stinger. "My dear cousin, you've made a terrible mess of your life. Look at you; you live in a world of make-believe. You don't have the prerogative to dangle the chairmanship of our company in front of your lover boy," he said with a sting of sarcasm in his voice. His cruel remarks stung her painfully. "What's the point? Stop dithering and get on with it," Rosemary said, sitting bolt upright.

Every nerve in her body was tense. Like a snake, Edward coiled up, ready to strike. "Listen, and listen well; don't arrogate to yourself the power to make decisions for the company. That's a top management decision to make. Don't play 'Baba Ijebu' with the family business," he said threateningly. Turning to face Tom, he added, "You're selfish, Major Tom or whatever you call yourself. You want to reap where you didn't sow. I know your type. You don't have any right to interfere in what is plainly a family matter," he said accusingly. His voice was choking with rage. It was apparent that rage was consuming him.

Tom took the criticism surprisingly well. He had to laugh despite himself. Looking Edward straight in the eye, he said, "Please give me a chance to explain. I must have been insane to agree to the idea of becoming the Chairman of the Board of Directors of Arunma Group of Companies. You alluded to selfishness. We've all been guilty of selfishness at some time in our lives. Look at what happened to your friend, Brigadier Peter, as he then was. Be humble enough to learn from your mistake. In my humble opinion, you were wrong in your assessment of the situation." "You don't need to justify yourself to me. I neither knew nor cared what had happened to Brigadier Peter. It would be sheer madness to trust a man like you, Tom. You are clever!" he gushed. His resentment towards Tom was manifest to all those in the ward.

Rosemary was slowly going insane. She jutted her chin out stubbornly. Tears welled up in her eyes as she was unable to keep back her tears. She could not keep the dismay from her voice. "Stop it! It's not fair. I've never felt so humiliated. And I don't know how you have the nerve to show your face after what you did. Please leave now!" she said with cold scorn. As Rosemary looked at Edward with contempt she contemplated him in silence. Addressing Dr. Stephen she said, "I need something to calm my nerves." In a strange way she seemed ennobled by her grief. Mrs. Brown was visibly displeased. "I wouldn't presume to tell you how to run your own business. But I find your behaviour this morning quite unacceptable. You've behaved with indignity towards your cousin who's not feeling well," Mrs. Brown said coldly. "Don't fuss, Mum, everything is all right. Tom takes up his duties as chairman of the Board next week. Edward's argument simply doesn't stand up to close scrutiny. After all, it's make-or-break time for the company," she said flatly as she now lay inert with half-closed eyes. Tom maintained his cool. "Edward, let's have done with this silly argument. Resentment and hate have eaten your heart. Justice will prevail over tyranny. You're totally without scruple. You should leave now," Tom said through gritted teeth as he struggled to rein in his emotion. "You don't need any special skills for the Chairman position, just plain common sense. You're so pretentious! Kindly keep your opinions to yourself in future!" Edward said. His manner was cold and distant. Smiling mischievously, he addressed Dr. Stephen; "I hope I'm not keeping you from your work." "You're contemptuous of everything I do Edward," Rosemary complained bitterly.

Dr. Stephen looked Edward up and down. "I find your attitude a little hard to take. You've thoroughly abused the professional courtesy I extended to you. Now leave immediately," Dr. Stephen demanded. Edward lingered, smiling mischievously. Dr. Stephen called the security guards. They grabbed Edward's arm and hustled him out of the ward. There followed a stiff silence in the ward as Dr. Stephen got mad and walked out of the ward. "I'm sorry for Edward's unruly behaviour. I'll talk to him seriously about it. You'll excuse me," Arunma said as she headed home. "I wish I could wave a magic wand and make everything all right again," Rosemary said regretfully. She was looking none too pleased. Her mother patted her hand consolingly. When the nurse finished with her routine she retreated to the Nurses' ward. There followed a short silence in the private ward. Rosemary was lost in thought. She knew Edward pretended to his family that everything was fine. He was too macho to ever admit he was wrong. Certainly he bore her husband malice. Her philosophy of life was to take every opportunity that presented itself. It was, admittedly, a mad idea to have entrusted everything to her husband as she had done. But then trust was a vital component of their relationship as in any relationship for that matter. It was the magic ingredient in their relationship. Even if it was a mad idea to do what she had done, she felt there might be a link between madness and creativity. She was jolted suddenly by her mother's voice.

"Let me go home, change and clean up. I'll bring you some clothes too. In the meantime try and get some rest. Will you like to eat some home cooked meal?" she said pleasantly as she rose up from the edge of the bed. "I'm not hungry, Mum. I wish I could wave a magic wand and make everything all right again. See what I have done to my husband. For months now he's been prostrated with grief," she moaned and whimpered. Tom drew nearer, held her hand and patted it consolingly. "Don't worry about me, honey. I'll be fine," he said pleasantly. A smile lifted the corner of his mouth. "It's only human nature to be worried about change. Change is inevitable. It is the only permanent reality. But then your kindness has restored my faith in human nature," she said appreciatively. He looked at her fondly. "Certainly, suffering has an expiry date. Affliction will not arise the second time. Time is a great healer," he said philosophically. She looked at him with great admiration as she contemplated him in silence. "Edward has always had a rebellious streak. I often wonder if he were reborn as an animal, which animal he would be!" Mrs. Brown said jokingly. At this they all laughed despite themselves. Mrs. Brown took her handbag and stepped outside. She hailed a taxi and headed home. As Rosemary dozed off, Tom went by the doctor's consulting room. The doctor reassured him that there was nothing seriously wrong with Rosemary. Tom was never able to heal the rift between him and Edward.

Time went by so quickly. Six days had passed since Rosemary was rushed to the General Hospital. It was a wet Thursday. The rain kept up all afternoon. At the Marina head office of Arunma Group of Companies, Tom paused outside the board room, collected his thoughts before entering. Curious faces looked up as he entered and sat at the head of the long conference table. Mrs. Adeola Ijebu, the Company Secretary and Legal Adviser stood up, scanned the faces of the executive and non-executive directors on the board of the company. "Our new board Chairman, a management guru, is the amiable husband of Rosemary Allison. He was, until recently, a Major in the Nigerian Army. He holds an MBA degree in Corporate Governance. Please, join me to welcome Mr. Tom Allison to Arunma Group of Companies," she said as the board room erupted in thunderous applause. Tom slightly bowed to acknowledge the encomium poured on him. "It's a rare privilege for me to be here today as acting Chairman of Arunma Group. Let's proceed with this extraordinary meeting. I'll like to hear your general observations and comments on the company. After that I'll sum up and give us a general road map for the company's economic and commercial interests," he stated simply.

There was a hand up. "Yes, please go ahead," he recognized the executive. "Sir, let me quickly give you a brief introduction of the company and those present here. Arunma Group has its base in Lagos and branches all over the world. We have five executive directors and four non-executive directors on the board. Our range of products includes petroleum, imports and exports, construction and general services," she paused and indicated that those present should introduce themselves. Introductions were made and the discussion started to flow. Unanimously the board ratified the nomination and appointment of Tom as interim board Chairman. But Edward was late to the meeting and so he did not cast his vote for or against the ratification.

"Oil prices fell to $105 a barrel. Share prices collapsed after news of poor trading figures. Our business needs to build up its customer base," the Company Secretary/Legal Adviser observed. Next to speak was the executive director, Finance and Accounts, Ozumba Chima. "The basic pay of the average workers has risen by 7 percent. Consumers will have to bear the full cost of these pay rises. At the moment there is widespread discontent among the staff at the proposed changes to pay and conditions. We cannot discount the possibility of further strikes," he stated. The Director, Marketing Communications and Brands, Adebayo Austin reported: "Our Company is a comparative newcomer to the software market. A new computer system has been installed at a cost of ₦250, 000.00. The good news is that all the statistical computations were perfumed by the new software system," he paused and quickly added, "Our Company has excellent customer relations. We need to explore direct marketing options. Over the next few months we will keep a close eye on sales."

Suddenly the boardroom door was flung open and Edward barged in on them. For a moment all eyes were on him as he took his seat near the Company Secretary. It was the turn of the Managing Director, Solomon Victor to make his contribution. "Our Company should divest itself of some of its assets. Profits really took a dive last year. We plan to make dividend payments of 50 kobo a share this year. Prices of our goods edged up 3% in the year to June. I must say that the economics of the ongoing projects are very encouraging. The main objection then to the plan was that it would cost too much. Notwithstanding anything to the contrary, our business needs to build up its customer base," the Managing Director finished at last. Tom scanned the faces before him and asked, "How do we improve our service?" It was Adebayo Austin who responded: "Our Service will be improved by batching and sorting enquiries promptly within 3hours. The customer has got us over a barrel. Either we agree to their terms or we lose our money." Edward was talking in subdued voice. "To this day, I still don't understand why Rosemary gave Tom the board chairman position on a plate," he commented in low tone to the Company Secretary sitting next to him. Arunma sat in silence enjoying the ebb and flow of the discussion. At last she added her voice: "Everyone is aware that the Nigerian economy is in recession. The current economic climate is not favourable to most businesses. The factory in Isolo is no longer economically viable. We need, therefore, to make substantial economies."

"What is the current financial standing or position of the company?" Tom directed his question to the Executive Director, Finance and Accounts. At this point, Edward edged his chair forward. Ozumba Chima responded: "The Company's financial position is robust. Financially, we are much better off than before. We have reduced overhead costs considerably." "All these reforms being touted will cost money. The ongoing projects need to be reviewed and costed in detail. But then I need a friendly loan to fund a pet project with high PR quotient. The money will go to finance a new Community Centre in Ajegunle," Edward said nonchalantly. Tom did not take kindly to this indirect request for loan by a non-executive director of the company. It was against company policy. "You're barking up the wrong tree if you're expecting us to lend you any money," Tom said coldly. Edward could barely conceal his disappointment.

He stared at Tom in disbelief. Tom's statement infuriated him and he let out a stream of invective: "You're a bastard! You've usurped a position belonging to my cousin. You've made her cry and suffer unnecessarily. Are you not ashamed of staying in your wife's shadows?" There followed a short silence as everyone was alarmed to hear a stream of abuse flowing from the mouth of Edward. Tom did his best to remain calm, but there was a distinct edge to his voice. "I've never minded basking in my wife's reflected glory. She's the only thing that makes life bearing. Even then, we all have our little eccentricities. Go purge yourself of the cancerous bitterness which is now devouring you," Tom admonished him. He stared at Edward fiercely. It was obvious to all that they loathed each other.

Edward stood up and hinted: "I've resigned my directorship. I'll be handing in my resignation letter today." The Managing Director quickly asked him, "If we were to offer you more money, would you stay?" "Not at all! Nothing will make me change my mind," he responded as rage consumed him. He got mad and walked out of the board room. There followed a stunned silence. Then it was broken as Tom summed up the discussion. "I apologize for that rude distraction. Let me now sum up our discussion. We need to work harder to remain competitive with other companies. We won the contract for the ongoing projects in the face of stiff competition. Our rival companies are now engaged in cutthroat competition. Arunma Group needs to improve its competitive edge. The cost of living has risen sharply. Our workers are our greatest assets. We should, therefore, endeavour to improve their living standards by paying those living wages. The meeting is now adjourned. Thank you for your time and contributions." As the directors filed out of the board room, Tom seemed to have overlooked one important fact. He was acutely aware that there was a danger of overkill if anybody planned everything too carefully. But more importantly he had not reckoned with the deep seated resentment which Edward bore towards him.

Arunma lingered for a few minutes to talk to him. Tears of anguish filled her eyes. "Sorry," she said with apologetic smile. "His unruly behaviour really made me angry. We've all got problems of one kind or another," Tom said. "You've got to help us tame Edward. Apart from anything else you're my in-law. You're a family," she pleaded. "As it stands, the human race has enough weapons to annihilate itself. Let's spice our world with love. Let's go visit Rosemary," he said as they left the board room.

17

The sun finally peeped out from behind the clouds. The evening sun beamed down on Tom and Arunma as they stepped into the lobby of the General hospital. Rosemary lay inert with half closed eyes. She sat up as she saw Tom and Arunma enter her private ward. Tom could see that his wife was plainly dressed and wore no makeup. She wore her hair in plaits. Arunma went and sat on the edge of the bed. She exchanged pleasantries with her cousin. As Arunma looked at her cousin up and down, she could see Rosemary had regained her sparkle. She looked surprisingly well. Tom walked to the small refrigerator sitting in a corner and took a bottle of water. He quenched his thirst with a long drink of cold water. Arunma's eyes settled on the bunch of flowers arranged on the table near the bed.   "It was very thoughtful of you, Tom, to send the flowers. What did you discuss at the board meeting today?" Rosemary asked with interest. "Oh, this and that," Tom responded as he sat on a chair. "How did you cope with the meeting on your first assignment as chairman of the board?" Rosemary asked, smiling. Her eyes sparkled with excitement. "It was a textbook example of how the game should be played. Don't forget I hold an MBA in Corporate Governance," Tom replied excitedly. "So I've heard," she intoned. Tom looked out of the window. Butterflies fluttered from flower to flower.

He sighed as he turned to face Rosemary. "Edward barged in on us while we were having the meeting. He tried to pour cold water on our plans to expand and reposition the company," Tom said regretfully. "With Edward, you should always expect the unexpected," she said thoughtfully. "Don't give it another thought, dear," Tom advised. The more she thought about it, the more depressed she became.

"Have you heard the one about Brigadier Peter?" Tom asked suddenly. "You tell me," Rosemary responded quietly. "His legal challenge to quash his conviction at the Court- Marshal was unsuccessful. He'll be away for 10 years in jail," he revealed. Rosemary did not say a word. She simply shrugged her shoulders. "Haven't you heard? Edward resigned his directorship today. He's planning to retire to South of France. I heard he's planning to get married to Annatu secretly, in Paris. You'll recall that she disappeared and was never heard of again. The last I heard of her she was living in Paris," Arunma revealed as she patted Rosemary's ankle consolingly. "Life hasn't exactly been a barrel of laughs lately. I wish them well," Rosemary said. Tom started getting up. He looked at Rosemary fondly. "I think I'll have a bath and go to bed," he said coyly as he went closer to Rosemary and put a protective arm around her shoulders. It comforted her to feel his arm around her. She smiled bashfully. Suddenly his phone rang. He answered it. It was Chief Agu. The trial would resume on Friday at 9 O' Clock. Rosemary bowed to the inevitable and resigned her fate to the court. She was lost in thought. Tom kissed her on the cheek as he took leave of her. Arunma hitched a ride with him.

Light beamed through the open window of the courtroom as the hushed courtroom waited for the judge to commence the proceedings of the day. Justice Adesina was seated and was busy scribbling away in the file before him. At last he looked up. "Call the next case," he said to the court clerk. The court clerk stood up and read the inscription on the cover of the robust file he was holding. "LD/11C/2014: Commissioner of Police versus Rosemary Allison," Rosemary was already in the dock. "My Lord, the accused is in the court," the court clerk informed the judge. "Appearances," the judge said.

The prosecution Counsel stood up. "With utmost humility, my Lord, I am Ayomide Olamide, Prosecuting Counsel, for the State," he said and sat down. Chief Agu stood up, adjusted his gown and said, "With the greatest respect to this honourable court, my Lord. I am Chief Agu, SAN. With me are Dan Okonta Esquire and Silas Etum Esquire; we appear for the defendant." He sat down. The prosecuting Counsel, Ayomide Olumide stood up and informed the court: "My lord, we will like to call Major Tom Allison as our first witness." Tom went into the witness box and was sworn on oath. The Court Clerk got close to the witness and said, "Raise your right hand and repeat after me. I, Major Tom Allison solemnly swear that the evidence I shall be give in this case shall be the truth, the whole truth and nothing but the truth; so help me God." Tom solemnly repeated as he held the Holy Bible in his left hand.

"My Lord, the witness has been sworn," the Court Clerk informed the judge. Justice Adesina was taking notes. The Prosecuting Counsel rose to his feet, looked at Tom and said, "Please state your name and occupation." "My name is Tom Allison. I am a Company Executive," he stated. Mr. Olumide looked surprised. "I thought you were in the Army. What happened?" he asked with curiosity. "My Lord, I was a Major in the Nigerian Army. I recently resigned my Commission because of this case so that I could stand by my wife who is the defendant in this case," he said flatly. There was murmur of agreement from the audience. "Very well, then, Mr. Allison. Please tell the court what happened on the 25th day of May, precisely on your wedding day," Mr. Olumide said as he adjusted his wig. Tom recounted what happened on that fateful day. "Are you aware, Mr. Allison that the defendant hit the deceased with a wooden club?" Mr. Olumide asked. "My Lord, it is not the case. The defendant did not hit the deceased with a wooden club or any other object for that matter. I was standing beside the defendant," Tom replied. "I put it to you that you're lying to this Honourable Court. You're trying to cover up for the defendant because she's your wife," Mr Olumide said accusingly. Addressing the judge, he said, "My Lord, I apply to treat this witness as a hostile witness."

"Counsel, you were well aware of the problem when you applied to have the witness testify for the prosecution. You have to accept the inevitable," the judge responded. "Very well my Lord. No further question for this witness, my Lord," he said. Tom was asked to step down. Other witnesses were called by the prosecution. Among them were Senator Adibe and Dr Edward Ote. The first exhibit was a wooden club which the prosecution claimed was the murder weapon. Some of the evidence the prosecution produced was highly suspect. The counsel for the defendant submitted that the evidence was inadmissible.

Chief Agu, counsel for the defendant cross- examined all the prosecution witnesses except Tom. It was after this that the prosecution closed their case. The defendant testified for herself. The prosecution Counsel cross- examined the defendant in a cold inquisitorial voice. The judge called for a short recess. When the court resumed, the prosecution made their submission. Counsel for the defendant also made a submission. Chief Agu stood up as he made his submission.

"My Lord, two elements, to wit: **mens rea** and **actus rea** must be present to establish a case of murder. There must be malice aforethought by the defendant. A murder weapon must be exhibited and admitted in evidence. Furthermore, the cause of death must be certified by a medical doctor who supervised or conducted the autopsy. In Lagos State, there is a coroner law which requires a Coroners' Inquest to be conducted to ascertain the cause of death as the deceased died in Lagos University Teaching Hospital, popularly referred to as LUTH. My Lord, it is clear from evidence of the prosecution witnesses and the submission of the prosecution that none of these elements had been established. To say the least, my lord, the prosecution went on a frolic of their own. They have nothing upon which they can build a case of murder. Not only is the evidence adduced by the prosecution not substantiated but it is manifestly unsustainable. The case of the prosecution is not only bad, my lord, it is incurably bad. Admittedly, the prosecution has failed woefully to prove its case. In the light of this, my Lord, I strongly urge this honorable court to dismiss the case of the prosecution in its entirety. It lacks merit; it is spurious and flies in the face of our jurisprudence. I further urge this court to discharge and acquit the defendant. May my Lord be pleased," he finished at last and sat down.

The judgment was reserved for Friday the following week. The defence counsel made a statement outside the court. Rosemary forced her way through the crowd of reporters as she was led away to the waiting Black Maria. Tears misted her eyes. Tom saw what was happening, but was powerless to see her husband and her mother one more time she spoke in an almost inaudible whisper.

The case came before Justice Adesina on this cloudy Friday morning at the Lagos High Court. A hushed court room listened as the judge read his judgment. The judge sentenced Rosemary to three years in prison for manslaughter. Her eyes misted over as she listened to the judgment. After the judge had pronounced the judgment Rosemary was whisked away and driven to the Kirikiri Maximum Prison.

Outside the court room, Chief Agu stood beside Tom. "The case of the prosecution doesn't hold together when you look at the evidence. The judge's legal reasoning simply doesn't stand up to close scrutiny. I believe there's been a miscarriage of justice. I'll file a notice of appeal immediately," he explained the situation. Tom struggled to get a hold on his anger. He felt disappointed. Throughout the trial he had clung to the belief that Rosemary was innocent. "Chief, it is best to treat the disease early before it takes a hold. Please act fast. I'm determined to fight the case. One cannot choose freedom for oneself without choosing it for others," Tom said with seriousness etched on his face. "We'll need some money to file the appeal against the judgment of the High Court," Chief Agu said. "That won't be a problem. I'll send a cheque to your office today," he said as he made for the parking lot. He filled the rest of the day closeted in his room, meditating. True to his words, Chief Agu promptly filed the appeal and the case was soon entered into the cause list. A few weeks later, the case came before three Justices of the Court of Appeal, Lagos Division.

That cloudless Monday morning, the doors of the Court of Appeal opened and appellants and their counsel began to file in. A hushed courtroom listened as the Chief Coroner of Lagos State gave evidence. Clerks transcribed everything that was said in court. The Coroner's verdict was 'death by asphyxia' by reason of breathing asphyxiating gases. Criminal negligence was identified as the key factor. The Coroner's evidence indicted the doctor on duty that fateful night Susan died.

Following the disclosure of the Chief Coroner, the appellate court ruled that the appellant could not be held liable for the criminal negligence of the doctor. The new evidence cast serious doubt on the guilt of Rosemary jailed for manslaughter. In a unanimous decision the appeal was allowed and the appellate court upturned the judgment of the court below.

Instigated by Senator Adibe, the Director of Public Prosecution gave notice of intention to appeal the judgment of the Court of Appeal. Once again, Rosemary, at the threshold of freedom, had her freedom taken away as she was driven in the Black Maria back to Kirikiri Maximum prison. Like a wounded tiger Tom fought ferociously for the freedom of his wife. The case would receive expedited hearing since it was the State which brought the appeal.

Following the evidence of the Chief Coroner at the Court of Appeal, the Chief Medical Director of LUTH on behalf of the Hospital management brought an action against Edward for criminal negligence and medical malpractice. Edward, in his written deposition admitted that the deceased developed complications after he performed surgery on her to remove blood clot in the brain. He revealed that the operation had a fifty-fifty chance of success. Unwittingly he confessed that he had mistakenly brought the cylinder containing the asphyxiating gases when the oxygen cylinder ran out. The court found him guilty of criminal negligence and medical malpractice. His medical license was immediately withdrawn and he was sentenced to seven years in prison.

Senator Adibe heard that Edward's legal challenge about his conviction was unsuccessful. He felt he needed some adventure to spice up his life that lately had been enmeshed in misfortune. He joined an adventure tour to visit the Niagara Falls. When the tour got to Niagara Falls, having nothing to do that evening, Senator Adibe got into a moored boat and lay down in it to rest. Rocked by the current, he fell asleep. Swaying in the current, the boat finally worked loose and began to drift downstream. Spectators on the shore, seeing his great danger, shouted loudly to waken him. Still asleep, he was rapidly swept towards the falls.

At one point the boat came to rest against a rock that protruded in midstream. Seeing their chance, the bystanders redoubled their efforts to awaken the sleeping Senator by shouting loudly, "Get on the rock! Get on the rock!" In the swirling water, the boat with its sleeping passenger soon cleared the rock and headed for the fall. At last Senator Adibe, waken by the thundering roar of the great cataract, plunged helplessly over the fall to his death. Arrangements were made to have his body flown back to Nigeria for burial.

In Paris Annatu waited anxiously for Edward week after week until she learnt of his imprisonment. By the end of three weeks she had abandoned all pretence of being interested in the marriage of convenience which Edward had spun. She gave out a substantial part of the money under her custody to medical charities. Thereafter she entered the convent and took the oath of Chastity and Poverty as a nun.

In spite of his disappointment, Tom managed a weak smile as he looked at himself in the mirror. He flew down to Abuja as soon as he heard the case would come before the Supreme Court at the Three Arms Zone, Abuja. Inside the sprawling Mansion at Maitama district he sorely missed Rosemary. Arunma had travelled to the UK to visit her parents and to intimate them of the misfortune that befell Edward. She felt it her duty to tell her parents personally.

The driver had brought the new Mercedes Benz jeep to Abuja the same day he flown down to the city. It was into this jeep Tom entered and was driven by the driver to the Supreme Court. Inside the hallowed chambers of the Supreme Court, he could feel the rich red and deep rug which covered the floor of the apex court as he walked in this bright Monday morning. When the case was called, the Justices did not waste time in dismissing the appeal. They unanimously upheld the decision of the Court of Appeal. The lead judgment was read by Justice Gabriel Onyeogara. In the Obiter of the ruling, he copiously alluded to Jurisprudential pillars in the Nigerian Legal System.

"We must strive to build a society where justice and equality prevail. It is true you cannot erase injustice from the world; deliberate miscarriage of justice is equally pernicious to our legal system. There is practically no difference between the two options. In the Nigerian Jurisprudence, a person is presumed innocent until proved guilty. Therefore this court must presume the innocence of the respondent until it has proof of her guilt. All through the trial at the courts below, there was no shred of evidence that the respondent had been incriminated in any way. The burden of proof of guilt rests on the prosecution. That burden does not shift unless evidence is adduced to incriminate the accused. In the case before us, no such evidence could be cited. It is our considered opinion that this case should not have been taken to the trial court in the first instance. We unanimously uphold the ruling of the court below. We also dismiss this appeal with substantial cost awarded to the respondent who has suffered needlessly. I hope my brother Justices will deliver their concurring judgments and arrive at the same conclusions which I have made. This is my judgment." He summed up his lead judgment.

Chief Agu congratulated Rosemary on her regaining freedom. For her, this was one of the biggest weeks in the racing calendar of life. As she looked at Tom, she felt it was impossible to calculate what influence he had on her life. The storm of misfortune had passed but its damage would linger. Chief Agu delivered his words in slow, measured cadences as he made a statement to the Press outside the court. Mrs. Brown took a cab straight to her daughter's sprawling mansion to prepare sumptuous lunch to celebrate the occasion. She was overjoyed at the outcome of the case.

Outside the Supreme Court, Tom and Rosemary climbed onto their brand new Mercedes Benz jeep and sped away with journalists in hot pursuits. The couple drove home in silence as they left the National Assembly Complex and Federal Secretariat behind heading in the direction of Transcorp Hilton Hotel. At the junction they turned right into Gana Street and drove towards the sprawling mansion. As Rosemary looked at the glove compartment, there was a sticker pasted on it. The words, "I love you" were written inside a big red heart. She could feel her heart pounding in her chest. Moreover, she could hear a still small voice say, "Let your heart rule your head."

As the Mercedes Benz jeep came slowly to a halt on the driveway inside the sprawling mansion in Maitama district of Abuja, Rosemary turned to her husband, smiling coyly with joy welling up inside her. She said:
"Take my heart,

It belongs to you

My heart is delicate,

Handle it with care,

Nourish it with affection and love."

Her voice was soft and cajoling. Tom was deeply touched by her powerful burst of emotion. Impulsively, he responded:

"I'll bathe you in the affection of my love;
 I'll treat you with tenderness and care,
 My heart is all yours to take,
    Life is meaningless without love." As they alighted from the jeep, they walked up the driveway, locked hand in hand and entered the sitting room. Inside the sitting room, Tom held her hands tenderly. He gazed lovingly at her face. The radiance of her beauty still shone, untainted by her troubles. "Let's go away for a weekend. What do you say?" Tom said cheerfully. "No objection, my Lord," she said excitedly. "Destination-Bonn, Germany," he announced pleasantly. "That's perfect, my darling," she said beaming with smiles. She couldn't have been happier. Tom caressed her face with tenderness. Rosemary threw her arms around his neck. He pulled her gently towards him. They held each other close. Without further promptings, they whispered endearments to each other as their eyes held and locked each other without flinching. At that point she felt healed by his love. Gently, he took her in his arms and kissed her passionately on her full lips. Suddenly he swept her up into his arms and carried her into the bedroom, whispering sweet nothings in her ears. She was alive with happiness.

A rush of joy pulsed through her body. For an instant, she knew her heart was safe with him. Naturally she gave herself wholly to him, letting go of all inhibitions as the heat of passion and stream of love washed over her. That night they made passionate love. It was the first time they had made love. She looked back now to that fateful day in May and strange though it might sound; she was pleased it was all over as a great sense of relief flooded over her.

Made in the USA
Middletown, DE
31 January 2019